CHASING
the Big Leagues

break away b🚲ks

Series editor, Michael Martone

CHASING
the Big Leagues

A NOVEL

BRETT BAKER

Indiana University Press

This book is a publication of

Indiana University Press
Office of Scholarly Publishing
Herman B Wells Library 350
1320 East 10th Street
Bloomington, Indiana 47405 USA

iupress.indiana.edu

Manufactured in the United
States of America

Library of Congress Cataloging-
in-Publication Data

Names: Baker, Brett, author.
Title: Chasing the big leagues / Brett
   Baker.
Description: Bloomington, Indiana :
   Indiana University Press, [2019] |
   Series: Break away books
Identifiers: LCCN 2018055194 (print) |
   LCCN 2019002282 (ebook) | ISBN
   9780253038951 (ebook) | ISBN
   9780253038920 (pbk. : alk. paper)
Subjects: LCSH: Baseball stories.
Classification: LCC PS3602.A58488
   (ebook) | LCC PS3602.A58488 C43
   2019 (print) | DDC 813/.6—dc23
LC record available at https://lccn.loc
   .gov/2018055194

ISBN 978-0-253-03892-0 (paperback)
ISBN 978-0-253-03895-1 (ebook)

1 2 3 4 5   24 23 22 21 20 19

Rights to "Diana Might" courtesy of John Schwab and Will Toney.

This novel is dedicated to the

FABULOUS BAKER BOYS: BRIAN, BUKIE, AND BUTCH

who taught me how to love the game of baseball
even before they taught me how to play it.

Acknowledgments

I WOULD LIKE TO THANK ALL OF THE WONDERFUL PEOPLE who offered me help and encouragement over the many years I needed to finish this novel, including Matthew Miller, Michael Mejia, and my family, both immediate and extended, for being there in the early years when support was hard to come by; Sandy Huss, Dr. Richard McGraw, Dr. Dwight Eddins and Dr. Ralph Voss for their insistence that there was a novel in this story; Eric McPherson and Mark Brobston for being dedicated readers and decades-long friends; Rick Brown for his generous technical support; Angelique Dunn and Carol McGillivray at Amnet Systems, as well as Ashley Runyon, Peggy Solic, Rachel Rosolina, Michelle Sybert, and Dave Hulsey (and the entire team) at Indiana University Press for their tireless effort and attention; and Melinda Castillo for her typo hunting, her Spanish expertise, and the adventure of a lifetime. Finally, a special thank you to Michael Martone, the kind of friend and mentor every writer should be fortunate enough to find.

CHASING
the Big Leagues

I HATE THE WORD SCAB—ALWAYS HAVE. IT SOUNDS LIKE THE noise your cleats make when you walk across gravel. A scab is something hard and ugly, something nobody wants, but when you got to have one, you got to have one. I never thought of us as scabs and I wouldn't want you to think that either. I guess that's what got me started going through my old notes, reading what I wrote back then, five years ago now though it feels like maybe a week. I know I didn't get everything down, so I'll try to fill in some of the blanks, stuff I remember but I didn't think was important then or I just didn't have time to put down the first time.

Can't say for sure why I think it still matters. Everyone else has pretty much forgotten. Still, I want to get down on paper what it felt like to be there with all the excitement and confusion. I want you to know how important it all seemed at the time, no matter how dumb it probably sounds now. You know that old saw, "The best you can do is the best you can do"? Mostly I just want you to understand that, if this was the best we could do, we made damn certain that it was us at our best.

You might ask how I can still recall so much about things that happened all those years ago but the funny thing is, I've never tried to remember. I just can't seem to forget. You might also wonder what difference it makes. How can writing about it now change anything from back then? The short answers are: none and it can't. But it might make a difference for you, in how you see and think about us. And maybe writing it down will make a difference for me, too. Or maybe, if it's true what they

1

say—that the older you get, the better you were—then maybe I just want to revisit one more time that glorious season when my best friend and I made it to the very top of the world, that sterling silver spring when the two of us made it all the way to The Show.

MONDAY, FEBRUARY 6, 1995

One hundred years ago today George Herman Ruth came into this world. If Ty Cobb epitomized the ideal baseball player at the turn of the twentieth century, then Babe Ruth arrived representing everything a ballplayer shouldn't be. He drank and smoked; he was a womanizer, a showboat, a prima donna. And yet people loved him. Newspapers of the time carried special articles on the sports page entitled "What the Bambino Did Today" right beside the box scores. He single-handedly changed our national pastime from Cobb's small-ball, one-base-at-a-time game into tape measure home runs and victory laps around the field. Ruth hit more dingers, appeared in more movies and advertisements, made more money, ate, drank, cussed, laughed and screwed more than anybody thought a ballplayer should, or even could. He was a media darling before the advent of TV or radio. He was a rock star before there was rock. In short, Babe Ruth was The Shit.

Ninety-nine years, six months and six days after the Bambino's birth, Major League players collectively decided that they too were The Shit. On August 12 last year the players' union declared a strike, and they haven't played a Major League game since. The Great Depression, two world wars, even an earthquake weren't enough to stop the World Series but last October they decided to skip it, all because of a labor dispute.

As a result, the suits who own the Major League teams voted last month to start the '95 season with replacements. It seems like a sorry little ploy to get the union players to back down, or maybe make a few bucks back from all the dough they've lost since the strike started. Whatever the reason, Major League scouts have been crossing the country trying to pull teams together so they can hold spring training like usual this March.

Of course, the union players, along with the media, most of the fans, several coaches and even one owner have all gone on record saying the idea sucks. Replacement baseball, they say, simply cannot be allowed to happen. The Toronto Blue Jays' radio network has already announced that they won't broadcast any replacement games. Tom Cheek, who's been calling their games on radio since the Jays broke into the league in '77, told a Toronto newspaper that he'll return to the microphone, and I quote, "when Ed Sprague, not some furniture mover from Oshkosh, Wisconsin, is playing third base."

Word gets around fast. I only found out myself last Saturday. Chris Buckley, a talent scout for the Jays, called to tell me they liked my try-out. They want me at third when spring camp opens in three weeks. So I guess Tom Cheek was talking about me. And yes, I have been moving furniture the last three years since college. But I'm not from Oshkosh, Mr. Cheek. I'm from Columbus, Ohio. And I have a name, sir: Jonathan Alders Standen.

Please, call me Jake. Everybody does.

"The game has gone to shit," I remember Tall Boy saying one night at his place. "And you and I are the toilet paper."

"It's your own fault," I reminded him as he carried dirty dishes to where Karen stood at the sink. "If you hadn't hit those dingers in the semis, none of this would be necessary."

Senior year our high school team made it to the state tournament. Though we lost by a run in the semifinal to a team from Dayton that we should have crushed, the Minnesota Twins drafted our star shortstop, Brian "Tall Boy" Sloan, one week after graduation.

"Don't start with me." Brian set the dishes in the sink and stood beside his wife. "You know who wears the pants in my family."

The Blue Jays called Tall Boy when they first started looking for replacements. Karen was the one who suggested I go along to the tryout. *Suggested* is maybe the wrong word. Karen is what you'd call a strong-willed woman, the kind who, even at seven and a half months pregnant, gets indignant when her dinner guest offers to do the dishes.

"You brought the wine," she said, and held up a finger when I tried to protest.

I sipped my drink in silence a moment, watching Brian rub his wife's shoulders. She closed her eyes and leaned into the massage, a dishrag dripping in her hand.

It was also Karen who answered the phone when the Jays first called. In Tall Boy's version of the story, she had already booked a hotel room five blocks from the tryout complex in Cleveland before she got around to telling him about it. In Karen's version, Brian asked about the details four times (What exactly did they say? Did they sound serious?) before he agreed to go.

"We've been down this road before," Karen said, turning back to the sink of dishes. "I know it would have eaten at Brian if he didn't at least give it one more chance."

We don't talk about it much anymore: about how Tall Boy had already started dominating double-A ball in the Twins' farm system by the time I'd used up my eligibility at Ohio State; about how that same summer his little brother went out riding on his new moped and got sideswiped by some drunk driving home from the bars. Nobody blamed Tall Boy when he took the rest of the season off to help his folks get Shawn to all those physical therapy sessions—nobody but the Twins, I guess, since they forgot to invite him back when the next season rolled around.

The Blue Jays offered Brian a contract on the spot after our Cleveland tryout and asked me for a number in case they wanted to get in touch. Three weeks later, Buckley called.

I got up from my seat to gather what was left of the dishes from the table. They had set a place for my dinner date, one of the secretaries from the U-Haul office, but at the last minute I decided just to spend the evening with Karen and Tall Boy, so I called and canceled the date. I didn't think it was that big a sacrifice. Brittany was the kind of girl who should never leave the house without her tits. There'd be no reason to talk to her if she forgot them.

"Nobody's holding a gun to your head," I told Tall Boy at the sink. "You can always tell the Jays to keep their signing bonus and stay here driving Pepsi bottles around town."

"Fuck that," he answered, wrapping his arms around Karen's belly. "For another five grand I'd trade places with her in the delivery room."

"Deal," Karen agreed.

"Just remember," Brian told me. "If the union guys cave and they reach an agreement, they'll ship us both back home fast as you can say *scab*."

In the weeks leading up to our trip to the Blue Jays' camp in Florida, I was surprised how little most people seemed to care about Tall Boy's and my leaving. It's not as if we went around City Center Mall shouting that we were going to be replacements but when you quit your job and break your lease with three weeks' notice, you have to tell a few people what you're up to, whether you want to or not. Still, no one threw us a going-away party; there was no send-off at work. Everyone kind of assumed we'd be back in a week or two, like we were just going fishing or something. One guy at U-Haul came right out and asked me, "You don't think they're really gonna let you play, do you?"

I didn't see why not. I'd read in the paper where 1,300 guys showed up at a replacement tryout for the Atlanta Braves. They all got sent home because it rained. Another 1,200 showed up for a California Angels' tryout and they signed nine to contracts. I'd never seen so many players under one roof before we went up to Cleveland—I heard there were 500 at the indoor facility where they held our tryout—and they signed three others besides Tall Boy and me. Even beating odds like that though, we had no guarantees. We knew from the start that we would have to go to Florida and earn a spot on the team. It just seemed like a lot of trouble to go through if the owners had no intention of putting us in uniform on Opening Day.

FRIDAY, FEBRUARY 17

I broke it off with Brittany tonight. I told her Tall Boy and I were going to Florida, and when she said she wanted to come along, I told her that was impossible. Then she asked if she could visit, so I told her we'd be staying at the team hotel and I doubted that we could have visitors popping in unannounced. Then she asked would I call her every few days and I told her we should probably just wish each other luck. Surprised me how pissed off she got. Christ, I hope she hadn't fallen in love. I thought I'd made my intentions perfectly clear from the start: going out with her was the obvious alternative to not going out with anyone. She was just something to do.

When she got to her car for the grand exit, she said something laugh-out-loud funny. She so clearly wanted it to sound cutting but it only came out sounding like B-movie dialogue. With just the right mix of hurt pride and fuck-me-no-fuck-you anger in her voice, she yanked the car door open, turned to me and announced with a regal sweep of her arm, "You don't know what you want."

Of course I do.

I want to stop dating women who are sixty-six inches tall and one inch deep. I want to quit working forty-five-hour weeks for twenty-five-hour paychecks. I want driving fifty-five in the passing lane to be a capital offense. I want days to last twenty-eight hours so I can stay out till three and not feel like crap when the alarm goes off at seven. I want more women to wear those half shirts that ride up so high you sometimes catch a glimpse of the creamy, curvy undersides of their breasts—because that's the Promised Land; there's your Valhalla; that's the cleavage you don't get to see for free. I want people who are cruel to animals in this life to come back as dung beetles in the next. I want baby boomers to finally admit that they're just as full of shit as everybody else, because the same generation that rose up singing madrigals of peace, love and brotherhood in the Psychedelic '60s came to power in the Me Decade '80s, purposely picking the Muzak of greed and selfishness that was playing when my generation stepped on this elevator. I want people to stop giving so much credit to fuckups who eventually get their acts together and start giving more credit to people who were never fuckups in the first place. I want conviction and heartfelt desire to be enough. I want to retire to a little place with some woods near a river and own a large dog that I'll name Max. And when I'm old and gray, I want to gather my little grandkiddies up on my knee and show them the page, point to the exact spot between Jerry Standaert and Pete Stanicek, where my name will appear forever in *The Baseball Encyclopedia*.

The night before we left, my mom invited Karen and Brian over to the house and cranked up the wok for a round of her famous stir-fry. Tall Boy has been a part of our family routine so long that I forget exactly when Ma stopped introducing him as "Jake's best friend" and started calling him "my other only son." After dinner I cleaned out the fireplace, and we had a few drinks in the living room while I started a fire.

We talked for a while about Karen and the baby, about good ways to pass the time during a two-day road trip, about whatever. Like the

6

faithful Buckeyes we are, Brian and I grew up rooting for the Reds in the National League, the Indians in the American, so of course Mom and Karen gave us grief about going to Florida to play for a team from Canada. We didn't put up a fight. Everyone knew this was different. It was like if you spent your whole life a proud Ohioan but while you were on the road you bought a winning lottery ticket in Indiana. Would anyone refuse the windfall because it didn't come from your home state?

Eventually Karen and Tall Boy begged off another drink and put on coats to head back home. The Blue Jays had sent us vouchers for plane tickets but we figured driving a rental for weeks on end would get crazy expensive, so we cashed out the vouchers and were using the proceeds as gas and food money for the trip down. Since Karen would need their car, Tall Boy and I were driving my old Chrysler to Florida. We made final arrangements for me to pick him up in the morning, then Mom and I waved good night from the porch as they walked through the snow to their car.

I was already out of my apartment and had stashed all my stuff in the basement at Mom's house, so I spent the night there. I couldn't even remember the last time I'd stayed over, and I was kind of dreading it this time for all the usual reasons. After eighteen years under her watch, I wasn't looking forward to feeling like a pent-up teenager again. But the old bed was more comfortable than I remembered, or maybe it was just uncomfortable in all the places I knew to avoid. That night I got some of the best sleep I'd had in weeks.

My room was pretty bare—I had years ago boxed up all the trophies and pictures and crap that prove a kid grew up in a room—but taped to the back of my door, there were still two faded posters of Johnny Bench and Joe Morgan. As I lay in bed that night under the steady gaze of my Hall of Fame heroes, it wasn't that hard to connect with the boy I once was in my old room. Like the punk kid who had put up those posters, I couldn't have said for sure what would happen beyond the middle of tomorrow. I couldn't tell you about love or longing, didn't know need from desire, wasn't sure about the stars or the cosmos, the order of the planets or even the order of the alphabet. But the answers were out there, mine for the asking, and I would find out soon enough.

No one sets out to be a server; nobody aspires to bus the banquet of possibility. If you dare to dream at all, the only dream worth having is that life is a smorgasbord set out for the best and the brightest, and there's a seat at the head table reserved just for you. That's the point of waking up tomorrow. I knew it as a kid same as I knew it lying there in my old bedroom the night before our trip. The point is not to find out if your dream is true, but to find out exactly what it feels like when it finally comes true.

SUNDAY, FEBRUARY 19

We caught several sports talk shows over the radio on the drive down. Everyone was talking about Sparky Anderson, the guy who skippered Cincinnati when they won back-to-back championships in '75 and '76, and then managed Detroit to a title in '84. Needless to say, being the first guy to manage a World Series winner with two teams in different leagues gets you respect, so it was pretty big news when Anderson announced on Friday that he's walking off the job rather than coaching Detroit's replacement team this spring. One talk show even played a quote from Anderson's press conference. "There ain't no place in baseball for replacement players," Anderson said. "The one thing that will never leave me is integrity. It's the one thing money can't buy."

I always liked Sparky and I still think he's a hell of a manager, but that business about integrity struck a nerve with me. It's nice to have standards and morals and all, but isn't integrity at least in part when you go out and do the work a company pays you to do, no matter how you feel personally about the job? Nobody ever asked me how I felt about the clientele we moved at U-Haul. I never walked off the job because I thought somebody's furniture was too ratty or smelly or wasn't up to my standards as a mover. I always did the work they assigned me because I said I would, and they relied on me to be true to my word. Maybe my definition will change if I make it in the bigs, but for now at least, that sounds like integrity to me.

We got to Clearwater this evening and found the Howard Johnson's where the team is staying. It's a fifteen-minute straight shot up Route 19A from the hotel to the Blue Jays' camp in Dunedin, a town with a two-block Main Street and no daily paper. The Blue Jays had sent us a packet with directions to the HoJo and the spring training facility. For some reason I thought that meant there would be someone waiting for us in the lobby, to say hello and maybe show us around. When we checked

8

in though, the guy at the desk just marked our names off a sheet he had behind the counter, gave us a couple of keys, and that was that. Brian and I unpacked, scouted out the area, and spent some time just walking around trying to stretch our legs after eighteen hours in the car. We didn't see anybody who looked like they were with the team.

At first I was a little worried about cash—it surprised me when the desk clerk said we owed $26 a night for our room—but then Brian reminded me of the food per diem. Our contracts are all conditional bonuses until the season starts: $5,000 for signing, which they'll pay in mid-April; another five grand for making the Opening Day roster, payable May 1; and then league minimum, with a big termination bonus if the strike ends after that. On top of everything though, they'll give us $78 a day for meal money.

I did a little math. If I worked a forty-hour week with no overtime as a Pack and Load Crew Chief for U-Haul, my salary per day came to $77.50. When I told Brian he laughed, gave me a high five.

"Welcome to The Show," he said.

The morning after we arrived, Tall Boy and I went over to the stadium, a preemptive strike of sorts to meet some of the players and coaches before the first full-team practice the following day. As it turned out, we hardly talked to anyone. Pitchers and catchers arrived in camp on the sixteenth and they were all on the field working out with the coaches when we got there. We did meet one coach in the clubhouse, Carl Assenmacher, a guy with the deepest, scratchiest, two-packs-a-day smokiest voice I've ever heard. Assenmacher seemed a little preoccupied when we came in, and after shaking our hands he told us to go see the main office secretary about getting our pictures taken. Brian and I traded glances; we had no clue what he meant.

"Pictures for the media guide?" I asked.

"Naw, hell," Assenmacher grunted. "Pictures for your ID cards. No offense fellas, but you replacements are all strangers to us. You'll need IDs so the security guys can tell you from the paying customers. If you don't have your cards they'll probably make you buy a ticket to get in." Assenmacher paused a second before adding, "If that ever happened, we'd reimburse you for the ticket."

I couldn't tell if he was joking or what; the guy never cracked a smile. Tall Boy and I said thanks, then wandered off in search of the main office.

Eventually we found the place, a cool, carpeted set of rooms in a low building outside the stadium. A sweet older lady in a gray sweater with the Blue Jays' insignia over the left breast made cards for us both while we waited.

It may sound stupid but when the secretary gave me my ID—a laminated, wallet-sized card with my name and picture above the words "The Toronto Blue Jays Major League Baseball Organization"—it hit me for the first time that I was there, in South Florida, as a professional ballplayer. This wasn't like when I was a kid saving up my money to buy some overpriced "authentic" jersey from a sporting goods store. This wasn't like when Tall Boy and I used to run around Little League practice pretending to be our favorite players from Cincinnati's Big Red Machine teams of the '70s. This was the real deal. We were about to begin spring training with a Major League club.

And as I realized all this, another thought occurred to me, a thought that hadn't crossed my mind since the first time I entered a game as a freshman at Ohio State. What if I can't do it? What if, after all the practice, and all the coaching, and all the games with all the teams over the years, I prove beyond a shadow of a doubt that I have no business being here? Try as I might, I just couldn't stop thinking: What if I suck?

"Good God," Tall Boy exclaimed, pulling me up out of my thoughts. "This picture's even worse than my driver's license."

The secretary smiled. "The security boys should start to recognize you in a few days. If you have any problems before then, just tell them to call me. I'll ID you in."

TUESDAY, FEBRUARY 21

Our first full-squad practice. I'm not sure just what I expected but whatever it was, today wasn't it. I guess what surprised me most was the silence. Every team I've ever been on, from Little League all the way through college, first practices were always loud, raucous, celebrations almost. You see old teammates, friends from school, people laughing and yelling across the field to one another. Today the whole place was silent.

Makes sense, I guess. Nobody here knows anyone else. Even to the coaches we're hardly more than names on a roster. The team manager, Bob Didier, told a reporter that he'd never seen twenty-five of the thirty-seven players in camp before today. I was one of those twenty-five. Then again, before today I'd never even heard of Bob Didier.

Turns out Didier managed the Blue Jays' triple-A team in Syracuse last summer. In a normal year a number of minor leaguers would come to spring training with the union players, but because of the strike the Jays decided to hold separate camps for the replacements and their regular minor league guys. The Jays' big-league manager, Cito Gaston, is working with Didier's minor leaguers at another complex a few miles from here and we have a minor league manager running our camp.

I assume in a normal year they start out the first day of full squad by holding orientation meetings with coaches and the general manager, but the closest we came to any of that was when Coach Didier gave a little speech before we took the field for the morning warm-up.

"Gentlemen," Didier said in the clubhouse, "I don't know how long you're gonna be here. I don't know how long I'm gonna be here. But for now we're all wearing the uniform of the Toronto Blue Jays, and I consider it the job of every man in this room to do his personal best to make sure we live up to the challenge we've been given. Together we can give this organization a team to be proud of. Let's get to work."

Under different circumstances Didier's speech could have been a rallying cry, like we should've been waving hats and calling out "Huzzah!" to show our support, but the room stayed quiet. Someone popped a fist into the palm of a glove. Metal cleats scraped over tile by the shower stalls.

Coach Assenmacher cleared his throat. In a voice like someone dragging an infield with a stretch of chain-link fence, he called out: "Pitchers and catchers, head for the warm-up mounds. Outfielders are in the batting cages. Infielders, come with me."

We carried that silence like the rest of our equipment up the clubhouse tunnel and onto the field. Other coaches started calling for the players they had charge of. Assenmacher told us to just spread out along the infield and get warmed up. The grass was still damp from a morning dew.

Brian flipped a ball to me and skipped backward until we were facing each other from about fifteen yards.

"Almost forgot," he said. "We're defending champs."

He jerked a thumb over his shoulder and I looked up. A Labatt's sign above the scoreboard beyond the center field wall proclaimed: "Canada's Favorite Beer Salutes Canada's World Champions."

The Jays won the last World Series, played in '93.

There were no fans in the seats as we loosened up and only a couple of reporters waited in the section behind the dugout to interview Coach Didier. The place was eerie, it was so quiet. The smell of recently cut grass hung over the field like a fog. I threw Brian the ball and, together with the rest of the infielders, we fell into an easy rhythm of pitch and catch, a rhythm the two of us have shared since we were seven. We gave a brief try at chatter, the usual banter of getting warmed up, but eventually we let the silence of the morning envelop us, only broken by a soft grunt as one man threw and the staccato pop of the ball as it landed in his partner's mitt. By the time I was loose I had forgotten all about the empty seats. It was enough to be surrounded by the grunts and the pops, and the silence in between, where gloves hung open, suspended, waiting.

There had been some speculation that union players might form picket lines outside the fields where the replacement camps were being held, and I wasn't sure just what we would do if we ran into a confrontation at the ballpark—but there was nobody. As we pulled into the parking lot outside the stadium that morning I realized how dumb I'd been to worry about it. We were talking about a group of men who made hundreds of thousands, even millions of dollars a year. They weren't about to get up at eight in the morning, drive to Dunedin and stand around waving signs hoping to gain public support. If any union players were in Florida that day, the only thing to get them out of bed that early would have been a tee time.

We practiced till about three that afternoon, mostly just conditioning, a little hitting, and some infield/outfield drills. I was nervous at first but after an hour or so I started to feel all right. In terms of what they expected from me, this was like any other practice I'd ever been to. There were a couple of guys who made some nice plays. Tall Boy looked as good as anybody, hitting liner after liner in the batting cage. Overall I felt like I could hang with anyone on the field, talent-wise.

When they let us go for the day, Brian and I joined some of the other guys for an hour in the weight room. It was nearly five by the time we hit the showers, changed clothes and went out for a bite to eat. In Ohio whenever we had an evening free we would usually wind up talking over some pitch and catch or going to a batting cage, but when your day job requires being around a ball diamond for seven hours straight, you look for something else to do at night. Tall Boy wanted to call Karen, so after dinner we went back to the hotel and mostly lay around. I wasn't going to admit it but I was pretty sore, and it felt good to just flop down on the bed and take a load off.

While he was on the phone I started watching some nature program on TV about the ocean life around this ice pack on the edge of the Bering Sea. They had these walruses, a big group of them stretched out along the ice shore. The narrator was saying how, even though the walruses rest and take care of their young on the ice, they're much better adapted to living in the sea. You could see the truth of it in the pictures they showed. On land the walruses were all clumsy and fat, slopping around and bumping into each other. But in the water they were so graceful and quick. They would dart around and do barrel rolls, chasing after fish or one another. It was like they were two different animals, depending on where they were. And then it occurred to me: I know just how that feels.

In everyday situations, if I'm moving somebody's stuff for U-Haul or I'm out in public somewhere, I feel slow and awkward, unsure of myself and my role. But on a ball field I know exactly what to expect and what to do. I know the rules of the game and how to use them to my advantage. At a bar or restaurant I loathe looking up to find someone staring at me; I assume I've got something in my teeth or my zipper is down. But between the first- and third-base lines, I want people to watch, want them looking at me, because that's the one place in the world where I'm as good as anyone. I know when to hurry and when to ease up, when to stab or dive or slide. I'm strong and quick and sure. I'm as graceful as a walrus in the ocean.

Of course Brian didn't hear me thinking any of this. All he heard, as he was hanging up the phone, was my final conclusion.

"I am that walrus."

"Goo goo ga joob," he answered.

The facility where the Blue Jays hold spring training has more names than it knows what to do with. A squat little sign on the corner of Beltrees Street and Douglas Avenue claims the place is called Grant Field but about a hundred yards from that sign, in big white letters across the facade of the park, it reads: "Dunedin Stadium." Nobody seems to know why. Right across Douglas sits a VFW and the Dunedin Senior Citizens Center. So far it's been difficult to tell the hottest spot in town; on any given afternoon the vets and the old folks have as many cars in their lots as we have at the ball field. During morning practice you can hear shouts and squeals from children on the school playground that sits just beyond the left field wall.

From the parking lot there's no mistaking the stadium for anything but the spring home of Toronto's Major League franchise. A giant blue-jay head in profile, Toronto's insignia, is emblazoned across the outside of the park, with a smaller version of the same painted on the side of the ticket booth. Just to the left of the ticket windows, on the fence leading into the stadium, are signs painted in Toronto blue and white bragging up the team's dominance in recent years: American League East champs in 1985, '89, and '91; World Series champs, '92 and '93. Along the tile grandstand wall as you enter is another blue and white sign. Written all in caps it reads, "PLAYERS FROM DUNEDIN TO 'THE SHOW.'" Beneath that runs a blue and white stripe, an honor roll a good fifty feet long of all the guys who played here as minor leaguers on their way to the bigs. Below Dave Weathers and Mike Timlin, just to the right of Pat Hentgen, is a circle painted like a baseball listing the man I was signed to replace: Ed Sprague. Even if I take his job for good, Toronto fans will always remember Sprague as a hero in the Jays' 1992 World Series title run. He came off the bench in the ninth and knocked a pinch-hit home run off Jeff Reardon to beat Atlanta in game 2.

To think that three weeks and two feet of snow ago Brian drove a Pepsi truck and I was lifting hide-a-beds for a living. Now here we are playing ball all day in a beautiful stadium in front of 6,200 brand-new, empty seats. I'd never seen carpet in a locker room before this week. Every morning they have fruit and coffee waiting when we arrive; free lunch catered in the players' lounge in the afternoon. Strain a muscle or feel tight after practice? Just sit in a whirlpool while the trainer gives you a rubdown. Toss your sweaty, grass-stained laundry in a giant canvas catchall and tomorrow you'll find your entire uniform spotless and folded neatly in your locker. They even have shampoo and disposable razors set out in the showers when we finish for the day. And the ball diamond—Jesus. Every inch, every millimeter from home plate to the farthest stretch of center field is manicured, immaculate. Not a weed, not a rock, not a bad hop in sight, only pampered dirt deep as you please and grass like a lawn-care commercial.

I'll never understand how the union guys walked away from this job. Every day I pass "THE SHOW" sign coming in and I think: How fine would that be? To be listed there in the cool shade of the stadium overhang for anyone to stroll by and see; to have a circle representing you among guys who hit game-winning dingers in the World Series; to have your name in bold letters, side by side with players who might someday be in the Major League Baseball Hall of Fame—how fine would that be?

By the end of the first week things were starting to loosen up around camp, guys talking, comparing notes, connecting teams and teammates in common. One of the first to start talking with Tall Boy and me was a pitcher named Adam Prince. Prince was the only guy in camp who had made it to The Show as a union player. He was called up briefly by Seattle during late-season roster expansions in both '90 and '91. Players refer to those temporary promotions as "a cup of coffee." Because Prince had two with the Mariners, everyone at camp called him Folgers.

Tall Boy and I walked into the clubhouse one day before practice to find Folgers standing in the middle of the room, a half-eaten banana in one hand, wearing nothing but a ball cap and a jockstrap.

"How you boys doing this fine mornin'?"

He reached out his free hand to shake. We didn't know it at the time but Folgers was the kind of guy who shook hands like young lovers kiss: fervently and often.

"You two sure do stick close," he said. "You knew each other from before?"

Tall Boy explained that we came down from Ohio together.

"That's good. I like when my infielders know each other as friends. They work together better that way. It's a harmony issue. Far as I'm concerned the perfect infield would be four boys from the same town. Hell, the whole defense could be made up of guys related to each other. Imagine that? I'm from Decatur, Alabama, myself."

I noticed a small yellow wad of gum stuck to his pinkie finger. Folgers took a bite from the banana and caught me looking at his pinkie as he chewed.

"It's that nicotine gum," he said without my asking. "Works just like the smokes do: the first piece in the morning is a dream come true, then you spend the rest of the day chewing your fool head off trying to get back the feeling the first one gave you. I started chewing to quit the smokes. Now I can't quit the gum. The bastards didn't help me do anything but switch who gets my addiction money."

He paused for a moment to swallow a bite of banana.

"Speaking of which, either of y'all like Chinese food? I can't lay off the stuff. Found the sweetest little Chinese place not far from the hotel last night. Egg rolls just melt in your mouth. I'll take you over if you want. Knock your socks off."

Another pause. More chewing.

"On that pop-up yesterday," Folgers said to Tall Boy. "That's your ball. If I'm in the way you just call me off. I'll get the hell out of there."

"No, you were fine," Brian answered. "I was just gun shy after kicking that one during the double play drill."

"As long as somebody catches it," Folgers agreed. "I wouldn't be too worried, by the way. About making the team, I mean. You're as solid as anybody out there."

Then he looked at me and I thought I noticed a slight hesitation before he added, "Both y'all. You guys look good. Just play your game."

Folgers finished his banana and tried a hook shot at a trash can with the peel. He missed by at least a foot.

"That's why I play baseball," he said. "You fellas be sure and grab you a little something to eat before practice. You know what they say: breakfast is the most important meal. Nobody plays good on an empty stomach."

With that he shook hands again and walked to his locker to get dressed for practice. It came as no surprise when the players unanimously voted

Folgers team captain two weeks later. Roy Campanella once said you need to be a man to play big league ball, but you need a lot of little boy in you, too. Folgers seemed a natural-born spokesman of both boys and men.

Maybe the union guys have played enough by the time they reach The Show that they don't need spring training for anything more than light conditioning, but I haven't been in organized ball for three years and I sure need the practice, if only to help develop the calluses required to play every day. After one week here at Dunedin I can safely say I'm sore in more places than I ever remember from college ball.

On my left hand I have open blisters at the base of three fingers, a split in the skin on the inside of my right thumb and a growing numbness in the heels of both hands that feels like I've been working an eight-hour shift on a jackhammer, all from swinging a bat eighty to a hundred times a day. Yesterday on a hook slide my pant leg tore, giving me a pebbly scab about six inches long that looks like someone sprinkled wet cinnamon down my left shin. From infield drills I've got bruises on my chest and left bicep; from my new cleats I have aching arches and a split toenail. I probably have more cuts, bruises, aches and abrasions than a classroom full of seven-year-olds in the elementary school behind the left field wall. If this is what a week of spring training can do, I can't wait to discover what a 162-game schedule is like.

We've been on or around the practice field six to eight hours daily and we're still a week away from even our first exhibition game. There are nine guys trying out for the infield and the team will probably keep five of us on the thirty-two-man roster for the regular season. Brian is definitely in at short and I think I've made an impression so far at third, though it's hard to tell with Coach Assenmacher. It's pretty obvious he doesn't care for us replacements, and when he makes a comment you have to sift through it, like panning for gold, to find any encouragement mixed in among the abuse. He takes a strange joy in testing us during infield practice, shouting out an opinion after each play. The crack of the fungo bat keeps tempo for his commentary as he runs us through our daily drills.

Thwack

Get in front of the ball, you pussy!

Thwack

Throw it low and hit 'im if he won't get out of the baseline!

Thwack

Yes—Yes—Yes. No! No! No!

Thwack

Ah Christ! You guys are slow and stupid.

I wasn't the only one who couldn't figure Assenmacher out. It seemed like more and more media guys entered the camp every day, and each one pumped the coaches for a fresh angle on "The Replacement Player Story." One day at lunch a reporter, new to camp, approached Assenmacher as he was sitting down to eat.

"Coach," the reporter asked. "What do you see when you look around this roomful of ballplayers?"

Coach dutifully looked to his left and right.

"I see a room full of men who still haven't forgiven themselves."

The reporter looked up from his notebook. "For what?"

Assenmacher had a baseball in his back pocket from the morning practice. He reached around to pull it out before sitting down.

"For loving a woman who didn't love them back."

He set the ball on the table in front of the reporter. It rolled off a seam, teetered a second between depressions in the tabletop and finally settled in a low spot beside a jar of mustard.

The reporter scribbled and scratched out, scribbled and scratched out.

That same lunch was the first time Tall Boy broke out one of his "would you rather" questions during spring camp. He usually throws them out as conversation starters but over the years they've taken on a life of their own. Sometimes they're gross, as in: "Would you rather screw a dead girl or eat a bucket of puke?" Sometimes they're obscure, like one he came up with in high school: "Would you rather be an art or a craft?" I thought that was a dumb one but he asked it several weeks straight because everyone kept answering "art." Finally a kid from the spec. ed. class answered "craft"—he probably didn't even know what art was—and Tall Boy retired the question.

"I've heard from both sides," he explained.

Occasionally his Would You Rathers were mean. A favorite of mine from that category he could only ask other guys, for obvious reasons: "Would you rather be a chick or a Chink?" That question didn't last long because when Brian asked Dan Delgado, the catcher on our high school team, Dan answered: "I'd rather be a Chink, because at least then I'd have half a brain."

"When you ask a racist, sexist question," Tall Boy said about retiring that one, "and you get an answer that's even more racist and sexist than the question itself, you've got to walk away. You can't hope for better than that."

Anyway, at lunch that Saturday afternoon Tall Boy asked the guys gathered at our table, "If you had to choose one or the other, would you rather have beauty or talent?"

"Are you implying I don't have both already?" Folgers wondered.

"If you had to choose one or the other," Tall Boy repeated, to remind us it was a hypothetical.

After years of being asked Would You Rathers I've come to realize that you need to examine all parameters of the question at hand, to prevent your answer from coming back to haunt you later.

"Is this a particular type of talent," I asked, "or a talent of our choosing? And is the beauty all-over, or just a specific kind of beauty? I don't want to be a foot model or anything."

"No, it's a beauty or talent of your choice," Tall Boy explained. "You can be Mel Gibson or Mel Allen. How about that?"

Folgers was working his way through a cup of pudding, and he took several spoonfuls before deciding his answer.

"I think I'd go with talent. I mean, being beautiful is sort of an all or nothing proposition. Either God decides you are or you ain't a beauty, right? But being talented—" He jabbed his spoon in the air for emphasis. "Now that takes talent."

SUNDAY, FEBRUARY 26

Because we play not just different but complementary positions, I can pull for Tall Boy without having to compete against him for a spot on the team. In fact, when we play together we have a built-in advantage over the other guys trying out for infield positions because we've played side by side so many years that we know what to expect from each other. I know the limits of his ability and he knows mine. Strictly speaking, I'm the one with the limits. Brian is a complement to any third baseman he plays beside.

There's a casualness to Tall Boy's game that drives me crazy. On the field he takes these huge strides, a latter-day Paul Bunyan in baseball spikes, and just when you think he's overrun the play he'll pounce, fluid as an alley cat, and scoop the ball with the softest hands you've ever seen. He has an average arm for a shortstop—I've always thought my arm was better—but he's so damn big it's impossible to knock him down if Brian is the relay man on a double play ball to second.

In the dugout I like to study the other team's pitcher, looking for any flaws or tip-offs in his delivery, but Tall Boy is a gabber. He'll play bench jockey, yelling out stuff to rile the guys on the field, or start in explaining one of his long, pointless theories to anybody willing to listen. If you didn't know better you'd think he wasn't paying any attention to the game at all. He once told me that when he's batting, even if there's a runner on second who can steal the other team's signs, he'd rather not know what pitch is coming next. I believe him. He has such a knack at the plate that he works best by simply reacting to whatever the pitcher throws.

Hitting, of course, is Tall Boy's forte. He stands in the box almost straight legged, bat cocked at an angle away from his back shoulder, and you'd swear any pitch over seventy miles an hour would blow right past him. But his step is a monster. He explodes through the ball and finishes in a neat little crouch, ready to spring out of the box and sprint to first. He's one of the new-wave shortstops in the Cal Ripken Jr. mold: a .290 hitter who can jack one with regularity. And the pièce de résistance, the one thing about Brian's game that I'd pay money to call my own: he's a switch-hitter with a dangerous swing from either side of the plate.

When I grow up I want to hit just like Brian "Tall Boy" Sloan.

I don't know why but nicknames on a baseball team are as common as stirrup socks. After our first week in camp, most of the guys had confessed to the nicknames they'd earned on other teams or we had collectively assigned new ones to those who wouldn't fess up. Some of them were obvious, a few obscure. There was Folgers of course, a middle relief pitcher from his days with the union players but the ace starter on our staff. One of the second basemen, Joe Hennessey, was a short, wiry guy from New Mexico. He had the strange habit of talking in exclamations, stressing everything he said like it was the punch line to a favorite joke. He owned up to the classic baseball nickname Hack because for the duration of his four years in semipro ball he was barely able to hit his weight. Then there was our right fielder, Clyde Voorhees, a surfer dude from California. He looked the part, too: tan, muscular, with perfect white teeth in a broad smile. We figured he could just as easily make the cover of a fashion magazine as he could make the team, so we all called him GQ. One of our starting pitchers, Miguel Martinez, wasn't even from the US originally. As a kid he came to the States with twenty other people from Cuba on a life raft with no food or water. He told us the trip took four days. Everyone called him Speedboat. One of our left fielders swore he didn't have a nickname and try as we might, we were never able to pin one on him either. Part of the problem was that he had one of the finest natural baseball monikers ever, received free of charge when Mr. and Mrs. Longo decided to name their future ballplayer Leonard. Talk about a name meant to be announced over a PA system: "Now batting—Lennn-ny Lonnn-go!" We finally gave up out of frustration and tabbed him the Player to Be Named Later.

All the guys assumed Brian got his nickname because he's six foot four. We didn't correct them. Actually he's had that name since high school, when his party drink of choice was Budweiser in the twenty-ounce cans. In the Midwest during the '80s, convenience stores sold the twenty-ouncers as single beers and everyone called them "tall boys."

Ever since we were kids, Brian has had a habit of doing things that both brag me up and embarrass me at the same time. When someone asked about my nickname Tall Boy said, "Are you kidding? Jake ought to be called *No Friggin' Way* because he does things at the hot corner you simply won't believe. He'll turn the DP, retie his shoes and break your sister's heart all before you've made it to first base. I've seen this man catch a full wineglass out of thin air without spilling a drop."

Honestly, the glass was only half full. One time the girl I dated before I dated the U-Haul secretary and I went out to a restaurant with Brian and Karen. Girlfriend got drunk and started telling a story with all these wild hand gestures, so it was just a matter of time before she connected elbow to wineglass. The thing went flying off the table tilted slightly sideways and I caught it on the stem, turned it right side up and put it back on the table without spilling anything. It was just anticipation, really.

"A full wineglass!" Tall Boy repeated to the guys in the locker room. "I wouldn't have believed it if I hadn't seen it myself. He has the fastest hands in the West."

We were standing about ten feet apart and to prove his point Brian turned us into a one-way juggling act, grabbing up and firing at me everything within his reach. In quick succession he threw a baseball, a roll of tape, a left-foot cleat, a balled-up pair of socks, a right-foot cleat, another baseball, an empty shampoo bottle, a catcher's shin guard, his hat, my glove, a jockstrap, and a third baseball. I caught and promptly dropped on the floor everything but the jockstrap, which I just dodged.

"Will you stop?" I finally asked.

Tall Boy shrugged. "Fastest hands in the West."

The guys all nodded, smiling.

My nickname came from our high school days too, and Tall Boy coined it himself. During our league championship game senior year, we were ahead by three in the last inning. The other team had a man on third with two outs when the batter hit a lazy, low fly ball down the left field line. Those little bloop shots, the ones that seem to be falling even before they reach the top of their arc, are known as dying quails. For my money a dying quail is the toughest play a third baseman has to make. You need quick reactions to read the ball coming off the bat, with a clean first step backward so your feet don't get crossed. Then you have to turn and look over your shoulder, keeping the ball in sight as you sprint away from the infield, like a wide receiver trying to track down a long pass. The problem is that the left fielder is watching the ball too, and he's running in as fast as you're running out. So it's not enough to get a good first step, or make a clean turn, or even have the speed to run the ball down. You have to commit yourself to the play at the crack of the bat and run balls-out, confident that either you or the left fielder will get there and make the catch before he slams into you blindside and bends your knee a direction it was never meant to go. Anyway, I did run the dying quail down that game our senior year and I was able to make the catch. I even avoided being blindsided, but as soon as I gloved the ball I stepped down a hole in the outfield grass, which sent me somersaulting over the sliding left fielder. When I finally stopped tumbling and still had the ball in my glove, it meant we had just won the league and were headed for the state tournament. Tall Boy, who had been chasing the play with me step for step, raced over and pulled me to my feet.

"Jake!" he yelled, loud enough for everyone to hear. "You're golden!"

From that day on, every time I've taken the field, those in the know have known me as Golden Jake Standen, third base.

MONDAY, FEBRUARY 27

The crowds at the stadium are starting to pick up, though the number of people in the stands on any given afternoon you could count between pitches during batting practice. They've been generally kind. You'll hear some lip now and again from a drunk or a punk, but it's nothing we can't ignore. The clubhouse guys assure us that spring training is always slow at first. Attendance will pick up once we start playing other teams at the end of the week.

Today I saw a kid sitting with a group of adults along the third-base rail, holding up a piece of cardboard somebody had scrawled on with Magic Marker. She was maybe ten—old enough to read the words, I guess, but probably too young to understand them. Her sign read: "This is real baseball." During a lull in practice I went over to say hello.

"Mister," she asked when I got close, "are you friends with Joe Carter? He's on this team, you know."

Carter had played out in real life every Little Leaguer's dream by hitting a World Series–winning home run in the ninth inning of game 6 against the Phillies in '93. I meant it when I told her that no, unfortunately, I'd never had the pleasure of meeting Joe Carter.

"Too bad," she said. "He's my favorite player."

The adults sitting around her were all wearing that tight-lipped, hope-my-kid-didn't-offend-you smile that parents of young children always seem to have on. Then I looked closely at her face. No jokes. No cynicism. Just a wide-eyed little girl who thought she might get to meet her baseball hero today.

"He's one of my favorites, too," I said, and I slipped a practice ball into the glove on her lap before jogging back to third.

Some days though, the few fans who do show up are a few too many for the sake of team pride. This afternoon during the intrasquad game there was a play on a ball to the left-center-field gap. The left fielder did well to track it down but then uncorked a monster toss that sailed over Brian's head as he ran out to get the cutoff. The second baseman was checking the runner coming around first, so he was turned the other direction when the ball came flying in and smacked him on the back of the head. It was actually a hell of a throw. The second baseman went down face first and was out cold a good five minutes. They carted him off to the local emergency room, where rumor has it he received several stitches and some heavy-duty aspirin. They told us the injury didn't look too serious but they would keep him in the hospital overnight to monitor the swelling.

The old cliché is true: you hate to see any player get injured, and of course everyone is hoping he'll come out okay—but, still. He is listed as a utility infielder, meaning he could make the roster at any infield position. If he can't return because of a concussion or whatever, that's one less guy I have to beat out for a spot on the team.

That Monday was a busy one for freak injuries, in part because the morning was warm but also because Coach Assenmacher had a maddening habit of making the same players run a drill over and over until everyone involved got it exactly. We were working on bunt defense with pitchers and infielders, and after five consecutive reps he still wasn't happy with a play on the right side where Folgers had to cover first. Then on the sixth, instead of following Assenmacher's bunt down the line like he was supposed to, Folgers simply fell off the pitching rubber and collapsed. When we reached the mound he was breathing heavy, sweat pouring down his face.

"Is it just me," Folgers asked, "or is it really dehydrated out here?"

Brian and I grabbed an arm each and EVAC-ed him, soldier style, to the trainer's room.

Of course the reporters ate it up. By the time we knocked off for the morning and made it back to the clubhouse, the newspaper and TV guys had swarmed Folgers by his locker. He looked pretty pale but seemed better. He gave us a wave as Tall Boy and I passed the mob. That night even ESPN did a short piece on Folgers, complete with clips of his days pitching for Seattle and the locker room interview.

And that's the one thing none of us ever talked about, though we all saw it in the papers and on TV: the sports commentators saying what a joke we were; how pathetic that a bunch of plumbers and roofers and furniture movers were there to replace the union guys. But every man on the Blue Jays' replacement roster had a solid baseball résumé. Many had pro experience from just a year or two previous. Walk through the clubhouse and you'd see hints of the history we all brought to the team. The lockers were huge—normally jammed, I'm sure, with all the stuff the union guys get free from sporting goods manufacturers. But with us there the lockers were mostly empty, and sitting on the shelves or hanging from the hooks were duffel bags and practice T-shirts representing almost every pro league in the country: Asheville Tourists, Toledo Mud Hens, Birmingham Barons, St. Paul Saints.

The sportswriters refused to admit that there was genuine talent on the replacement teams, players who had Major League skills in one aspect of the game or another. But we did have tools. The main difference between us and the union guys was that they play the game with three or four or five tools: maybe they hit for power or percentage, have sprinter's speed, boast a giant fielding range with a cannon for an arm. Most of us only had one tool.

My tool was made out of leather and fit over the left hand.

The afternoon of our injury-plagued practice, Coach Assenmacher ran infield drills right before we called it a day. His favorite drill was to grab a featherweight fungo bat and challenge each infielder with repeated grounders until you made a great play or took one in the chops trying. Either way, if he beat you or you beat him, Assenmacher never showed any emotion. He'd just grab another ball, yell out "next man!" and smoke a grounder somewhere else.

I was the last infielder to take balls that day and Assenmacher didn't bother hitting me any three hoppers. His first stroke was a liner in the hole that I snagged with a stab to my left. By the third ball he was giving it everything he had. There were maybe fifty people in the stands and they caught on pretty quick to our little battle. With each stop I made, they clapped and cheered, calling out my jersey number.

On the eighth ball Assenmacher hit an absolute rocket, a sinking line drive straight down the third-base line. When you're trying to field a ball moving as fast as Assenmacher hit that one, you literally don't have time to think through your options. You just let your reflexes take over and hope the assumptions you make about the ball's speed and trajectory turn out right. It looked like the ball would bounce in front of the bag, then rise at roughly the same angle as it headed for left field. That meant it should be shin high when it reached the point where I'd have the best chance to glove it behind third base. I started the play maybe fifteen feet from the foul line, so there was no way I could get my body in front of the ball before it would be past me. Instead, I took a slide step with my right foot, a crossover with my left, and launched myself toward the foul line.

As I left my feet, the ball did something I wasn't expecting. Instead of hitting the dirt in front of third, it thumped off the soft middle of the bag itself. The good news was that the padding took some of the steam off the line drive, giving me an extra fraction of a second to react. The bad news was that the ball took a bigger bounce than I'd anticipated. Rather than converging shin high, the ball and I would meet when it was about rib-cage height, and rather than me needing to fully extend my arm in front of me, the ball would actually be above my head. I was already committed to my lunge so as I flew through the air I shot my glove up over my head to where I thought the ball would be. Because I was airborne, the act of moving my hand from shin to waist height caused my whole body to spin clockwise about a quarter turn. Just as I was about to hit the ground, I felt the ball catch hard in the palm of my glove.

I doubt this counts as having a sixth sense but I've always been able, in the middle of a fall, to guess the fastest way to get off the ground and into position to make a throw. Once I had the ball in my glove, I realized that my midair quarter turn meant I would land on my right shoulder with enough momentum to spin one full rotation, and instead of facing the third-base dugout, I would end up facing almost directly toward home. I went into a shoulder roll and pulled my knees in so when I rolled to where I was facing the ground again my elbows and knees were under me. I pushed myself off the ground and up onto my left knee, with my right leg straight out behind to stop my momentum. Just for show I grabbed the ball out of my glove and fired a low liner to first base on one hop.

I hate to brag, but seriously—from the stands, that play had to look cool as shit.

The rest of the infielders, spectators themselves, whistled and clapped with the people in the seats. I heard one woman in particular, her voice a half note higher than the rest.

"God," she exclaimed, and then added, "Damn!"

When I looked over she seemed embarrassed, but I couldn't tell if it was from her inadvertent cursing or the fact that I'd heard. Regardless, she met my gaze with a steady look back.

"Nice play, Third Base," she called out.

Pretty brunette. Great smile. She was sitting alone, just above and a little left of the dugout, closer to the field than most of the other spectators. It was the usual spot for a player's girl to sit. *Somebody's wife*, I decided.

Assenmacher yelled, "Bring it in!" and picked up his gear. I tipped my cap bill and nodded to the woman, slapping little clouds of infield from my uniform as I jogged to the dugout with my teammates.

TUESDAY, FEBRUARY 28

We played another intrasquad game this afternoon. In a normal year with the union guys they have over fifty players in uniform during spring training, but since there are only forty guys in camp now and they'll be cutting us down from here, they didn't schedule any split squad games with other teams during the preseason. We found out why today: both sides were short on players, especially fresh pitchers. It didn't last but six innings. Felt great to do something besides run infield drills though.

There's a physical joy in fielding a chest-high two hopper three steps to your left, and that joy begins at the crack of the bat. As you see brown specks fly up from the home-plate dirt apron on the first hop, you already know where the ball will be once it gets to you. There's no hurry as you come out of the crouch and make your move left. Running is unnecessary—only rookies and fools would charge the short hop—just slide step and close, slide step and you're there as the ball takes its second bounce and rises to meet your glove. You register that familiar pull as it catches in your glove pocket, and you understand even before you reach in how those 108 stitches will feel when you grip the tight red seams, as if they matched the grooves in your fingertips like gears in a cog.

When your feet come together again your right cleat is already planted, already beginning the quick, explosive burst that will be your throw to first. You feel your muscles clench and release as the power rises up from ankle to calf, calf to quad, quad up through your back and then down the shoulder to your arm, a harnessing of all the energy of earth and sky. When you finally, fully uncoil, you stand perfectly balanced for just an instant on one leg, watching as the white streak connects your hand to the first baseman's glove in an arc so low it could be an arrow fired across the field instead of a baseball. You already know from ten thousand other throws to keep it down—anything over letter high and the first baseman's stretch is wasted. This time, though, he won't even need to reach. The play takes four, maybe five seconds pitch to putout, but from the instant bat meets ball, you are as certain as gravity that at the plate could be the fastest man on the planet and still your throw will beat him by a step and a half. It's a promise and a fulfillment, a complete conflict, climax and conclusion as natural as sex and as comfortable as the deep sleep after.

Folgers had recovered nicely from his dehydration spell but you wouldn't have known it from his pitching that day. He struggled with his control, which is a problem for any pitcher but especially for him. Folgers was well beyond the point in his career where he could blow fastballs by anyone, so having no control on his finesse pitches meant that he got shelled. He gave up five walks and four runs before they put somebody else on the mound at the end of the third.

According to pitchers and the fans who love them, a perfect game is when no opposing batter reaches base from start to finish. It doesn't matter how many strikeouts or pop-ups or grounders the pitcher induces; as long as no one gets on by hit, walk, or error, it's considered perfect. As far as fielders are concerned though, the perfectly pitched game would be three pitches every inning for nine innings, resulting in twenty-seven batted balls that make twenty-seven outs. We like pitchers who challenge hitters to swing the bat because walks and deep counts take a lot of time, and it's difficult to stay focused when your pitcher is having control problems. Still, you absolutely must stay focused when you're defending along the base paths because we infielders deal with a slightly elevated sense of occupational hazard: our lives are in danger. That may sound like hyperbole, but I'm serious. The pitcher's mound is sixty feet, six inches from the plate, and a third baseman playing regular depth stands roughly one hundred feet from the batter. Factor in a 90 mph pitch and a 100 mph bat swing and it's no stretch to say a baseball can travel from the pitcher's hand, off the hitter's bat, to one inch from your face in under two seconds. For obvious reasons then, you need to be on your toes, literally, for every pitch. I tend to lean forward on the balls of my feet and point my toes in a little just as the pitcher releases the ball because that gives me better balance to go either left or right. If one half inning of control-problem pitching takes fifteen minutes to play, that's a long-ass time to stand crouched and pigeon-toed over the course of a nine-inning game.

In the third inning, as Folgers struggled through yet another batter, Brian and I heard something you don't normally expect to hear in the middle of a ball game. Lenny Longo, the Player to Be Named Later, began singing in left field. At first I thought it might be musical sarcasm, Lenny's way of telling Folgers, "I'm so bored out here I'm doing show tunes to stay awake!" But he wasn't singing loud enough for anyone but Tall Boy and me and maybe the center fielder to hear. I'm not even sure he was conscious of doing it because when I glanced back between pitches Lenny stood with one leg set in front of the other, free hand in the palm of his glove, the very picture of outfielder concentration as he awaited Folgers's next delivery to the plate. He just also happened to be singing.

I was going to say something to him about it in the dugout during our next at bat, but then I thought better of it. For one thing his singing was helping my concentration by getting me out of my own head, giving me something else to focus on between pitches besides my aching arches. More to the point though, it wasn't just idle, tuneless humming. It was beautiful. I don't think I've ever heard anyone sing so softly, so well.

29

There was a power behind his voice, like an opera singer, that made you believe he could have filled the stadium and drowned out the fans if he were suddenly to throw open the vocal cord floodgates. But beyond that there was a certain joyful timbre in his tone, like a smile was planted somewhere deep inside his windpipe, and that smile came out with every note he sang. I honestly would have paid money to hear him sing on stage but thanks to Folgers's control problems, we were getting a private performance for free.

Lenny sang his way through several tunes that game, mostly country and western by the sounds of them. It wasn't my preferred music, but with that voice he could have sung acid rock lyrics and made them sound like lullabies. The one I remember best was a love song of sorts.

Diana Might

I asked Annie and she didn't say
A single word. She just walked away.
Susie said that she was true.
Linda laughed—ha!—not with you.
I never ever lowered my sights.
I moved on into the night.
I took a chance. I made an advance.
Now I think Diana might.

Diana might! I think we're close to the fuse.
Diana might! Blow away my blues.
Diana might! I hope she doesn't refuse.
Diana might, Diana might, Diana might!
We're wrapped together so tight.
Diana might! We might explode tonight. . . .
Here in this dim light
I think Diana might.

Cindy slapped me. Brenda booed.
From the way Alice acted I may get sued.
Teresa treated me like I wasn't there.
I kept on tryin'; I didn't care.
When I fine-ly saw Diana walk in
I knew that I had to try again.
Now I'm alone with her every night
And I think Diana might.

Diana might! I think we're close to the fuse.
Diana might! Blow away my blues.
Diana might! I hope she doesn't refuse.
Diana might, Diana might, Diana might!
We're wrapped together so tight.
Diana might! We might explode tonight. . . .
Here in this dim light
I think Diana might.

THURSDAY, MARCH 2

Had a full morning of practice with an intrasquad game in the afternoon, but everyone seemed a little flat. I think we were all just anxious: our first exhibition game is tomorrow against the Pirates. Like any other spring season, these games won't count for anything, but that doesn't mean they don't matter. Even during a normal year with the union guys, when a Major League team has an open position on the roster, they identify the players who have a shot during early spring practices and then make their final decisions based on who does what during the exhibition season. This year isn't any different, except that every position is an open position on the roster.

If the union guys are worried about us, you wouldn't know it by the negotiations. The players' rep, Donald Fehr, said in an interview yesterday that Bud Selig, the acting commissioner and mouthpiece for the suits, isn't serious about negotiating and that the union is prepared to walk away from the bargaining table in Tempe, Arizona, if they don't make substantial progress by the weekend. As far as anyone can tell, they haven't made substantial progress on anything since the strike started seven months ago.

We shouldn't be too surprised that the union players aren't taking us seriously; the owners aren't much better. We've heard reports that some teams left their Major League spring training facilities empty and have their replacement teams practicing on secondary fields or at minor league camps nearby. Some teams haven't even specified which players they signed for the replacement teams so the union guys won't know the replacements from the rest of the minor leaguers. The owners claim it's for the protection of the replacement players but it's a fine line between feeling protected and feeling like a redheaded stepchild.

My boys in Cincy have royally screwed their farm system trying to figure out what to do this spring. The Reds wanted to field a replacement team made up of regular minor leaguers, so they stocked their spring training camp with forty-four players from their farm system. That put the minor leaguers in a bind because the union has already said anyone who plays during a replacement game, even in an exhibition, will be considered a strike breaker and thus barred from joining the union if and when that player makes The Show after the strike. Naturally the suits in Cincinnati decided to make matters worse by giving their players an ultimatum: if they refused to play replacement games, the minor leaguers were told they would be sent home. Not fired, mind you, just sent home. But everyone knew that refusing to play would land you on a shit list of players who were "unwilling to act in the best interests of the organization." Good luck getting a serious shot at making the Major League club if your name ends up on that list.

What's a poor minor league slob supposed to do? You don't want to piss off the organization because without it you're out of a job. But you don't want to piss off the union either—even though as a minor leaguer the MLBPA doesn't represent you at all—because what happens when you do finally make it to the bigs and none of your teammates will talk to you since you've been branded a scab?

Because the exhibition season starts tomorrow, this morning was crunch time for the Reds' minor leaguers. The result was already the lead sports story by the time we turned on the TV in the clubhouse at lunch: exactly half the Reds' players decided to stay and play out the exhibition season; the other half walked. I completely understand the decision made by all forty-four of them.

All of this resulted in the most bizarre news yet. Because Cleveland has extra replacements in their camp, they offered a suddenly shorthanded Cincinnati team five players in exchange for "future considerations," which in baseball jargon means we'll scratch your back now if you'll scratch ours the next time we get an itch. Thus, the Indians and Reds made professional baseball history today by conducting the first transaction ever to involve replacement players, and the deal was a trade of five guys for none.

Though it was as nice a ball diamond as I'd ever played on, Grant Field at Dunedin Stadium had some quirks to it that the team was asked to address as the exhibition season approached. There was talk right from the start that we might not be allowed to play in Toronto if and when our regular season began. It had something to do with a local law against strikebreakers taking jobs while unionized labor was negotiating a new contract. So when they started inspecting Grant Field for its flaws, they did so with full knowledge that Dunedin might be where we played out our regular season schedule as well.

First and foremost they realized that the lighting, while good enough for the single-A Dunedin Jays who played there during the Florida State League season, was too dim for Major League night games in March. Instead of upgrading the lights however, they just rescheduled all our home games to start at 1:05 in the afternoon. That was fine by Tall Boy and me, as we had fallen into a daily routine from the previous two weeks of practice. Get up by eight o'clock for a morning workout, practice or play till midafternoon, then hit the weight room till we knocked off around dinnertime. Other than the midnight curfew the team imposed during the first few weeks, it was a lot like being back home working nine to five.

Some of the field dimensions weren't up to snuff, either. There's a mandate requiring the backstop at all Major League parks to be at least sixty feet from home plate and at Dunedin it was only fifty, but changing that would have meant reconfiguring the entire field, so it was left alone. Also, the wall down the right field foul line was only 315 instead of the Major League–minimum 320 feet from home plate, but in right a ten-foot-high chain-link fence topped the eight-foot wooden wall that ran the length of the outfield, so they decided the extra height made up for the lack of proper distance and left that alone as well.

As part of the old contract with the union guys, all Major League diamonds except Chicago's ivy-famous Wrigley Field are required to have padding on the outfield walls. Since we weren't union though, they didn't worry about that rule at Dunedin. Just as well in my opinion, because padding would have covered the colorful signs painted along the fence, the one detail about that brand-new concrete-and-steel complex that suggested an old-time, throwback ball field. In among the usual signage for oil change shops and pizza places was my favorite: a billboard for a local restaurant enticed readers to "Try Molly Goodhead's grouper sandwich!" Simply changing *grouper* to *groupie* provided Tall Boy and me with endless one-liners about the actual services provided by the sultry-named Miss Goodhead.

The most drastic change required of our spring training home was due to its most unique feature. The powers that be decreed that the warning track would have to be "softened" with dirt, since the original track was made up of crushed seashells. It wasn't as strange as it might sound at first blush. The shells were ground to a fine powder, and though they were a bit rough against the skin of an unsuspecting outfielder, why waste dirt when you could use an unwanted by-product of the Tampa-St. Pete beaches fifteen miles away?

Ultimately, the only significant change they made was to raise the foul poles down both lines an extra twenty feet. How that change addressed any of the other problems with the field was a mystery to all of us. Still, the ballpark, like our team, seemed as ready as it would ever be for the exhibition season.

That night before our first game I got antsy with nervous energy, so while Tall Boy made his regular call home to Karen, I started packing my duffel with the things I'd need for the next day. Along with an extra T-shirt and socks in case it was hot, a new pair of batting gloves I'd bought for the occasion, and a change of clothes for the bus ride back after the game, I made sure to put Mike Schmidt in the side pocket of my travel bag.

At the start of my junior season at OSU, Tall Boy sent me a Mike Schmidt rookie card, mint condition, encased in plastic. Schmidt had made all-American at third base for Ohio University before starting a career with the Phillies that would take him all the way to Cooperstown. On the back of the card Tall Boy had taped a note that read, "If this bum can make it from college ball in Ohio to the bigs, what's your problem?" I stuck the Schmidt card in my locker before the first game of the season, more as a reminder of Tall Boy's thoughtfulness than anything else. That afternoon I scored three runs, went four for five with three RBI, and made seven putouts from third base. It was hands down the best game of my college career. Needless to say, I didn't play another game without Mike Schmidt sitting somewhere in my locker.

I've always thought it was a little too pat to say that ballplayers are superstitious by nature. Superstitions are for old ladies and simple minds. Only a fool believes that throwing salt over a shoulder or avoiding black cats can somehow convince the fates to change the way things are supposed to turn out. Shit happens because shit happens, and hexes or curses or good luck charms have as little effect as making the sign of the cross before stepping into the batter's box. I seriously doubt God gives a damn if you advance the runner or strike out looking.

But, still. Those same fates, or God, or whatever it is that watches over baseball had been mighty kind to Mike Schmidt in his career, and baseball is built around tendencies. If a person tends to have a good game with a certain baseball card tucked in his locker, why take chances?

FRIDAY, MARCH 3

A short practice this morning, then took a bus to Bradenton for our first exhibition game against Pittsburgh. McKechnie Field, where the Pirates hold spring training, is a beautiful place to play ball. I'd guess it opened just a few years back—the locker room was clean and modern—but the park itself has an ancient, grand look. Along the top of the stadium is a giant white facade, and dark-green seats are lined up under a matching green patchwork of metal overhangs. It looks like something out of a Hollywood movie about baseball in the '20s. One of the Pirates' players told me they had bunting and balloons along the field railing for their opener against the Twins yesterday. And the clubhouse guys were right: there must have been 1,500 people in the stands, ten times the biggest crowd we've had for any practice at Dunedin.

The game itself was pretty loose. None of the coaches seemed too uptight about winning as much as just seeing how we played together. A lot of substitutions and double switches between innings. We lost, 3–2. From here on we'll play exhibition games most every day until the season starts in a month.

Pittsburgh's pitching seemed a lot like ours. Nobody threw ninety-nine miles per hour. They were mostly guys with good control, throwing mid- to upper-80s. Brian got a hit, scored a run. I played third for five innings: popped out, struck out, then sat out.

I know some people think that baseball is dull and that it looks easy to anyone who doesn't know the game, but Ted Williams was right: hitting a ball thrown with the intention to deceive you, using a round stick of wood not three feet long, is the hardest skill there is in any sport. Ask Deion Sanders or Michael Jordan which game is the toughest to master. If an NFL wide receiver only catches three of every ten passes thrown his way, he'll be riding the bench all year long. If an NBA player only sinks three of every ten shots he takes, he'll be selling insurance next season. But if a guy in The Show fails to get a hit 69 percent of his trips to the plate, he's probably having a career year.

I batted sixth in the lineup today. There was a man on second with one out when I came up in the fourth, Pittsburgh leading 2–1. I've always been a count hitter; it just makes sense to go up ready for a particular pitch, maybe a slider that forgets to slide, and if you don't get it, you take the first few. That way you can see what kind of stuff the pitcher's got and look for a fat one if you get him deep in the count. I started out that way, and the pitcher nibbled at the plate. First pitch: fastball low and inside. With a guy on second, my job is to drive in the runner or at least move him over to third. No need to fish for low pitches inside, so I let it go for ball one. The second pitch was up, but I wasn't expecting another fastball—strike, inside corner.

Now I'm ready to take my cuts. With a one-one count on two fastballs in, it's a fair bet that the next pitch will be off-speed and away. The runner on second is our right fielder. He's got good wheels. With me in the right-hander's box it makes the catcher's throw to third more difficult, but in this situation—down by a run and a pitcher with a quick delivery on the mound—my guy won't try to steal third. Still, it is the exhibition season. A sacrifice bunt or even a run-and-hit are possible. The third-base coach gives me the "swing away" sign.

The next pitch is outside, as I expected, but he surprises me with another fastball. It seems like a mistake since I'm trying to slap one to the right side to move the runner over, but the speed fools me. I only get a piece of it and hit a weak squibbler foul of first base. A ball and two strikes. Time to get conservative, protect the plate.

This is the same pitcher and catcher who got me to pop out to end the first inning so they should remember the third pitch of that at bat, when I got a slider down but over the plate. I've always liked sliders. You can spot them right away because the rotation it takes to throw one forms a white dot surrounded by spinning red seams in the middle of the ball as it comes in. If you see the dot, you can anticipate where the pitch is going, and if you know the location, you've got the advantage even before you've started to swing. In my first at bat I drilled that slider down the right field line, landing just foul about fifty feet beyond first. He doesn't want to give me that pitch again. Plus he's ahead in the count so he can waste one if he wants. I'm guessing fastball up and in.

With all the things I try to keep in mind when I'm at the plate, I sometimes forget the golden rule of hitting: think long, think wrong. The guy threw me a thigh-high slider on the outside corner, just the way I like 'em, and I missed it by a foot. Strike three, fuck me, sit your ass down.

Where are you when I need you, Mike Schmidt?

Despite all their bitching to the contrary, pitchers have every advantage when it comes to the pitcher-hitter matchup. As a hitter all you have is a bat, a helmet, and any information the guys who have already been up to the plate can bring back to the dugout. But how does the sentence "His fastball is really sinking today" compare with all the advantages a pitcher has?

First, only he and the catcher know what pitch is coming next, and the pitcher doesn't even need to think that through if he doesn't want to; the catcher can call the type and location of every pitch the entire game and the pitcher just has to throw it. Plus, the pitcher can scuff or cut or grease the ball any one of a hundred ways to make it dance or dive at the plate. What's a hitter going to do, put more pine tar on the bat for extra distance? And of course the pitcher has seven other guys behind him, and the catcher in back of home plate, to help when the batter puts the ball in play. When you're the hitter, forget the team concept. It's just you against the world, baby, and the world can't wait to see you fail.

Even the way baseball announcers talk about the pitch count is predisposed to favor the pitcher. Everybody knows you need four balls to earn a walk but the pitcher needs just three strikes for an out. Yet what do announcers say when you have a two-ball, two-strike count? They call that *even*, as in: "The count is even at two and two." Bullshit. That ain't even. Three balls and two strikes is even. Two balls and one strike, one ball and no strikes—that's even. With a 2-2 count you're still two balls away from a free pass but just one strike shy of being branded a defensive specialist.

37

There wasn't any rah-rah stuff after the game, no coach's assessment of how we played and what we should work on for next time like we got in college. Everyone just showered and changed, then packed up for the trip home.

On the bus back to Dunedin Tall Boy was his usual pain-in-the-ass self. He knew I was pissed about my hitting—I had left three runners on base in a game we lost by one—so he decided to yank my chain by telling the guys sitting around us about his mother's scouting report on my batting skills back in the day.

The two of us were on the same teams every summer growing up, so of course Mrs. Sloan had watched me play all those years right beside her son. She even got to know most of the girls I dated at school but in the spring of our senior year I started seeing someone from another district. Mrs. Sloan caught me talking to this mysterious new girl between innings at one of our games and she quizzed Brian about it as they drove home that night.

"That's Candi," he told her. "Jake's new girlfriend."

"She's pretty," Mrs. Sloan said.

"She won the Miss Teen Ohio pageant last winter."

Mrs. Sloan seemed surprised. "Jake's girlfriend won a pageant?"

"Yeh."

"A beauty queen is dating Jake?"

"Yeh, Ma. What's the problem?"

Mrs. Sloan was quiet a moment, puzzled.

"But why?" she finally blurted out. "He can't hit."

As it turned out, Mike Schmidt came through for me at Saturday's game in a way I hadn't expected. We played Pittsburgh at home and won, 7–5. I started and stayed in through the fifth. I was a little better at the plate: grounded into a 4-6-3 DP my first trip up, but in my last at bat I hit a sacrifice, scoring the runner from third on a long fly to left. Then, as I was jogging back to the bench, I saw her again—the "goddamn" woman. She was sitting by the railing just to the outfield side of our dugout. When I caught her eye she gave me a wave.

"How you doin', Third Base?" she called.

Coach Didier made some switches, changed pitchers and put another guy at third after our turn at bat. I was done for the day so between innings I walked over to where she sat.

"Which one is yours?"

The afternoon sun was full in her face and she squinted down at me. "I'm sorry?"

"Your husband," I explained. "Figured a pretty woman, sitting alone by our dugout in spring training, must be married to some lucky stiff on my team."

"Oh." She looked away and then back. "No. Just had the afternoon off, so I thought I'd come see what a replacement baseball game looks like."

"Just like the real thing, without all those home runs and great catches to get in the way."

"You've made some nice plays. It's Jake, right? Or no—" She cleared her throat and did an imitation of the PA announcer. "Jake-ake-ake, Standen-den-den."

"Number eighty-three in your programs." I tipped my cap. "Number one in your hearts."

She offered a hand across the railing. "I'm Sadie."

I was prepared to make small talk, had in fact a repertoire of opening lines collected from years of talking to women beside baseball diamonds, but she seemed willing to keep the conversation going without any of my standard prompts.

"I was wondering about that," she said. "Is it normal for major leaguers to wear jersey numbers in the seventies and eighties?"

It was a loaded question; she knew her stuff.

"Naw, they were saving these numbers, wouldn't let the union guys touch 'em. This way it'll be easier to retire our jerseys. You know, when we all wind up in the Hall of Fame."

Sadie nodded, still smiling. "You guys play every day?"

"Play? This is work! I'm at the office right now." I made a motion to straighten my tie, found my hand empty, shrugged. "Most every day. We're in Plant City tomorrow and I think Clearwater day after, but if you're free Tues—"

She cut in before I could offer up my comp tickets.

"I work afternoons during the week."

I glanced back toward the field. The next inning was about to start and Assenmacher had already barked at some of the guys for wandering around while the game was on.

"I better get back," I told her. "It was nice meeting you."

She replied in such a clipped way that I couldn't mistake it for anything but a dismissal.

"Likewise," she said.

I nodded and smiled, jogging back to the bench before Assenmacher could notice I was missing. I wasn't hurt or even surprised really. Under the best circumstances my success rate with women at the ballpark is about equal to my success against right-handed pitching: a tick over .250, give or take. The only way to handle a called third strike is to shake it off and be ready when your next at bat comes around.

Then again, Wally Pipp proved that a wise ballplayer should never make assumptions. At the end of the next inning one of the clubhouse guys came into the dugout and handed me a note.

I'll try to make it Tuesday. If not, how about next weekend? and then a phone number. At the bottom she had signed it: Sadie Holder.

I ducked my head around the side of the dugout but she was already gone.

MONDAY, MARCH 6

We beat the Reds 5–3 on Sunday, then lost to Philly in Clearwater this afternoon, 3–2. I was part of a late double switch; played third the last three innings, one at bat, grounded out to short. Season to date: eight at bats, one single, one sacrifice, one RBI, one run scored.

It was odd to find myself in the game against Cincinnati Sunday. For maybe the first time since we started playing other teams, I understood what some of the naysayers have been saying about replacement ball. I tried to get excited at the sight of those uniforms, the stitched red C on the white caps they wore for the game, but I couldn't pretend this was the same club I cheered as they won the '90 World Series by sweeping Oakland in four straight. There was no Barry Larkin making diving stops at short, no Chris Sabo playing a gritty third base in his space goggles, no

Jose Rijo and the Nasty Boys throwing aspirins in from off the mound. There was plenty of talent on the field, and it was a tight game all the way to the end, but mostly they were a collection of guys you never heard of, much like the team I play for.

Still, the game's the thing. Even the coaches are starting to loosen up in the clubhouse now that we're playing every day. Before today's game Coach Assenmacher walked to the middle of the locker room, stood up on a chair and officially declared Folgers the magistrate of our team's monkey court. Some of the guys (me included) didn't understand, so Folgers and Assenmacher explained the pro ball tradition.

Each team polices itself, handing out five- and ten-dollar fines for things like missing the team bus or swinging at a pitch when the third-base coach gave you the "take" sign—any bonehead mistake made on or off the field during the season. Folgers said it was all done in fun, the point being a few laughs as much as the money the court takes in, which he'll use for a party or maybe gag gifts for the coaches, whatever we all decide on at the end of the season.

Folgers's first act as monkey court judge was to name me "Official Timekeeper of the Game That Has No Clock." I was very honored, and I promised my constituents I'd perform the appointed duties to the best of my ability. Tonight I'm making a cardboard sign for above my locker that will read: "DAYS TILL WE'RE LEGIT." I've already checked the calendar. On April 3, twenty-eight days from now, the Blue Jays are scheduled to open the season against the Seattle Mariners. If the strike is still on and we're still here come day 28, we'll be honest-to-God Major League baseball players.

They say the first responsibility of a soldier in the field, not only for his own benefit but for the sake of his brothers in arms, is to take good care of his feet. It makes sense when you figure that a guy can't be much of a foot soldier if his feet are shredded from blisters and fungus. On a ball diamond my biggest hygiene priority has always been to protect my pits from chaffing because, including pregame warm-ups, it's not unusual to get sweaty in the field and then sit long enough to cool off again eight or ten times a game. You won't be much of a third baseman if it hurts every time you raise your arms to catch or throw. With that thought in mind

41

I walked back down the tunnel of the visitors' dugout prior to the Phillies game on Monday to change my undershirt after we had run through our warm-ups. When I entered the locker room I could hear someone at the urinals in the far corner of the clubhouse.

"Vamos, que se hace tarde!" I heard someone call out. "Vaya!"

As I got closer I saw a crown of curly black hair just visible above one of the walls dividing the urinals. It was Miguel Martinez, our Cuban-born pitcher.

"Speedboat?" I called. "Aren't you pitching today?"

The divider was about five foot tall, and Speedboat was maybe five foot three in cleats. He made a half turn in the stall and I could see one eye peeking over the urinal wall.

"Golden Jake!" he called back. "Sí, I am pitcher, but I can't go! I can no do it!"

We had played three games already but Speedboat was a starting pitcher. I hadn't thought about it till just then, but he was making his first appearance against live competition. Maybe this was the pitchers' version of stage fright.

"What do you mean? You don't want to take the mound? Does the crowd bother you?"

"No," he answered. "The crowd es no problem. I mean I can't go! I have no pee. My insides want to go but here I am, and—no pee!"

"You've got to be . . ." I started, and then trailed off. I knew he wasn't kidding. Like many people in the middle stages of learning a second language, Speedboat didn't really know enough English yet to spend much time mincing his words.

"Help me, Golden Jake!" he called out.

I was stumped. The thought occurred to me that, if we were playing in Dunedin, I could call the old folks' home across the street from the stadium and ask what they do when their patients have this problem, but we were in Clearwater and there were no geriatrics nurses in sight. Still, I had to think of something. The game was about to start, and there would be no time to get another pitcher warmed up.

"What can I do? Tell me how to help."

"I don't know!" Speedboat cried out. "Es the worse. Do something!"

Speedboat's cleats made a metallic clomping sound against the cement floor as he hopped from foot to foot. That gave me an inspiration. We were in a locker room after all, and the one thing other than sex that always made me want to go was close at hand. I walked to the nearest sink.

"How's this?" I asked hopefully, turning the faucet on full blast.

For a moment all was silent except the sound of running water. Then Speedboat let out another cry.

"Es not enough! Keep trying!"

In a panic I ran along the wall of sinks, cranking the handles at each faucet. When I reached the last sink I kept on going right into the shower stalls. I didn't have hands enough to both turn the water handles and aim the showerheads. The first blast knocked off my hat, and by the time I had all the showers going, I was half soaked. A cloud of billowing steam followed me out of the stalls when I reemerged from the shower room.

The crown of Speedboat's head bobbed merrily above the urinal wall.

"Jake!" he sang out. "It works!"

Considering I was already wet, I decided to go back and turn off the showers before changing my clothes. When I emerged a second time from the shower room, there was Speedboat in the middle of the clubhouse, a grin across his tan face.

"My friend, you make me want to go." He stood on his tiptoes and clapped me on both shoulders. "You are truly golden!"

With that he turned and clomped out of the room, up the tunnel to the visitors' bench and out into the bright sunshine, where the national anthem was just starting over the PA system.

TUESDAY, MARCH 7

Played the Reds again this afternoon in Dunedin, lost 4–3. I was at third for five innings, two at bats. Grounded into a fielder's choice my first time up, then hit a clean single to center in the fifth. Before his first pitch to the next batter, the pitcher made a pickoff move to first. I dove back in and was safe by a half foot, but the ump shot me down. He was out of position and didn't see my hand hit the bag. Assenmacher was the first-base coach and he gave the ump some hell. Between innings I heard him make a point of telling Coach Didier that it was a bad call; I had been safe.

I've often wondered what drives someone to be an umpire. It's a strange job, if you think about it. As prerequisites go I might actually be good at it, since one of an ump's most difficult tasks is to anticipate the flow of play and get in the best position to make a call on the close ones. I think the same anticipation I've developed from years as a player would help me to do it as an ump. But I also think an umpire's job is like being a politician: no matter how serious you took the work or how effectively you performed your job, you'd go to the office each day knowing that at least half the people out there would hate you for your decisions, even the ones you got right.

Umps do receive grudging respect from players on the field. It's a lot like how you treat cops or court judges; you may not like the person or what they have to say, but you'd better honor the authority because they can make your life miserable if they want. Most players call the umps "Blue"—as in, "How many outs, Blue?"—because that's the standard color of a professional umpire's uniform. There's an ascending scale of respect in addressing umps though, depending on how much you want them to consider your side. If you need a moment after skinning your knee sliding hard into a base, you might ask, "Time out, sir?" Disputing a ball-strike call, an appeal players universally try to avoid for its potential to anger an ump, requires even more solicitude. I once heard a catcher ask the ump after he called a close pitch a ball: "Was that strike high or outside, Mr. Umpire?"

I've been thrown out of a game exactly once, because I forgot the connection between ump-address and ump-respect. My junior year at Ohio State, I'd already had a crap game—0 for 3, plus an error in the field that cost us a run—when the ump called a strike on a borderline pitch. The pitcher then threw the exact same thing and got the exact same call, so I let the bat slump off my shoulder and bent down, asking as I looked over the mysterious strike zone, "C'mon, Ump. What are you, blond?" I thought it was a pretty good line but the guy working the plate that day actually had blond hair, and he was not amused. "That's it," he said, pointing to the dugout. "You're gone."

Umpires can also surprise you in good ways, when you get a glimpse at the man beneath the uniform. In Sunday's game against the Reds in Plant City, I scored from second on a hit to center field. I was busting ass down the third-base line when the home-plate ump passed me, jogging in the other direction to be in position if a play at third developed. He said just one word but it was unmistakable, the meaning perfectly clear: "Cadillac," he told me, and repeated it to make sure I heard. "Cadillac." He knew that because the play was behind me I couldn't see where the ball was, but he wanted me to know I could ease up and still score. Considering players pull muscles, even blow out ACLs simply by running full speed when their legs aren't sufficiently loose, I thought that was a generous piece of information for him to pass along. And if you only had one word to offer, what better word would express the thought that the hard times are behind you and you can coast in from here? Cadillac.

I got a chance to talk to some of Cincinnati's players around the batting cage before today's game. These are the same guys who defied the players' union by staying on with the team even though, as part of the Reds' minor league system, they'll be branded scabs if the strike ends. No one came right out and said it but I got the impression they were a little pissed at the attitude of their coaches toward the whole replacement experiment. One guy told me their manager, Davey Johnson, had taken to leaving practice in the mornings so he could go fish in a little pond behind the left field wall at their park in Plant City. They were all laughing about the fact that, no matter how the strike turns out, at least they got to meet a celebrity; earlier in the week the Reds signed Pedro Borbon to a contract. Borbon had been a star pitcher for Cincy during the Big Red Machine days in the '70s. Someone said he was forty-eight years old.

One guy told me this story he'd read in the news from back home about Opening Day in Cincinnati. It was a tradition for a military officer to come down from Wright-Patterson Air Force Base in Dayton and sing the national anthem during Opening Day ceremonies. This year though, the Department of Defense decided that they wouldn't send a singer as they didn't want to appear like they were choosing sides in the labor dispute. I asked him if, since it already was a tradition and they weren't going to send someone this year because of us, didn't that mean that they *were* choosing sides?

"Fuck the fly boys," my buddy said. "I just want to play ball."

We had an afternoon game scheduled with the Rangers on Wednesday but by eleven o'clock the rain was coming down so hard everyone knew we were looking at a rainout. We weren't allowed to leave though, until the umpires officially called the game, so we sat around the clubhouse most of the afternoon waiting for the obvious. At one point while we were still picking over the lunch spread, I heard Folgers say, "No shit!" and then he turned to Tall Boy and me.

"Gents, our esteemed colleague from Cuba here says he doesn't know how to play poker. Have you ever heard of anything so un-American in your life?"

Folgers and Speedboat had been assigned the same hotel room when they checked into spring camp with the rest of the pitchers and catchers. Though they made a strange pair, there was something apropos about the oldest and youngest players on the team being put together. They were already close friends.

"Oh, Speedboat," Tall Boy agreed. "You're gonna apply for US citizenship, right?"

Speedboat nodded.

"Poker questions will be on the test."

Speedboat looked nervous. "Really?"

"Not to worry, son," Folgers said, producing a pack of cards from somewhere deep in his locker. "We're here to help."

I was happy to join in Speedboat's poker initiation. You can play beside a group of guys an entire season before getting to know them as well as you can after a few hours of cards. We freed up one of the tables holding the lunch buffet, and Hack Hennessey joined us as we sat down to play. While Hack explained to Speedboat the difference between a straight and a flush, I asked Folgers about his time in pro ball.

"Not much of a story really," he said. "Though there's plenty of plot. I married the prettiest girl in town right out of high school and started pitching at a junior college in Athens, Alabama. A scout from the Braves came by to catch a game one time. Just so happens I struck out thirteen that day. Next day I've got a contract in one hand and a bus ticket to God-knows-where, South Carolina, in the other. You ready to give it a try, Speedboat?"

Folgers scooped up the cards laid out in front of Hack and began to shuffle.

"Dollar gets you in the game, gentlemen. So I spent three seasons in the Braves farm system, then got traded to the Brewers. I think I was in double-A by then. I was there four weeks and they shipped me to the Mariners. They moved me up to triple-A and sent me to the Cubs. Cubs sent me down to double-A and then traded me back to the Mariners. No, wait—was that the Cubs or the Mets? Ah hell, who can remember? Somewhere along in there it seemed like I stopped pitching for any one team in particular and found myself in the rotation of the Journeymen All-Stars. Have fastball, will travel."

We played the first hand and sure enough, Speedboat won. Beginner's luck.

"So you started out a power pitcher?" Hack asked.

"You know it." Folgers nudged Speedboat with his elbow. "Didn't we all?"

Speedboat just grinned.

"At the age of eighteen I could throw you seven innings of ninety-five-mile-an-hour heat and then give you twenty one-armed push-ups after the game. Coaches all told me I was gonna be the next Nolan Ryan. Shitfire, but I sure wanted that to be true."

Speedboat won the next hand as well and I figured the lessons had worked.

"These are real dollars I'm losing here," I protested. "Quit giving him all the good cards."

Hack again: "So are you trying to tell us you ain't Nolan Ryan?"

"I did my damnedest to be just like him," Folgers answered. "He was one mean SOB on the mound, the kind of guy who'd get in your face if you got so much as a single off him. And he'd make you think the next time he might just stick a fastball in your ear as payback. It'll shock you boys to hear this, considering the mild-mannered pitcher you see before you now, but I started out like that, too—all piss and vinegar. It got me all the way up to The Show with Seattle, that attitude. Then my wife left me. After eight years of minor league travel and minor league pay, she leaves me the first time I get called up."

"Ouch," Tall Boy sympathized.

"What's worse," Folgers continued. "The very next season she started dating this procession of milquetoasts, ya know? I don't mean they were fags or anything, but the guys she was going out with, they were definitely on the tofu side of manly. That just got under my skin. There I was on the mound in the Kingdome acting like I was some hard-ass flame-thrower, and I couldn't even win my own wife away from these froufrou boys. And the whole time I'm wondering—who am I putting on this dog-and-pony show for? I wasn't Nolan Ryan. I wasn't mad at anybody. I just wanted my wife back.

"So after the second call-up they tell me I'd lost the fire, that I needed to go down to Calgary for another season. When you've been in the minors as long as I had, they won't tell you when it's time to quit. They just stop giving you reason to hope. I'd already spent part of four seasons in Calgary; I knew nothing good was gonna come from a fifth. That's when I decided to hang 'em up."

"And the wife?" Tall Boy asked.

"Divorced me so she could marry a real estate agent in Portland."

"At least you got us," Hack said.

Folgers smiled. "Shitty trade."

We played another hour or so, swapping money and stories back and forth. Folgers got on a losing streak toward the end and just after he'd lost a big pot, one of the clubhouse guys came down the tunnel from the field.

"That's it," he announced to the room. "They just called it."

Folgers, dejected, threw his cards on the table. "Well damn, boy! We've been waiting to hear you say that all afternoon. Where were you thirty dollars ago?"

It was about five thirty when we got back to the hotel. I decided to give that brunette I'd met at the field on Saturday a call. She hadn't shown up to Tuesday's game and I didn't want to wait till the weekend just to talk to her again. Besides, I figured out a long time ago that girls like it when you call unexpectedly to ask them out. It's a matter of appearing eager without being threatening. Makes them feel like you've been thinking about them—which, of course, you have.

I didn't know if she lived alone or what, so when a woman answered I asked for her by name: Sadie Holder. Thank God she wrote it down with her number. I suck at names.

"I'll see if she's in," the woman said. "May I ask who's calling?"

"This is Jake Standen. We met, umm—I play for the Toronto Blue Jays."

I almost bit my tongue on the last part; it came out sounding so pretentious. Still, it was true. In fact I think that was the first time I'd ever identified myself that way: *I play for the Toronto Blue Jays.* I was going to have to get used to saying that.

The woman said "Oh!" and gave a quick laugh. "Hi, Jake Standen. This is Sadie. I'm sorry; I didn't recognize your voice."

"Ah, the old fake-roommate trick. Used it myself many a time."

"How are you?"

"I'm hungry. Any chance I might buy you dinner tonight?"

She laughed again. "So much for small talk. Isn't it tradition for the boy to banter idly a moment before he invites the girl to dinner?"

"I'm saving all my idle banter for the first course. Will you be having soup or the salad this evening?"

"Dinner sounds good," she said. "But I have to run some errands first. How about if you call me back around seven o'clock?"

"How about if you call me when your errands are done?"

"How about I call you when my errands are done," she echoed.

"Around seven o'clock?"

"Around seven o'clock."

So our conversation over the railing at Saturday's game hadn't been a fluke. I liked the way she talked. It seemed like I could throw anything her way and she would pick right up on it. I gave her the hotel number and our room extension.

While Tall Boy made a call back home I hopped in the shower, which did me no good because when I came out he was through talking with Karen and wanted to go for a run.

"Why didn't you say something before I got cleaned up?"

"Don't panic, Golden J," he answered. "Showers come free with the room. You'll take another when we get back. Let's go."

49

I figured I had an hour to kill and a date to look forward to, so I agreed. We headed out to a school a few blocks away that Brian had discovered the day before. The sign by the entrance claimed the place was a middle school but it must have been built as a high school, because it had a full-sized track around a football field in back that they left open for the community to use after school hours. There were maybe two dozen people walking and jogging the asphalt oval as we started our run, but once the sun went down most of them left and eventually we had the place to ourselves.

Tall Boy is one of those freaks who actually enjoy working out. I've never minded hitting the weights if I have somebody to lift with, but running is a different story. The only part I like about running is when I get to stop. Tall Boy knows this of course, so he tortures me by starting out slowly and then upping the pace every half mile. We ran four miles that night and by the last lap he was so close to sprinting I couldn't tell the difference. He can be a real ass sometimes.

We walked another lap to cool down from our run, and then Tall Boy said he wanted to do a few wind sprints. I told him that sounded sadistic and headed back to the hotel. When I got in, the light on our phone was blinking. I had to read the directions printed along the side of the phone to figure out how to listen to voice messages.

"Hi, Jake. Sadie here. It's seven o'clock and you're not in. Where did you go? I'll be around another fifteen minutes or so, and if I don't hear from you I'll probably head out again. Sorry I missed you."

The radio clock on top of the TV read 7:24.

When I dialed Sadie's number and got her answering machine, I said all the right things—it was my fault; sorry I was late; call me back; I still want to do dinner—but I knew it was useless. She had given up on me and found something else to do with her evening.

I was pissed off but I couldn't decide who exactly I was pissed at. True, it was dumb of me not to leave the track sooner because I knew it was getting close to seven. But if Tall Boy hadn't dragged me out to go run, I would have stuck around the room and been there when she called. And if he hadn't tried to kill me by sprinting the last lap, I wouldn't have needed to walk a quarter mile to cool down and I could have gotten back to the hotel on time.

On the other hand, it was a little unsettling how quickly Sadie had written me off. Did she have that many Wednesday dinner date offers to choose from? Maybe she thought I wasn't really interested so she was ditching me before I had a chance to ignore her. That seemed unlikely though, since I was the one who had called in the first place. I realized she knew as little about me as I knew about her, but I didn't think it would've been that hard for Sadie to put herself in my shoes. It wasn't like I had a life in Dunedin, Florida, beyond spring training. If she was afraid I would stand her up, what else did she think I was going to do? Besides, I thought she was a baseball fan, and like I said on the phone, I played for the Toronto Blue Jays. Didn't that fact in itself buy me more leeway than a quarter of an hour?

Fuck. Fifteen minutes. What was up with that?

THURSDAY, MARCH 9

We lost a wild one to the Cardinals today in St. Petersburg, 4–3. I played the first five innings, went oh for two from the seven spot. It was just as well I got taken out because our pitcher got into a beanball contest with the St. Louis pitcher toward the end. Coach Didier gave the ump so much hell he got tossed out of the game. That may have been the replacement ump's fault as much as Didier's, though. Lost in all the talk about the players' strike is the fact that the owners have locked out the Major League umpires this spring due to a different collective bargaining dispute. A group of local college and independent league umps have been working our games.

In the fourth inning the Cards' third baseman crushed a dinger that was still rising as it cleared the left-center wall. When he came up to bat again in the seventh, our pitcher drilled him with a fastball in the ribs. I was sitting a few feet down the bench from Coach Assenmacher when he turned to Coach Didier.

"That'll be trouble."

"Who do you think they'll go for?" Didier asked.

Assenmacher thought it over a second. "Longo."

It's standard practice for teams to protect the best hitters in their lineup, and the Cardinals knew our pitcher had beaned their biggest batter on purpose as retaliation for hitting the home run. So logic dictates that the Cards' pitcher would in turn throw at our heavy hitter, in retaliation for the retaliation. Our big bat is Lenny Longo, the left fielder. Sure enough, when Lenny went up to the plate the next inning, he took a fastball right above the knee. The umpire did what he was supposed to: he warned both benches that he would run the next pitcher to throw at a batter. But then our next hitter went up, their pitcher sailed a ball past his ear and the ump didn't do anything. Coach Didier started riding his ass after that and by the top of the ninth, the ump was so frazzled that he missed a call on a close play at home to end it. Didier went out to argue, and the ump promptly threw him out of a game that was already over.

I know it sounds weird but when Lenny got hit on the knee this afternoon and went sprawling on the ground in pain, I was jealous. He's our cleanup batter, the four man, the guy most likely to hit a homer whenever he steps to the plate. More important though, is the respect that that power commands. It means that he is comparable, on our team at least, to every power hitter who ever played the game. If we had been playing the Atlanta Braves, circa 1972, and our pitcher purposely hit Hank Aaron in the ribs with a fastball, the Braves' pitcher from that '72 team would have done the exact same thing as the Cardinals' pitcher did today: bounce one off of Longo's kneecap. That's what made me jealous. How cool would it be to have someone consider you your team's equivalent of Henry Aaron?

Call it the dream of the have-nots, the thing that sends me to sleep with visions of Elysian Fields dancing in my head: if I had three wishes I'd trade all three to be as good with a bat as I am with a glove. I want to be so scary in the box, other teams intentionally walk me with the bases loaded. I want to be so deadly dangerous, they pitch around me during batting practice. Just once, I'd love to be the guy they hit on the knee on purpose.

Even though Lenny was our cleanup hitter, that didn't make him our team's MVP. Far from it. The fact that he hit the ball so hard so often was about the only reason he was on the team. He was a complete liability in the field, which of course is why Lenny played left field.

Most casual fans never realize it but a change takes place in the out-field around the time you reach college- or entry-level pro ball and start facing batters who can hit with power to any field. Instead of hiding your weakest-fielding, slowest-running defender in right field like they do in Little League, every team above the high school level puts their gimp in left. The logic is simple: other than the occasional freak play, outfielders are never expected to make a throw to first base, and a throw to second or home is the same distance from either right or left field. But on a single or deep fly ball, few runners will challenge a left fielder's arm by trying to take the extra base at third because the throw from left to third is so short. Conversely, batters want to hit balls to right field to advance that same runner because the throw from right to third base is so much longer and more demanding in accuracy. It's simply intelligent baseball to put your fastest outfielder in center to cover all that ground, the outfielder with the best arm in right to make those long throws to third, and then your weakest-armed, slowest-footed bum, your Lenny Longo, in left—because that's where he can do the least amount of damage.

And while we're on the subject, making the most with the talent on your roster is the very reason why the designated hitter rule should be abolished immediately. It's not that the idea behind the DH—to create more fan-friendly offense while skipping the weakest hitter in every team's lineup—is inherently bad, but the practice of replacing the pitcher at the plate simply because that's not his forte runs counter to every-thing that is pure and good about the game. Even worse, the DH has done double damage by replacing one specialist with two. If you're go-ing that far, why stop there? Second basemen usually stink at the plate; give them a DH as well. Left fielders generally suck on defense, so how about a designated glover to replace them in the field? Catchers and first basemen tend to run with all the agility of broken boxcars; let them have a designated sprinter any time they hit something shorter than a home run. Pretty soon you'll have nine for offense, another nine for defense, and specialists for everything from hitting and catching to spitting and scratching. That would create some serious action for the unserious fan, right? It might be dumb-fan friendly, but it wouldn't be baseball. In fact they already have a sport like that. It's played with a "ball" that's pointy on two ends, by guys whose knuckles drag on the floor.

Everybody loves how baseball is so steeped in its own traditions but what could be more traditional than demanding that the way you made the team in 1920 should be the same way you make the team in 2020? Baseball was meant to be played by one guy at each position, in the field and at the plate. If you don't like the way pitchers bat then put a stick in their hands while they're still in the minor leagues and teach them to be better hitters—or just pay pitchers who can also hit like the more valuable players they are. But don't soil my game by replacing a man who can't hit with a man who can't catch. End the DH. End of argument.

None of which is meant to say that Lenny Longo didn't deserve his place on our team. Hell, he would have been our DH if we didn't have a couple other guys even worse on defense than he was. But in addition to the towering shots Lenny hit so often, I was becoming addicted to the songs he sang in left field. His voice was to a tune what butter is to popcorn.

Lenny must have had a premonition about the pain his knee would endure later in the game against the Cardinals, because the song he trotted out in the third inning that afternoon was perfect for the occasion. That night in our hotel room, Tall Boy even suggested that we nickname him "Lenny Longo, the Leftfield Lounge Lizard," but I told him nah, too many Ls.

The S&M Song

There's a bar near a car
Painted polka dot and stripes.
When you're there you will hear
O' all the suffering in life.
Sam and Mame's is the name
Stenciled on the sign above.
When you go you will know
O' the true meaning of love.
Come join me down in S&M.

S&M! Put away your fears.
S&M! Make me cry real tears.
Whip me, spank me.
I know one day you'll thank me.
I'll see you down in S&M.

On the way you will say
You don't do that sort of thing.
Once inside you'll confide
That this place really does swing.
Just to see all the glee
On the faces who are there,
It will show why I go
For the fun so good you share.
Come join me at the S&M.

S&M! I really wish you would.
S&M! This love hurts so good.
Kick me, scratch me,
You know just where to catch me:
With all my friends in S&M.

SATURDAY, MARCH 11

Started our longest home stand of the exhibition season yesterday, four games in Dunedin, with a day off come Monday for good behavior. Lost to the Phillies 8–5 on Friday, then again this afternoon 2–0. In the two-game set I played eleven innings, went one for five, one single, four men left on base. So much for good behavior.

As a PR promo, the front office gave away tickets to today's game. They asked Folgers to round up a few of the guys to suit up early, stand outside the gate and greet the fans coming in. We felt like morons, but we tried to make the best of it. It reminded me of the summer I graduated high school, when I got a job at the new gas station in the neighborhood and as part of the grand opening they had me dress up in a gorilla costume. My instructions were simple: walk around and have fun, but don't be so friendly you annoy customers, and for God's sake don't scare the children. Actually most of the people I greeted today were surprised to see us out there, and they seemed happy to shake hands as they walked in. I even got asked to sign a couple of programs. Attendance was announced at four thousand plus.

I saw an article in the paper about the Seattle Mariners, the team we open against when the regular season starts May 3. Their manager, Lou Piniella, got pissed at the lack of hustle he was getting on the field and decided it was due to the amount of food his players were socking away during lunch, so he cut the rations each man is allowed to take from the buffet table. Imagine that: having to show your plate to a coach every day before you can sit down and eat.

The guys hold a little ceremony for me to hang a new number on my locker-room sign every afternoon before our games. Twenty-three days till we play the fatted Mariners. Twenty-three days till we're legit.

At one point in the middle of the Phillies game Saturday, Folgers came over and sat by Tall Boy and me on the bench. We watched the game in silence a minute and then, as our right fielder Clyde Voorhees stepped into the batter's box, Folgers said out of the blue, "I can't stand the sight of that son of a bitch."

Tall Boy and I traded glances.

"I mean, look at him," Folgers continued. "He's four inches taller, ten years younger and thirty pounds thinner than me. Whad'ya bet back home his family's rich and famous, too? That would make him everything I hate in the competition, all rolled up into one."

Within the confines of the baseball season, I never once met a teammate I couldn't get along with. I understood what Folgers meant about GQ, though. It wasn't enough that he was infectiously good humored, flashing a crooked, boyish grin whenever someone started talking to him. GQ was blessed with the kind of rugged, casual good looks that even other straight guys have to admit are appealing. On top of all that though, he seemed to be at his best when most guys are at their worst— which is to say when he sweated. After a few innings in the sun-drenched expanse of right field, GQ glistened in a way that hinted of a carefree life spent outdoors among sand dunes, open skies and sea breezes. I'm always startled when I look in the mirror because I never feel like I own the face staring back at me, but I doubt GQ ever spent much time worrying over his appearance. He had probably looked exactly like that since he was sixteen and will probably look the same, maybe even better, twenty years from now.

I hadn't gotten to know GQ that well yet, mostly because we played opposite ends of the field on defense and dressed on opposite sides of the clubhouse after each game. He seemed friendly enough though, and was usually one of the first guys on the dugout steps with a high five when you scored a run or made a solid play.

Hack Hennessey dressed two lockers down from GQ and knew him better than I did.

"He's a funny guy!" Hack reported with his usual verbal vigor. "He wants to be a TV sports broadcaster when this is over. That's why he mostly keeps to himself. He's practicing."

"Practicing what?" I asked.

"Talking!"

After that I kept an eye on GQ. Sure enough, while the rest of us would gather in our usual groups to play cards or swap stories before a game, you could always find GQ on a stool in front of the small black-and-white TV set in a corner of the players' lounge, running through the channels in search of a game he could narrate. It didn't seem to matter the sport, either. GQ seemed as eager to offer play-by-play for a women's bowling tournament as a men's basketball or baseball game.

"There he goes!" I caught GQ saying to the television screen one day while a Spanish-language station aired a Mexican League soccer game. "Number fourteen Villarreal takes the pass from the midfield stripe and is headed for the goal. Two defenders are in pursuit but I don't think they're gonna catch him. Villarreal pushes it to the top of the box. He plants, the shot—Goooal! Goooal! Villarreal slots the ball in the top left corner of the net, goalie Maldonado had no chance at making the stop, and Mexico City takes a two-nil lead in the sixty-fifth minute of the contest. That may just about finish it for coach Chewy Deal and Team Monterrey today."

I squinted at the TV. All the graphics were titled in Spanish, and the reception was so poor you could barely make out the players' jersey numbers, let alone any names written on their backs. Either GQ was a closet Mexican Soccer League devotee or he was making up the entire commentary, names and all, on the spot.

"Hablo español?" I asked over GQ's shoulder.

I was more than a little surprised by his response. Considering how little we had spoken to each other so far that spring, I wasn't even sure he knew my name.

"Well hello there, Jake," GQ said without taking his eyes off the screen. "Just joining me in the booth, ladies and gentlemen, is Golden

Jake Standen, rookie third-base sensation for the Toronto Blue Jays this spring. Here we'll get another look at that beautiful goal by Vasquez Villarreal as he bends the ball just out of the reach of Monterrey's goal-keeper, Jesus Maldonado."

A round of instant replays came on the screen, showing the goal in slow motion from several angles.

"No, as a matter of fact I don't speak any Spanish, Jake," GQ continued. "But your question reminds me of a funny thing that happened over the weekend. I was speaking with a mutual friend of ours—and one of your teammates on the Blue Jays—by the name of Miguel Martinez, and during our conversation I used the word *phonetics*. I should add here, folks, that Martinez is originally from Cuba, so although he's fluent in his native tongue, Spanish, he's still working to improve his English skills now that he's living in the States. Anyway, when Miguel asked me what *phonetics* meant, I told him it means spelling a word the way it sounds, like they do at the beginning of each definition in dictionaries. Naturally he asked me to spell the word, and when I did he told me, 'You know, Clyde, this is the problem with the English language: even the word *phonetics* is not spelled like it sounds.'"

I would have laughed anyway; that story sounded just like something Speedboat would say. But there was a draw to GQ's delivery that made me want to laugh directionally, so the people at home could hear me chuckling into the microphone.

The slow-motion replays of the goal were now over and the game broadcast showed players milling around the midfield, getting set for the restart. It was almost time for GQ to resume his play-by-play.

"So before you can get away, Jake, I'm sure our viewing audience would like to hear some insights into the Blue Jays' prospects this season. Have any thoughts?"

"Well, as all our coaches could tell you," I replied, "the core of our team is built around the five-tool talent of our starting right fielder."

"Yes, I've heard he's quite good," GQ chimed in, and this time we both laughed.

GQ was our starting right field the previous day when a batter hit a line drive down the first-base line in the fourth. It was a sure double as soon as it came off the bat. The best GQ could do was keep the runner on first from scoring, and he made a nice backhanded play to stop the ball as he was sprinting toward the wall. He just needed to hit Hack in short right field with the cutoff throw and the runner would have stopped at third. Instead, GQ spun around, doing a complete 180 to uncork a throw toward me. The ball sailed over Hack's head, skipped past the pitcher's mound, and I had to slide in front of the dugout to keep the thing in play. Not only did the runner score but the batter wound up at third. When we made it back to the bench at the end of the inning, Coach Assenmacher was standing guard on the top dugout step.

"Voorhees!" he yelled. "What in Sam Hill were you thinking on that throw?"

"Sorry, Coach," GQ replied meekly, flashing his grin. "My manager in Charleston told me once that if I could generate the momentum, I should try to make my throw directly to third on that play. In case the runner slips or overruns the bag."

"Momentum?" Assenmacher spat. "Momentum! Son, that pig may fly in the Carolina Coastal but up here you hit the cutoff man. Besides, I've seen your arm. You ain't that good—and don't let nobody tell you any different."

As the exhibition season wore on, we practiced together as a team less and less. That was fine in that it gave us more time away from the ball field, but some days, especially when you only got in for four or five innings, you'd find yourself with more energy at the end of the game than you knew what to do with. It wasn't uncommon for players to hang around afterward and run wind sprints or jog the outfield just to work off some steam.

After Saturday's game with the Phillies, while the fans were still filing out of the stadium, Tall Boy grabbed a ball and we spent about ten minutes throwing long toss to each other down the left field line. Eventually my arm got tired and I threw a couple that landed at his feet. When Tall Boy finally missed one, the ball rolled all the way to the wall. "I'm done!" he called as he started walking after it.

I turned to head for the dugout, and there she was; Sadie stood at the railing, eyeing me from under a wide-brimmed summer hat.

"Why is it," she asked as I walked over, "that the only time we sing 'Take Me Out to the Ballgame' is when we're already there?"

"Just make sure the fans you're sitting with are still on our side. Last couple games I thought I heard folks singing, '*If they don't win it's the same.*'"

"Big crowd today. I came late and had to sit way up near the top."

"I thought I saw you in the nosebleeds," I lied.

"Did you? I always wondered how much players can see from the field when they look up into the stands."

"Come on down and see for yourself."

I held my hands up as if to catch her when she came over the rail. When she glanced down at my outstretched arms, a smile spread across her face, as if I had said something wicked—a secret she harbored but couldn't bring herself to speak. I really thought she just might jump.

"The heart says yes," she answered finally, "but my skirt says no. You haven't thrown my number away, have you?"

"Still on the nightstand, right beside my teddy bear."

"I'll be home around six. It feels like a shorts-and-T-shirt night tonight. Don't dress too nice or I'll be embarrassed."

And that was it. No mention of Wednesday. No talk about our failed dinner date. Nothing at all about fifteen minutes.

Tall Boy walked up beside me. "What was that?"

Sadie reached the top of the stairs and disappeared down the walkway to the exit without turning around.

"That," I told him, "is why you're running alone tonight."

We met for dinner and then drinks. She was perfect for me. Not only a baseball fan, Sadie preferred beer to wine, wearing tennis shoes to dressing up, and talking across a game of eight ball to just about anything else you might do at a little dive bar together. It didn't feel like we were on a date at all. I was as comfortable with her as if I'd been hanging out with Tall Boy all night. I don't mean she acted like a guy; I mean being with Sadie was like being around one of the guys.

And my first impressions about the way we clicked had been right on the money. We talked about a thousand things—school majors and old jobs, worst dates and favorite childhood TV shows. No matter what subject came up, it felt like I could say anything to her, whatever popped into my head, without worrying about feeling stupid or getting laughed at. When she laughed, it was always with me. Sadie always got the joke.

In the middle of a pool game, she started telling me about a quiz she had taken in the back of a women's magazine at work. I thought it was just a little story she was sharing, but when she said she added up her score and it indicated that she may have an eating disorder, I could tell she was genuinely worried it might be true. Now I'm no dietitian, but there's no way Sadie had an eating disorder. She didn't have much to speak of top shelf, but I always suspected that on the right woman perky could be just as sexy as buxom. Besides, she had an ass to make an atheist thank God. She looked fantastic.

"Those things are such crap," I assured her. "They design those quizzes to make you worry about whatever they want you to worry about."

"How do you mean?"

"Well, they start by picking a buzzword or a hot topic, right? Overeating, binge eating, workaholics, shopaholics. And then they ask questions that all sound like they describe you. But the questions are always the same because they're based on the first self-tests, which were designed to make drunks admit they have a problem. 'Is it the first thing you think of when you wake up in the morning? Is it the last thing you think about when you go to bed at night? Do you think about it at odd times during the day and find yourself sneaking off to do it alone?'"

Sadie rested on her pool stick, taking in my spiel.

"I always take those quizzes too," I admitted. "But I switch whatever buzzword they're quizzing me on with the word *sex*. According to those tests, I'm a sex addict. Is it the first thing I think about in the morning? Of course! The last thing I think about at night? Hell yes!"

"Do you sneak off to do it alone?" Sadie asked.

"Case closed."

Together, we laughed and laughed.

If there was one drawback to the evening, it was the thin slice of untanned skin on her left-hand ring finger. Sadie caught me looking and didn't wait to be asked.

"We're separated," she said between pool shots. "It lasted three years, but he's been in Miami and I've been here since January. He said he needed to grow as an individual. Honestly, I don't even know what that means. I could've sworn when we got married that he was already fully grown."

61

I thought she meant they lived together in Miami but Sadie said no, she lived in the house they had bought in West Tampa.

"He does so much traveling that he could live anywhere in South Florida and it wouldn't matter. So he got an apartment there, and I got a job so I could stay here."

So she had a husband. That news stopped me for a minute. I've always had trouble picturing people my age doing things that would never occur to me, and marriage was up near the top of the list. We had been getting along so well all night that I'd forgotten we hardly knew each other. She might as well have been telling me that she was a Prussian princess. Sadie didn't offer any more details, and I got the feeling that I shouldn't press. At least she was being open about it. I decided to change the subject.

"That's the third time I've heard you mention your job, and I still don't know what you do for a living."

"That's because every time I tell someone they think I'm joking. You'll laugh if I tell you."

"I won't," I promised. "It can't be any sillier than wearing knickers and chasing a ball through the grass all day. What do you do?"

Sadie chalked up her stick and considered me through squinted eyes a moment.

"You know those commercials they show on TV during the afternoon soaps for the one-nine-hundred numbers? That's what I do."

"You make those commercials?"

"I answer the phone."

I still wasn't following. "And when you answer the phone, what do you say?"

"I say, 'Good afternoon. Thank you for calling Psychic Soulmates. What part of your future would you like me to tell you about today?'"

She was right; I thought she was joking, but I made damn sure not to laugh.

"How exactly does one become a phone psychic?"

"Well, first, you have to be psychic. The rest is pretty much like any other job: fill out an application, go through an interview, so on."

"And you're really a psychic."

"Of course I am!" She laughed. "Although mostly the job is just listening. You'd be surprised at how much people you've just met are willing to tell you about their lives. I'm like a therapist who works for a dollar ninety-five a minute. And if you learn to listen, it's not hard to figure out what people are like, what they want to hear from you."

"Give me a for instance," I suggested. "Tell me what I want to hear."

"You want me to give you a reading?" Sadie tucked a strand of loose hair behind her ear. When she spoke again, the tone of her voice had changed—measured and thoughtful. "Well, let's see, Mr. Standen. I think you studied history in school not just because you like the subject but because you always wanted to be a part of it. You feel like you've never had a chance to show your true talents, and you always dreamed of getting one more try to prove how good you really are.

"If other people see you as the tough, fearless type, that's only because the work you do requires it. You are capable of caring very deeply, but you don't get much chance to show your sensitive side, so instead you keep it bottled up and act the way people expect you to.

"You've been hurt by women, I can tell. But I don't think it was one big breakup that made you hesitant in love. I think it was a hundred little heartbreaks. A hundred times you've felt like this could be the one, and for a hundred different reasons it just never seemed to happen. You have a lot of love to give, and you're getting to the point where you're not sure you'll ever find the right someone to give it to. But don't give up hope, Jake Standen. Someday you'll find just the right person. Maybe sooner than you think."

When she finished I made a quick motion to scratch my nose, but really I was checking to make sure my jaw wasn't hanging open. How could she nail me like that in just one try? Was I that transparent? We had talked all evening, but it's not like I'd been pouring my soul out to her over every beer. I was certain she had talked at least as much as I had, but there was no way I could have fired off a description of her like she had just made of me. I tried to laugh it off with one of those that-was-a-pretty-good-trick kind of chuckles, but I swear I had goose bumps.

When they gave last call, Sadie turned down one for the road so I walked her to the parking lot. She said she was free for the afternoon and would try to make it out to our game the next day. When I got her safely in the car, she rolled down her window and waved, calling "Good night!" into the air as she pulled out of the parking lot. As I watched her car turn and merge with the traffic coming off a stoplight, it occurred to me that I couldn't imagine spending a better evening with a woman without any clothes winding up on the floor.

I've always thought that most people sleepwalk their lives away, just going through the motions week in and week out. You'll only meet a handful of people your entire life who are truly, fully awake, and you know them the moment you meet them because they experience every day in a state of absolute wonder. They glow from it, in fact. Sadie was one of those people. That night, the whole night of our first date, I couldn't get over how no one else noticed that Sadie alone was in Technicolor, in a bar full of sleepwalkers shaded black and white.

SUNDAY, MARCH 12

Dropped another one this afternoon, 3–1 to the Astros. We can't buy a win. We've lost six in a row and seven of nine so far this spring. I went four innings today, oh for my one at bat. To date: three for sixteen, two walks and a sacrifice, one run, two RBI. Good thing games can be won with defense, too—forty-three innings so far without an error.

At the start of spring training, somebody was tasked with the job of putting a stretch of tape with a name written on it above each locker to let us players know which one was ours. I should say two somebodies, since it's clear one person was reading the names aloud and whoever had the Magic Marker wasn't too worried about spelling. The tape above Brian's locker reads "Slone." They spelled mine "Standing." After today's game the guy two lockers down from me looked up to notice that the tape with his name was missing. "All right," he said. "Who's been screwing around with my stuff?" Just then Assenmacher appeared from out of the manager's office, reading off a clipboard in his hand.

"Williams," he called out, "Devereaux, Motts. C'mon in here a minute, will ya?"

I'd walked by the manager's office when the door was open enough times to know that three guys plus Didier and Assenmacher would make for a tight fit in that small room. They weren't overly concerned about comfort today, though. A minute later all three guys walked back to their lockers and began changing into street clothes. Everyone in the room seemed to figure it out at the same time. I looked over at Tall Boy. He made a quick gesture as if he had an itch—one finger across his throat. The guys had just been cut.

A pall settled over the room. Though a moment before the place had been full of chatter, suddenly it felt like the very first day of camp. The three guys didn't say a word, didn't even look around, and no one said anything to them either. By the time I finished my shower they had packed up their things and cleared out of the clubhouse.

There were forty players here by the end of the first full week of camp. In the three weeks since then I've gotten to know maybe half the team by name, most of the others by the positions they play. Williams was platooning in the outfield. Devereaux, my locker neighbor, was a relief pitcher. Motts was the utility infielder who got hit in the head by a ball and went to the hospital. Now they were just guys again, guys who needed to find a ride back to their old lives.

Is it schadenfreude or simple human nature to feel pity for someone else's shit luck yet joy because that same misfortune isn't yours? Naturally I couldn't help thinking: *There but for the grace of God.* And yet, as much as I worry about my hitting, I truly don't believe I'm a liability on this team. I know I'll get better at the plate through sheer repetition but even without more practice I'd bet that if you got all the third basemen in the world together for one giant tryout, I'd place somewhere among the four hundred best. I mean that sincerely. Six billion people on this planet, and I'm in the top four hundred. I know a lot of guys back home who are full of themselves for a lot of reasons, but how many of them can say that they'd make the top four hundred in the world in anything?

Thirty-seven players will be listed on the updated roster come Monday morning. Teams will be allowed to keep an expanded bench of thirty-two for the replacement season. I've already made the cut down from six billion. Five more cuts to go.

Even though my name was still taped above my locker, I had reason to worry that Sunday. Before every game Assenmacher stuck the day's lineup card on the wall beside the batting rack at the end of the dugout, and though I'd started most of our games to date, I always made it a point to look for my name before I began warming up. As it was still spring training, the coaches changed our lineup frequently, but on Sunday the only change from the previous day's game involved me: I was starting at third again but in the batting order against the Astros, I had been moved to eighth, right behind Hack Hennessey. In both the games I started before the previous Wednesday's rainout, I had been batting sixth in the lineup. Since then I had hit from the seven spot. To suddenly find myself slipping to eighth in the order was reason to worry indeed.

Most positions in the batting order have played a role that's remained unchanged from the days of Ruth and Gehrig. In baseball the team that scores first usually sets the tempo of a game and wins a majority of the time, so the goal of a batting order is to maximize your chances to score in any inning, with an emphasis on scoring in the first. Considering that even the best pitchers average at least one hit or walk per every three outs, if you want to score in the first inning, then that's where your best four batters should be grouped.

But simply putting your best four up top is not enough. The first four hitters should work together like the car transmission on a four-speed manual. The leadoff batter is first gear; he gets you going with a quick burst of speed. He should be patient enough to watch a few pitches, either drawing a walk or slapping a single to get on first, where his wheels can create problems for the defense through stolen bases and hit-and-runs. Your next hitter, like second gear, is also about speed, but he should be a little more versatile than the leadoff guy. A contact hitter with good bat control, your two man should be able to move the runner over with a grounder to the right side or find the holes in the defense created by the threat of your speedy runner already on base. Ideally you want your fastest, most intelligent base runners to be the first two men in the lineup. Though the cleanup batter gets all the macho press, you want your best all-around hitter batting third since he's likely to come up with at least one man on base and he'll always get to the plate in the first inning, no matter what the top two batters have done. Your three man should be a guy who can hit either a single up the middle or a banger off the wall depending on the traffic patterns around the base paths. Finally, your cleanup man is fourth gear. He's what you want when the bags are full of runners and you're ready to do some serious long ball traveling.

On great hitting lineups, the second four are sometimes a lesser version of the first—start with speed, end with power. On most teams though, especially when you replace the pitcher with a DH, you usually fill the final spots in descending order of ability: the five-hole batter is your fifth best hitter, the six spot is sixth best, and so on down the line. All of which is to say that my being demoted in the span of one week from the sixth spot in the lineup to the eighth was an unmistakable sign that the coaches thought I should be hitting better than I had so far.

The worst thing though, was that they were right. After all the batting practice of spring training and now nine games into the exhibition season, I still wasn't hitting above the Mendoza line. True, it was early yet, and a couple of good games could get my average up to respectability quick enough. Based on my at bats so far that spring however, I hadn't earned even the small amount of pride that comes from hitting in the lineup ahead of a second baseman named Hack.

I didn't see her at the stadium Sunday but when Tall Boy and I got back to our room around five, the phone light was flashing with a message from Sadie. "Hi, Jake," she said. "Sorry I missed your game today. I was thinking of going to see a band tonight that I've been hearing about lately. Want to come? Write this down." And then she told me how to find the place. I called her number but only got the machine, so I said I'd meet her there and hung up.

I had to smile at the thought of how straightforward Sadie's message was. Another guy might have gotten torqued that she didn't say how much fun our first date was, but if she hadn't had fun then, she wouldn't have called back now, right? I liked how she had a plan and then just cut to the chase. Let's go here; write this down. It drives me crazy when a girl says she wants to go out and then acts like she has no idea what she wants to go do, because then you waste ten minutes saying, "I don't know. What do *you* want to do?" I hate that shit. Give me a woman who knows where fun can be found and you're already halfway to having a good time there.

I followed her directions without any trouble, and Sadie was standing by her car when I pulled in the lot. As I got out, she walked over, smiled, and said, "You found me."

I was glad to see my golf shirt and khakis seemed about right on the dressiness over/under scale. Some women don't figure out their best assets until they don't have them anymore, but Sadie was rocking a white blouse and jean skirt above white canvas shoes and ankle socks—powerful advertising for a world-class ass and the legs to match. She looked great.

It hadn't occurred to me until we were walking in that I didn't know what band we had come to see. The venue was a pizza joint called Sal's, a little dive in Clearwater that sold food and Cokes up front and had a long, narrow bar and stage in the back. A flyer at the front counter claimed a band named Dancing Madly Backward Again was scheduled. Based on no other evidence but the guys who took the stage and the battered look of their instruments, it seemed clear their show would be far more about volume than musicality. I doubt I would have suggested this for a date but since Sadie had suggested it, I decided to just go with the flow. We were the oldest couple there by four or five years in a crowd of about fifty—lots of tattoos, body piercings, orange and metallic blue hair. While I bought a pitcher of beer at the bar, Sadie grabbed us a couple slices of deep dish, then we converged at a table by the wall in back.

Once the band got cranked up I was even less convinced that this was a great idea; the music was so loud we had zero chance to hear each other talk. After a couple songs though, I did start to enjoy just watching the band play. It was like something out of a documentary on the decline of our nation's youth. Four skinny, stringy-haired guys were jumping all over the stage, playing chords as fast as they could while the kids bounced around, crashing into one another on the cleared section of floor in front of the band. Occasionally someone would fling themselves up on stage and a guy in the group would shove them back down into the crowd. There was such a raw energy to it, as if everyone had been kept in a pressure cooker all week and this was their one chance to release some steam. It looked like fun to be in the middle of the throng, but I kept thinking, *Someone is going to twist an ankle or get their Achilles stepped on.* The suits who ran baseball had already declared that replacement teams couldn't carry injured players on a disabled list. A sprained ankle or tweaked Achilles could end my pro career tomorrow.

In the middle of one song, I felt a hand on the arm I had draped across my side of the table. I looked over in time to see Sadie draining her glass. She set it on the table with a thud I could feel but couldn't hear over the music, wiped away a beer mustache, and shouted with mock heroism, "I'm goin' in!" The next thing I knew, she was bopping with the crowd on the dance floor, crashing into people, twirling and spinning. For a moment I could see Sadie, hair flying, eyes flashing, and then I lost sight as the mob absorbed her. I got such a rush of desire and envy watching her dance, it felt like a baby heart attack. She was killing me in that jean skirt.

On the side of the stage between the band and the bar sat what looked like a dentist's chair, and every few minutes someone would climb up into it. There were two guys, must have been employees, who would then perform something best described as an in-person mixed drink. The first guy would hold up a bottle of margarita mix, unscrew the cap, and pour it into the mouth of whoever was lying back in the chair. Guy Two would then perform the same ritual with a bottle of tequila. When they finished pouring, they would swivel the chair a circle to the right, another spin back to the left, and then flip a lever that shot the person straight up into a sitting position. Twice I saw Sadie climb in the chair as a spiky-haired slam dancer threw money at the guys with the bottles. Both times she came up choking and laughing, margarita mix dripping down her chin. People in the crowd would then pump fists in the air, egging her on to dive back down into the melee. She never did, though. Amid the waves of bobbing heads and twirling bodies, Sadie was the picture of decorum as she deftly stepped off the stage and back onto the dance floor.

By midnight it was over. That seemed a little early but I guess even kids with metallic blue hair need to get to bed at a decent hour on a Sunday night in March. I was hoping Sadie would be in the mood for some coffee or frozen yogurt—we'd hardly spoken five minutes the whole evening— but she said she needed to be up early the next morning. It was probably just as well. My ears were still ringing from the show.

As we walked across the parking lot, I was expecting that moment of awkward uncertainty when the night is obviously over and neither of you is sure if this is the date when you have your first kiss. This was after all our second date, and if you're going to stay on the three-dates-before-sex schedule, it's important to clear all preliminary hurdles.

When we reached her car Sadie fumbled with her keys a moment before unlocking the door. "Who thought up the double standard that says men can go to a bar alone and nobody thinks anything about it, but women are floozies if they do the same thing?" She looked up and smiled. "That's the long way of saying I'm glad you came out tonight."

"Thanks for the invite. I always liked punk. I'm just surprised you do, too."

Sadie laughed as she ducked into her car.

"You're such a bad liar. Call me if you want to do something this week."

Before I could even say "How about tomorrow?" she started up the motor, waved to me behind her car window, and pulled out of the parking lot.

MONDAY, MARCH 13

Easy day today. A couple hours of practice and no game scheduled.

I've been thinking about Tall Boy's latest Would You Rather, the one about beauty or talent, and I'm fairly certain that as it applies to me his question is unanswerable. That's not to say I have any illusions; I already know that all my blessings in this life came from the talent bin rather than the looks department. It's not that I'm hideous or anything, but as far as tall, dark and handsome go, on even so small a sample as the Blue Jays' roster this spring, Tall Boy is half a head above me, Speedboat has better natural skin tone than I ever got from a week at the beach, and if GQ is a ten on the handsome-o-meter then I'm maybe a six, seven on my best days. Still, I'd be one ungrateful bastard if I got to the Pearly Gates and gave Saint Peter any grief over my luck with the ladies while I was down here. Hell, I'm the first to admit that half the women I've gone out with could have done way better than me. So how does such an average Joe wind up with so many lovelies in the old scrapbook? Most of the women I ever dated I first met beside a ball diamond, and for most of my life, whenever I've put on a uniform I was clearly one of the most talented guys on the field.

But don't bother asking if I feel bad somehow for using baseball as a way to date girls who were out of my league in attractiveness. Do you think they felt bad using their beauty to land a guy with an OSU varsity baseball jacket? Nobody involved was sorry for the trade because it was an equal trade, and that's my point exactly. Beauty as it relates to the women I've dated is the same as baseball talent is with me: it's what you use to get what you otherwise couldn't. Actually I think it would've been more unforgivable, for the ladies and for me, *not* to have used it to get what we wanted because athletic talent may be more than skin deep but, just like youthful beauty, it comes with an indisputable shelf life. So unless the stars line up just right and you win yourself a Golden Glove trophy or Miss Ohio sash while you still got it, there will be no way I could prove to my grandkids that my sixty-year-old body once possessed Major League reflexes, any more than one of my old flames could use her body at sixty as proof that she was once the belle of the ball. Tall Boy's Would You Rather is unanswerable because comparing beauty and talent is like comparing a pile of four-hundred quarters with a hundred-dollar bill. They may look different but, as far as the currency they represent, they're the exact same thing.

Beauty is talent, and talent beauty.

The coaches only scheduled a two-hour practice for Monday, and even that was mostly perfunctory. We spent about an hour running some drills, and then anyone who wanted to could take batting practice or shag balls in the field. I figured the bone-deep numbness in my hands would be better served if I took the rest of the day off, so I headed for the clubhouse. As I stood at my locker I heard someone walk behind me and go into Coach Didier's office. A moment later, as I was sitting down to unlace my cleats, I got the biggest scare of my professional career.

"Standen!" Coach Assenmacher called out. "Come in here a minute, will ya?"

I looked around the locker room. There were three or four guys in various stages of undress. They all seemed not to have heard, or maybe they were pretending they hadn't heard while thinking the same thing I was: Can a guy get cut for not taking voluntary BP? In the corner I saw Speedboat rummaging through his locker. Like the others, he was busy not looking my way. What about him? In two starts Speedboat had given up six runs on twelve hits and hadn't gotten past the fifth inning in either game. How could they cut me loose when a guy like that is our fourth starter? To think I could have been dancing with a beautiful woman last night but I declined, all so me and my pink, perfect Achilles heels could get cut the very next day.

And where the hell was Brian? Did Assenmacher wait until we were separated before calling me into the office? Was he afraid I'd try to hide behind Tall Boy, maybe drag him in there to testify that we came as a set, like matching luggage? We'd come down in my car together and were splitting the hotel bill. What would he do to cover expenses and get around town if I got sent packing?

I took a quick look above me. According to the tape over my locker at least, I was still Standing. With what little confidence that gave me, I drew a deep breath, walked to the manager's office and leaned in through the open doorway.

Assenmacher was sitting on the manager's desk, changing his socks. "You were gonna take some batting practice today, right?"

It sounded more like a statement than a question, so I nodded.

"I should have this thing set up in about ten minutes." Beside him on the desk were a video camera and some wires. "Don't start until I'm up there."

Standing behind the netting around home plate that served as a backstop for BP, waiting my turn, I felt a tide of embarrassment rising in me at the thought of having a coach film my swings. The guys might see it as the baseball equivalent of wearing a dunce cap. Luckily, Assenmacher got the equipment set up while GQ was taking his cuts so at least it didn't look too obvious. Besides, most of the guys on the field were talking and joking around, caught up in their own thing. Nobody seemed to pay us much attention.

While Assenmacher was still adjusting the camera tripod I decided to risk a personal question. "I thought you were the bench coach, Coach. What's with the video all the sudden? Working on a fallback plan for when you retire?"

Assenmacher grunted between glances into the viewfinder. "I work with minor leaguers, Standen. Bench coach, hitting instructor, wet nurse. In the minors you learn to wear a lot of hats."

Once GQ had finished, I stepped to the plate. I stretched and stalled a minute to see if Assenmacher would bark out some orders, tell me to

72

lay down some bunts or hit a few pitches to the opposite field. When he didn't say anything, I assumed my regular stance and gave it my best. My cuts were nothing special but I got a couple nice shots in. After about thirty swings I looked back to where he stood behind the camera. Assenmacher gave me a "that's enough" nod.

"Take some infield if you want," he said. "Meet me in the manager's office after lunch."

I hadn't planned on staying at the stadium past noon, but enough of the guys hung around on the field and later in the weight room to make the time go by quick enough. After I snagged a sandwich from the spread in the players' lounge I headed down the hall and knocked on the manager's office door. Assenmacher looked up, then waved me in.

An old TV sat on the top shelf of a metal stand on wheels, with an equally old VCR unit connected from a shelf below. Assenmacher turned on the set. White noise came blaring out as a static pattern raced across the screen. "Hit the lights," he instructed, thumbing at the remote control to start the tape and turn down the sound. The office was only big enough for two chairs on the visitor's side of the manager's desk so when I flipped the light switch and took my seat beside his, we were almost knocking knees. It was an awkward closeness, the same uncomfortable combination of authority and proximity as when a college prof stands in front of your desk while lecturing the whole class. The static picture went black and stuck there a second before the familiar backdrop of Dunedin Stadium's blue seats filled the screen.

"All right, Standen," I heard Assenmacher call from behind the camera on the video.

The camera focus adjusted as I stepped into the batter's box. The video me took a few practice swings, screwed my back foot into the dirt and assumed my stance.

"Now here's one thing," Assenmacher said from his seat beside me. "Look at the way you're standing. You're very rigid at the plate, like you got a rod stuck up your ass."

That was true. I had a tendency to stand straight legged, same as Tall Boy in the box. My right elbow was held out even with my shoulders and my bat was cocked slightly forward—not unlike the shadow man pictured on the red, white and blue Major League Baseball logo. And

73

just like that shadow man, high heat was often on me before I'd gotten the bat off my shoulder.

Assenmacher paused the tape and turned to me. "Think of your stance not as part of your swing but as a way to get the most comfortable to allow you to swing. Are you comfortable at the plate?"

I'd never really considered my comfort level as part of the batting process. I answered with a shrug.

"Forget show. Forget style. Forget whatever stupid shit they told you in college ball. Everything you do in the box should be designed to get the barrel of the bat through the strike zone and on the ball as quickly as possible. That includes your stance."

He mashed the Play button on the remote, and we watched me hack at several pitches. I had a hard time connecting the batter on the TV with the hitter I pictured myself to be. Although I'd seen tapes of games I had played in before—in videos from my college days and home movies Mom had made back in Little League—not once had I really studied how I stand or swing at the plate. Like seeing pictures of myself in my junior high yearbook, I struggled to believe I ever looked like that.

My step into the ball was short and choppy; my arms, hips and legs all seemed to move at different times and different speeds. On one swing my front shoulder flew open and I hit the ball straight into the dirt. On the next I finished with a huge uppercut, the ball zipping straight up out of the picture. I didn't just look uncomfortable; I looked downright clueless at the plate.

Finally the video me hit a solid shot. The *dock* of my bat striking the ball sounded large even on the tinny TV speakers. I remembered hitting that one during BP. The ball cleared the left-center wall on one hop.

"There," Assenmacher chirped, thumbing the Pause button. "That's more like it."

He fumbled with the remote until the tape rewound to the beginning of my swing.

"See how your motion is fluid on this one? First your step, then hips and hands, then shoulder, all in a row. One-two-three. That's what you need to do every time."

He hit the Fast-Forward button, and the tape zipped through several of my swings.

"There was another one I wanted to—" Assenmacher mumbled. "Oop, there it is."

We watched me take another cut, and my motion in the box was nearly identical to the one we had just seen. I remembered that hit as well. The ball went right back up the box, fifteen feet above the pitcher's mound and into center field for a clean single.

"Head down, eyes on the ball," Assenmacher said. "Tony Gwynn would be proud of that stroke. You know what to do, and these swings prove it, I think. But I also think you're too worried about mechanics to concentrate on putting the bat on the ball. I want you to try two things and leave everything else alone with your swing. First, unlock your knees when you get in your stance. Give your legs some bounce, like you're standing on the end of a diving board. That'll give you more balance when you stride into the pitch. Second, instead of holding your hands up here"—Assenmacher made fists of his hands and put them at his right shoulder like he was holding a bat—"hold your hands here, at your ribs. I think that'll help level your swing through the zone. It may feel funny at first but if you start hitting the ball in games the way you hit these in the cage, you'll stop worrying so much about mechanics and just start getting it done."

I kept waiting for him to dump on me some more. I couldn't remember Assenmacher ever saying anything to one of the guys on our team that wasn't at least half insult. After a moment of silence though, he seemed surprised I was still sitting there.

"Questions?" he asked.

I was afraid to open my mouth for fear of breaking the spell.

"One last thing," he said. "I want you to switch sticks. I noticed you're using a maple bat and you keep getting jammed. I bet your hands are sore as hell. You need a bat made from ash. They're softer. If you get jammed, the bat breaks and usually the ball goes foul. When you get jammed with the maple bat, your hands feel broken and you hit a dribbler that an old lady could field without a glove. You can tell the difference because the ash bats are the ones with the brand cut into the wood. Maple bats just have a sticker. Grab me when you take BP tomorrow and we'll make sure you're comfortable with the changes. See you in the morning."

I had to convince myself not to run as I got up and left the office.

On my way to find Tall Boy so we could head back to the hotel, I started thinking about the pointers Assenmacher had given me. They made sense in a simple way. He wasn't trying to change my swing wholesale, just a couple of quick adjustments—bend my knees, hold the bat lower. I had no problem with that. He even said he thought I knew what I was doing already. If it weren't for the numbness in my hands, I'm sure I would have gone out to the cage and cranked up the pitching machine just to see if I could put a couple line drives together.

That night Tall Boy and I met up with Folgers in Clearwater at the Chinese restaurant he had been telling us about since the first time we talked. It was in the corner location of a strip mall, just down from a four-chair barbershop and a Piggly Wiggly supermarket. The restaurant, named Trey Yuen, looked small from the outside but was surprisingly large and roomy inside. An intricately carved set of folding panels, the kind people used to dress behind in old movies, separated the waiting area near the cash register from the dining area beyond. Folgers waved to the stooped old man sitting behind the register counter as we made our way inside. The old man nodded in return. He told us business was slow so we should just go seat ourselves.

As we claimed chairs around a circular table, a young Asian woman in a flowing dress appeared from behind swinging kitchen doors and glided across the carpet.

"Three bowls of egg drop soup," Folgers told her as she passed out the menus, "and three beers."

The waitress nodded, gliding back to disappear again behind the kitchen doors.

"I think I'm gonna propose to that señorita," Folgers said. "We're perfect for each other."

"How can you tell?" I asked.

"Because every time I come in here, she never says a word."

"And that's your idea of a perfect woman?"

"That's my idea of a perfect relationship. How many times have you been with someone and everything seems to be going along fine—and then it just falls apart? You know why that happens? Because you start talking. I figure if you can find a woman who doesn't talk to begin with, you can't screw it up."

"That's not a wife," Tall Boy told him. "You're describing a pet."

"Even better," Folgers agreed. "Nobody gets married because you've found the perfect mate. You get married when you find the compromise of your choice. Everybody settles for their spouse. You might say 'I do,' but what you mean is 'Close enough.'"

"Spoken like a jaded ex-husband," Tall Boy said.

Folgers put a finger to his lips when he spotted our waitress approaching with the drinks. She was cute: maybe twenty years old, jet-black hair, arms as thin as bat handles. Folgers smiled a big, foolish grin as she put our beers down and glided back to the kitchen.

"Ah, she loves me," he mused.

"I dunno," I said. "She didn't speak to me at least as much as she wasn't speaking to you."

Folgers picked up a beer and turned to me. "So how'd you manage to last this long without some woman baggin' and taggin' ya? Usually third basemen are the first ones to go."

"Jake went to college," Tall Boy answered, as if that explained anything.

"That's right. What was your major?"

I told him I'd earned a BA in American studies.

"That's a degree? Never heard of it."

"It's one part sociology, one part lit and one part history major—but only the last four hundred years or so, and just the stuff that happened in this country."

"What's a bachelors' degree in American studies good for?"

"It prepares you for either pursuing a master's degree in American studies, or moving furniture."

"Damn," Folgers said. "I gotta get me one of those."

The waitress appeared again with our soup. After she took our dinner orders Tall Boy excused himself to go wash up and walked down the hallway beside the swinging kitchen doors. I ate about half my soup before realizing Folgers hadn't touched his yet.

"It's a bad sign when the guy who ordered the appetizer isn't eating any of it."

"Sorry. Just have a little upset stomach. I'm waiting for these to kick in."

He held up a small brown prescription vial and shook it, making a soft rattle with the green pills inside.

Tall Boy appeared from the restroom hallway and walked back to our table.

"I have a theory," he announced as he sat down. "You know how I know there's a God? Because everything you have to do for survival feels good."

I held up a hand. "Please don't tell me what you were just doing in the bathroom."

"It's true," Tall Boy insisted. "I mean—sex is the obvious one, right? You have to do that to keep your genes in the pool, and to make sure we do it, God made it feel great. But even the everyday stuff feels good. If you're really hungry, haven't eaten all day, a plate of saltines and a glass of water is like a feast. If you haven't taken a dump for a long time, when you finally get to take one it feels wonderful. Even puking, after you've chugged a dozen beers and the room is spinning and you think you're gonna die. Then you finally hurl and you feel a hundred times better. The fact that doing those things helps keep us alive proves to me that there's a master plan in place—but to make them feel good, too? That has 'God' written all over it."

Folgers was nodding but I wasn't going to let Tall Boy off that easy.

"Puking and crapping are your ideas of good dinner conversation?"

"They're natural body functions," Brian pointed out. "Don't pretend you're above talking about them."

"Thought about 'em, talked about 'em," I agreed. "I'm just saying, at the dinner table I try to be less indiscreet."

Folgers slipped into a hillbilly southern accent. "Indiscreet?" he asked Tall Boy. "What's they-at?"

"It's a five-dollar word that means Jake thinks I'm an asshole."

Folgers turned back to me. "It's some of that there book learnin' you got in college, ain't it? Teach me some more."

I drained the last of my soup and declared, "Fuck both you fucking fuckheads."

"Aw," Folgers said. "I already knew that one."

We had ordered individual dinners but when they came each dish was more food than any one person could eat, so we just left the plates in the middle of the table and sampled from all of them. I ordered a pepper steak and noodles combo but ended up eating more of Folgers's sweet and sour chicken. Tall Boy's order of ribs was excellent as well. Everything I tried was delicious, spicy without drowning in spices. As Folgers had promised, the egg rolls that came after dinner were divine.

"Admit it," Tall Boy said, patting his bloated belly when he'd finished. "God was on this table tonight."

I told him, "I think that's what the G stands for in MSG."

Folgers fished a pack of cigarettes from his pocket and grabbed an ashtray from the next table over.

"You boys mind?"

"I don't mind," I said, "but I thought you were on the gum."

"I am, but nothing beats an old-fashioned smoke after a good meal. I think that's the main reason I took a liking to this place. Damn near nobody lets you light up in a restaurant anymore. First time I walked in and saw ashtrays on the tables, I knew this place was for me."

He lit his cigarette and let out a satisfied sigh of smoke.

"The trick," he continued, "is to not buy a pack in the first place. If you don't have cigs, then the gum is enough, but if you got 'em, you smoke 'em."

"Isn't that the same trick to quitting cold turkey?" Tall Boy asked.

"It is, but at least none of Mother Nature's little creatures are in danger when I'm out of smokes and I have the gum."

"And which species are endangered when you got nothing?"

"Every one I see."

When the check came we all threw money in a pile, and I went for a quick restroom stop before we left. While I was in there I noticed two faded scrawls on the tile above the urinal where I stood. "God is in your hands," the first one read. Underneath that someone else had written, "Better call home then cuz yo mama's gonna find religion tonight!"

Which came first, I wondered: Tall Boy's unifying theory of monotheism, or his translation of Chinese-restaurant men's-room graffiti?

Folgers had gone out to run errands before we all met up at Trey Yuen, so we were following his car on the way back to the hotel after dinner when Tall Boy asked, "How old do you think he is, anyway?"

"Folgers? Mid, maybe late thirties. Why?"

"He just seems kinda young to have arthritis."

I was surprised too. "Folgers has arthritis?"

"He's taking some meds for it. Popped a couple little greenies while we waited for you in the john."

"Arthritis at thirty-something," I said. "Bummer."

"Hope I die before I get old," Tall Boy agreed.

TUESDAY, MARCH 14

Our day off paid off, as we won at home today 6–5 against the Marlins. Great game. I started on the bench but was in by the fourth, went one for three with a single and a run scored in the sixth. Both my other at bats were at 'em balls, too: stroked a drive into right that the guy caught at his shoes, and my eighth inning fielder's choice up the middle would have been a single if they had been playing at regular depth. The second baseman was pinching in toward the bag because there was a runner on first.

My at bats felt good but I earned my per diem in the field—made the play that ended the game, in fact. In the top of the ninth we had two outs when the Marlins got a guy on first with a walk. The next man up drilled one down the left field line that landed two feet fair and rolled all the way to the wall. Brian went out to get the relay, but our left fielder throws as wild as he runs slow. I could tell when he let fly from the left field corner that the ball would sail over Tall Boy's head. The runner from first was making the turn for home, and I figured it wouldn't make any difference whether the batter wound up on second or third with two outs if the tying run scored, so I left my bag and started running to cut off the overthrow. Just as it landed about ten feet from me, I realized that the direction I was running—toward center field—would make it hard to get anything on the throw if I were trying to get it home, so I purposely overran the ball, or rather the place where I knew I would meet the ball, by a half step. Then I planted my foot, started my turn, and put my glove out to snag the ball as it hopped past me on the left. All in one motion I pirouetted, grabbed the ball from my glove and whipped it toward home.

The universe has a strange way of slowing down in the middle of a play like that. I'd guess it took all of two seconds for me to make the relay, but that was time enough to realize that if my throw home wound up off line, it would probably tail left, first-base side, because of the momentum of my turn as I threw, so just as I released I put a little extra pressure on the right side of the ball with my middle and ring fingers, as if I was throwing a weak slider from forty yards away. Sure enough, the ball sailed a little up the first-base line as it headed toward the plate. It bounced about three yards beyond the pitcher's mound, and the spin I put on was enough to make it skip slightly right, hopping waist-high to the catcher just as the runner reached home.

Despite all my heroics, the guy would have been safe easily if he had just gone into a slide. Maybe he was too close to the plate to change his approach, or maybe it surprised him that I'd gotten the ball anywhere near home to begin with. Whatever the reason, instead of sliding, the runner lowered his shoulder, plowed into our catcher, and they both went tumbling into the umpire—who was way out of position to make the call on a close play at home. All three jumped back up at the same time. When our catcher pulled the ball from his glove and held it up, the ump made a big, sweeping punch in the air. Game over, good guys win.

While my throw was in midflight toward the catcher, I realized that the batter had held up at second base to see how things turned out on the play at home, so I took off to re-cover my bag. I was still sprinting to third when the catcher fished the ball from his mitt and the umpire ended the game with his big punch out. Every person in the stands seemed to jump out of their seat at the same time to celebrate the call. I figured it would be bad form to stop running just to take in the applause, so I slowed to a jog but kept on trotting until I reached the dugout. I only looked up when I got to the top step. Today's attendance was announced at 2,500, and I swear every man, woman and child was on their feet cheering as I looked around.

Am I sorry about the labor dispute that put me on the field this afternoon? Fuck no, I'm not sorry. I drove all the way from Columbus, Ohio, to make that game-ending throw today. For just the chance at a repeat performance, I'd happily drive home and the same route back tomorrow if I thought that fool would forget to slide again.

Twenty days till we're legit.

It was probably my old man who taught me that the best players let their game speak for itself, and leave hotdogging and smack-talking to the rookies and the homeboys. He never put up with a lot of showboating on the rare occasion when we'd go down to the elementary school field so he could hit me some grounders or throw pitch and catch. It wasn't that he would yell, but if you did too much prancing around after stopping a hard liner at your feet, he'd be apt to hit the next ball twice as hard at your chest.

"Don't act surprised that you made the play, Johnny," he'd call out. "Everyone will think you got lucky."

For me, growing up, a professional baseball game seen live and in person represented the height of conspicuous consumption. My father was a Depression-era baby, a member of the luckless generation that spent its adolescence in the shadow of the hardscrabble '30s. The lessons he learned about thrift and an honest day's work, he would never recover from.

"When I was your age I tried to train my dog to live without food or water," he would say, grinning at his own skinflint joke. "Almost did it too, till he up and died on me."

Invariably I would slip our collie Pharaoh the end of my hamburger or the heel of the bread loaf, just in case.

Dad worked forty a week in the Western Electric plant near the airport, stringing together wires that would eventually become the insides of telephones. The job fit my understanding of the father I knew: the intricacy of the circuits and the attention to detail needed in making all those wires work in harmony must have spoken to his love of order and precision. Still, working the line at Western was menial and repetitious, and at an early age I understood without having to be told that by the time he made it home at night—wrinkled from the heat of the soldering machines and worn down by the demands of the floor foreman whose orders he had to follow—my father would be in no mood to play catch or help me restring the webbing on my glove. Most evenings after dinner I biked over to Tall Boy's house, where we would listen to Marty Brennaman and Joe Nuxhall call Reds' games on the radio in his garage or throw grounders to each other till we'd retired nine innings' worth of imaginary batters.

I can still remember the sugar-high jolt of surprise when one evening in the summer between first and second grade my father brought home tickets to a Columbus Clippers game. I wasn't even sure he liked baseball, and I knew for a fact that he hated spending money. This was, after all, the same man who never threw away old newspapers because we could tie up a stack of them to use as a substitute for logs in the fireplace, thereby saving the going rate of twenty dollars per cord of wood.

"They had a deal at work," he told Mom and me, skipping over an explanation that the Clippers, Columbus's new triple-A team in the Pirates' farm system, held regular family-night specials for most of the big corporations in town.

That Saturday night Franklin County Stadium was packed with Little Leaguers in their uniforms and parents chasing after loose toddlers. The best seats we could find in general admission were under the stadium awning, well above the visitors' dugout.

"This is perfect," my father said. "All the first baseman does is catch the ball. But over here we can watch the left side of the infield work. Here's where the action is."

Dutifully, I kept my eyes on the shortstop and third baseman all game, watched as they positioned themselves for each pitch, noticed how the third baseman picked pebbles off the dirt apron around the bag before each new inning even though the field was pristine, having just been renovated for the Clippers' arrival that spring.

My father kept a running commentary through most of the game, only rising from his seat for a home run in the fifth and a hard grounder down the line in the seventh that the Clippers' third baseman took off his chest but was unable to make a play on.

"You see that, Johnny?" He nudged me with his elbow. "I told you these guys are good; just one promotion away from playing in the bigs."

"But Dad, he didn't even get the out."

"No, but if he lets that ball get by, the runner on second scores." My father pointed toward the sprawling cemetery beyond the left field wall, as if the ball might have hopped the fence and could be rolling among the tombstones by now if the third baseman hadn't done his job. "All of his teammates were counting on him to keep that one in the infield, and he didn't think twice about stopping it with his body. That's his responsibility, and he saved the run."

Duty, sacrifice, dependability—these were the ideals that made the game interesting for Jonathon W. Standen. Even at seven years old I thought my father was missing the point of baseball, but if those ideals were enough to get us out of the house and into seats forty rows above my hometown Clippers, I was willing to put up with his bullshit.

The phone rang not long after we got back to our hotel room following the Marlins game. I didn't even hear a hello.

"Jake! That was the most amazing throw. You won the game!"

"Sadie? You were there?"

"No, I watched it on NBC's *Game of the Week*. Yes, silly, I was there. How did you—"

"Wait," I cut in. "Why didn't you come down to say hi?"

"I got there late and didn't want to be a bother. But don't interrupt me; I'm praising you. That was fantastic! That play earned you dinner, anywhere you want."

"I only know a couple restaurants in town. I'm new here, remember?"

"Name a place," she said. "I'll even come pick you up."

I thought it over for a minute. I'm not one for eating the same food every day, but they had a pretty big menu, and everything I'd tasted yesterday was terrific.

"Do you know a Chinese restaurant called Trey Yuen?"

"Sure, just down from the Piggly Wiggly. Is six thirty too early?"

So I had a couple hours to kill before my date.

Our hotel room was nice enough, with a little kitchenette and two double beds separated by a nightstand. For a couple days running though, it had been bugging me that the corner on my side near the window was very dark. The ceiling light was fairly dim and the reading light above my bed wasn't bright enough to reach into the dark corner by the chair, which was where I liked to sit when I was reading. Tall Boy thought I was nuts but I decided to go out in search of a lamp while he headed for the middle school track to run some laps.

I wasn't impressed with the selection I found at the big-box store not far from the hotel but as I was getting ready to leave I saw a lamp on a high shelf that looked just right. It had a black base and black shade, with a looping gold trim pattern running along the top and bottom. It seemed a little jazzy for our otherwise vanilla hotel room but I figured, screw it. It was my lamp for my corner and if I liked it, to hell with matching the decor.

I brought the lamp back to our room and set it on the end table beside the reading chair. When Tall Boy came in from his run, it was the first thing he noticed.

"Call the cops," he said. "Somebody broke into our room and dumped their crap in the corner."

"I just bought it. It's kind of cool, don't you think?"

"It's kind of something." Brian peeled off his sweat-soaked T-shirt. "It gives the room a certain Hugh-Hefner-at-the-Playboy-Mansion, beautiful-babe-on-a-waterbed-in-the-middle-of-the-living-room feel. Except this isn't the Playboy Mansion. And you got no waterbed. And there's no woman here. And you ain't Hugh Hefner."

I didn't tell Tall Boy about my date but when he finished showering, he cleared out of the room without me having to ask. In a weird way I was glad. Other than that time at the stadium after the Phillies game when she was leaving as he was walking up, Tall Boy had never seen Sadie. I had to admit I wasn't sure I wanted them to meet—not yet, anyway. Brian and I had never once fought over the same woman, and I didn't want Sadie to be the first. He was married after all, with a kid on the way. If I lost this woman to a guy in that situation, my ego might never recover.

I had given her the room number before we hung up, so there was no call from the front desk, just a knock on the door when she arrived.

Sadie had her hair swept back from her face, held on the sides with what looked like little yellow daisies. It wasn't all that dramatic, but there was something in the way her cheekbones stood out that I'd never noticed before. The trick with the hair clips I would have thought of as a teenage-girl thing but on Sadie it somehow made her look regal, like a queen gone a-Maying. Usually when you date someone for a while you get used to how they look, but every time I set eyes on Sadie, I was surprised at how much I had missed the last time. She looked stunning.

"So this is where they put you guys on ice between games," she said as I stepped aside to let her in. "It's very Howard Johnson-ish."

"I know. I even had to buy a lamp to make it look more like a sloppy bachelors' pad."

She glanced at my lamp, then did a 360 to take in the room.

"Hmm," she said with a shrug. "Hotels."

It crossed my mind that, with Tall Boy out of the room and this being our third date and all, there might not even be a need to go to the restaurant. But then I remembered that we only had a sort-of date at the pizza place so technically this was our second and a half date. I thought: *Christ, things are getting complicated, and I haven't even kissed her yet.*

"So I've waited long enough." I motioned to the lamp again. "What do you think of my new purchase?"

"Oh, sorry. Are we fishing for compliments now?" Sadie appraised my acquisition. "I thought you were joking about buying a lamp. Don't these rooms come furnished anymore?"

"They do, but that corner needed more light. I like it: black lamp, gold trim—very chic. What do you think?"

"And you bought this, huh? Meaning you paid money for it?" A smile fought its way across Sadie's face. "It's interesting. It has a certain—how do the French say?—'I do not know what.'"

"Am I sensing a less-than-positive reaction to my lamp?"

"You know the song that goes, 'I'm turning Japanese, I think I'm turning Japanese, I really think so'? That song is about this lamp."

"It's not that out of place, is it?" I wasn't about to tell her that Tall Boy hated it, too. "I think it's all right."

"No, it's fine. It's really different." Sadie could only keep her smile down for a moment. "You don't think they made any others like this, do you?"

"Okay, forget the lamp. It's an ugly lamp. Sorry I asked about the lamp."

"I'm only teasing," she said, and then she did the sweetest thing. Sadie reached over and lightly stroked the hairs on my arm, like she was smoothing ruffled feathers. "You're not mad, are you?"

How do you get mad at someone who was quickly becoming the prettiest woman you've ever known?

We drove in Sadie's VW to Trey Yuen. Everything was so similar to the previous day that it might have been one hour after Tall Boy, Folgers and I left instead of twenty-four: same hunched old man; same dividing panels; same empty dining room; same cute, mute waitress.

I ordered soup and beers for both of us, and the waitress disappeared behind the swinging kitchen doors. When I turned back, Sadie was beaming at me from across the table.

"No, really. That was an amazing throw."

"I got lucky."

"Your throw was skill," she corrected me. "It was lucky that the runner forgot to slide."

I don't know if it was because she understood the details of the play as well as she did or if it was just the wattage of her smile beneath those amazing cheekbones, but I had to look away for a second to keep from laughing like a schoolboy.

"You really know the game," I finally said. "How did you learn so much?"

"My father used to take me to spring training games all the time when I was little. That was a long time ago though, before they became such a big deal."

So far that spring the largest crowd for one of our home games was the day they gave tickets away: four thousand people. Even at dinky Dunedin Stadium that hadn't filled two-thirds of the seats. We both realized it at the same time.

"Well, I mean before—"

"I know what you meant." I took the opportunity to change the subject. "You've never mentioned your father. Is he still . . . ?"

I finished with a shrug so she could answer any question she wanted: Is he still living in this area? Still a good guy? Still walking the planet?

"He lives in Pensacola with his new wife. I only see him a couple times a year but we talk every few weeks." Sadie paused when our waitress appeared with the soup and beers, then began again once we had given our orders. "I really loved those times with my father. I think that's the main reason I've been going to your games this spring—just to remind myself."

I wondered if maybe I should resent that. Did she mean she hadn't been coming out to see me? I liked the way she said "your games," though. I decided not to go there.

"And Mom?" I asked instead.

"Bad subject. We don't get along so great."

"Was it something that happened in particular, or just mothers and daughters and Freud?"

"No, it was something very in particular." Sadie took a spoonful of her soup and nodded in approval at the taste. "When I was fifteen my parents and I were traveling on vacation. We had one of those big RVs everyone used to own, remember? Anyway, it was late and I was sleeping in the middle of the front seat. My dad was driving, and she was on the passenger side. I guess a deer ran out in the road or something, we never really did figure out what it was, but Dad swerved, we ran off the road, and the RV flipped over on its side—my mother's side.

"Everybody broke something, and we all wound up in the hospital. Dad broke his wrist and his leg, and I broke my back. It was one of the thorax bones. You know the ones on your spine that look like little angel wings? Believe it or not, I was only in the hospital about four days, and then I had to wear a brace for a few weeks and that was it. I was fine after that."

It wasn't a funny story, but I had to smile at the part about the wings. That made perfect sense to me. She might have broken them, but who wants to drink beer with an angel? I just liked the idea that at fifteen she had angel wings, unfettered and whole.

"And what did Mom break?"

Sadie frowned. "Her personality, I think. She wasn't buckled in, and she smashed her head against the dashboard. They had to open her skull to relieve the swelling. And when they sewed her back together, she was the same woman—same face, same height, same clothes, everything—but she was a completely different person. I don't know how to describe it. She stopped laughing and smiling. She wasn't interested in doing family things. She stopped coming to my school events. She just didn't care about anything but herself."

"I've never heard of anything like that. Are you sure—" I didn't mean to put her on trial, so I stopped for a second to reword my question. "Did your father notice the changes, too?"

"Did he ever," she said with a sad laugh. "They got a divorce about a year later. That's when I saw him last, in fact—when he got remarried this past Christmas in Pensacola."

I could tell Sadie was uncomfortable with the details of her story, but I was fascinated by the telling. It reminded me that she had been alive for decades before we met, and every time she told me more about herself, I couldn't wait to find out the rest. She was like a wonderful movie full of intrigue and promise, and I was already hooked after just the opening scenes. But with that realization came another: you couldn't rush things with a woman like Sadie; the stories she had to share needed to unfurl at their own pace and in their own time.

I changed the subject to lighten the mood, and her smile came back quick enough. She liked my stories about the team, so I told her everything I could remember about the last few days in the clubhouse. She paid the check as promised, then even put up a brief protest before letting me chip in for the tip. By the time we were parked outside the hotel it was well past nine.

"What are the chances I can buy you a nightcap in the lounge?" I asked.

"I'd love to, but I have to go. I promised a friend that I'd cover her shift in the morning."

"Can you make tomorrow's game? Business woman's special. All working girls who know one of the players get in free."

"I can't. I'm sorry." She shifted her car from park to neutral, the international sign for someone who needs to hit the road. "I should be able to make it Thursday, though. So you'll only have to play great without me for one game."

I got out of the car and walked around to her side. I've never been shy with the ladies and I would have given money to kiss her good night, but I just couldn't. It didn't seem right. She wasn't the kind of woman you pushed things with. They just had to happen.

I forgot, of course, that Sadie was a Psychic Soulmate. She reached through the open window and pulled me down to her.

"Thanks for a lovely evening," she said, and we kissed. "Have a good game tomorrow. Break a lamp. I mean, a leg."

She smiled and waved, and then she was gone.

Another solid day at the plate: one for three, doubled to right center and scored in the fourth. Didn't help. We lost 10–6 to the Red Sox in Fort Myers.

My two-bagger today hit the warning track and bounced over the wall on one hop. It always drives me crazy when someone refers to that play as a "ground rule double." That may be the dumbest thing anyone has ever said about anything. Ground rules are specific regulations that only apply to the field you are playing on today, due to special circumstances related to those grounds. This is why there's a ground rule at Wrigley Field that describes what happens if a batted ball gets lost in the ivy growing on the outfield wall. No other stadium in the MLB has ivy on the wall. Yet every home field of every professional baseball team in North America has an outfield wall. The rule book states that if you hit a ball over the outfield wall on the fly, you get to touch all the bases and score. Nobody in the history of the game ever referred to it as a "ground rule home run." It's an automatic home run—and if you hit that same ball over that same wall on a hop, it's an automatic double. Let's all try never to get that wrong again, shall we?

At the request of the players' union, the National Labor Relations Board issued a complaint this morning against the owners for unfair labor practices in connection with the owners eliminating salary arbitration after the MLB contract expired last winter. The sports talk shows are saying this will lead to the NLRB filing an injunction on behalf of the union guys in US district court to have the old, expired contract put back in place. That could end the strike as far as the players are concerned but then lead the owners to lock the players out until a new agreement is reached. In other words, you can't temporarily quit because you're temporarily fired. All of this after the players' union rep, Donald Fehr, and the owners' rep, Jerry McMorris, agreed at a press conference last week that, and I quote: "The replacement players, not the striking major leaguers, likely will be on the field Opening Day." Things look better with each passing week.

None of which has kept the local press from laying into us every chance they get. I think they've come up with every possible variation on our team name in the papers. Some of them are dumb, some are actually funny; they all sting a little. So far this spring we've been called the Not So New Jays, the I've Got the Blues Jays, the Replacement Jays, the Free Jays, the E-Jays, the Egre-Jays, the Oh Jays, the No Way Jays, the Go Away Jays, the Not Ready for Prime Time Ball Players, the Sad Jays, the Scab Jays, the Sorry Jays, the Sub Jays, the Toronto Waiters and Bartenders Association, the D Team, the F Troop, and "those guys in blue with the bird on the uniform."

Nineteen days till we're legit.

Looking in a mirror outside the locker room showers that Wednesday, I was shocked by the image reflected back. My hair was growing bushy in back, was smooched down across the front, and was standing almost straight out on the sides. I'd reached the point every player reaches at least once every baseball season: I had developed permanent hat hair. Basically you have two options—walk around looking like there's an invisible bowl pushed down on your head, or cut the front and sides short so there's no extra to stick out and get funky when you have your hat on. Though in Ohio I'd gone entire seasons without worrying about it, I thought that this spring, here in all this Gulf coast humidity, I should try to keep my 'do under control. So when we got back from Fort Myers after the Red Sox game I headed into Clearwater to look for a barber. I drove around for twenty minutes but the only barbershop I found was the one in the strip mall between Trey Yuen and the Piggly Wiggly, so I gave up the hunt and just went there.

Because the shopping center itself was almost brand new, I wasn't surprised to find the barbershop cleaner and better lit than the ones I frequented back home. Instead of the standard collection of framed photos, bowling trophies and tin Coke signs on the wall, the shop's waiting area featured padded chrome seats and posters of beautiful people in hairstyles so au courant that only a model could get away with wearing their hair like that. The usual smells of tonic and shaving cream mixed with a sweet scent I couldn't quite identify and wasn't expecting to encounter at a barbershop—plug-in air freshener maybe, or suntan lotion.

An old Chinese woman, in the middle of cutting a guy's hair when I walked in, smiled and motioned toward the farthest station lined up along the wall. Behind that chair stood a skinny Asian kid who looked all of fifteen. He was absorbed in the work of sharpening a blade on a strap.

"He take you now," the woman told me in a heavy accent.

Both sidewalls were lined with mirrors, each reflecting its opposite, and my head whirled with a vertigo sense of peripheral infinity as I walked past the old woman and her customer. I sat down at the chair in front of the kid but he didn't seem to notice. Behind me I could hear him sharpening, dragging the razor back and forth over the strap. I was about to turn around when the woman said something in Chinese and the kid put the blade down.

"Okay," he said, touching my shoulder.

A moment passed before I realized he was waiting for me to speak. I told him to leave the back alone, straighten it out if it needed it, but mostly I wanted to get a cut above the ears and about cap-rim high in front.

"Okay," he said again, and I thought maybe I'd heard his entire repertoire of English. That was fine. I hadn't come in for scintillating conversation, just a trim. I settled back for my haircut.

He started to hum a tune I didn't recognize and snapped his scissors twice before beginning on the back. He paused several times in the next five minutes and I kept expecting him to move around to the sides, but he continued to snip away behind me. When he took a short break and walked to the sink, I was sure he'd come around to the front. Instead, he picked up the razor he had been sharpening and began to scrape it down my neck. He had worked the blade to a fine edge. After two or three passes I could feel the nape of my neck tingling. Several more swipes and still he showed no signs of stopping. Finally I had to lean forward to stop him.

"Dude," I said. "You don't need to do much to the back. I mostly want the front cut."

"Okay."

He shortened his strokes, making tiny swipes down my neck, but continued working on the back for several more minutes. By this point my neck was raw. When I was certain one more scrape and he would carve through to my Adam's apple, I leaned forward again.

"No, really," I said. "That's enough on the back."

The old woman, who had finished with her customer and was watching us from her chair, said something sharp in Chinese. When the kid answered I was surprised to discover his only accent was that of a Florida teenager.

"I'm not," he said. "I'm just trying to get it straight. Look at it. His hair is stupid. It won't sit down in back."

The old woman covered the distance between her chair and mine in four quick strides.

"You no say that! You do what customer want. He want you quit, you quit!"

She turned to me and bowed very gracefully. "You hair not stupid."

"Umm," I said. "Thanks?"

She shooed the kid out from behind the chair and took his place. "Short in front, top of ear, yes?"

I nodded and she picked up the scissors, going to work on my left side. I closed my eyes and listened as she carried on a conversation with herself over my bowed head. "Customer not stupid," she murmured between snips. "You stupid one." At one point she stopped in midclip to yell out, "You stupid!"

The kid shouted something in reply, but he was in a back room somewhere and I didn't catch the words.

I don't know if she was giving me the usual treatment or special attention to make up for the torture I'd endured, but after she finished with the trim, she brought a warm towel, lightly scented with lemon, and placed it over my face. Then she got out one of those vibrating electric massagers that strap over your hand, and she went to work on my back and shoulders.

As I lay there with the towel draped over me and the massager thumping away on my shoulders, I began to consider my last few games. I still had my errorless streak going, but what excited me was how my at bats seemed to be improving. I had a hit in both of the last two games, including a double. Even my outs had been solid shots that just didn't find a hole. It wasn't exactly a streak to rival DiMaggio's but I was feeling way more comfortable in the box. I pictured myself in my stance, hands at my ribs, knees unlocked, leaning slightly back and shifting my weight forward as the pitch started in. Assenmacher's pointers were a help, but they weren't that dramatic a change. What else had I done differently between our game three days ago and two days ago?

We'd had a day off on Monday. That was the same night Folgers took Tall Boy and me to Trey Yuen—the same place, of course, where Sadie bought me dinner last night. The more I thought about it, the more I thought there might be something to that. Dinner two nights in a row at a restaurant I'd never even heard of before, followed by two good games the next afternoon. There might be something to that.

By the time the old woman finished, I'd been patted and primped, powdered, shaved and massaged. I was so relaxed my upper body felt like Jell-O. I gave her a five-dollar tip on a twelve-buck haircut and headed down the sidewalk for a quick round of sweet and sour at Trey Yuen.

THURSDAY, MARCH 16

We got shut down 5-2 by Texas in Port Charlotte. A seventh-inning dinger by Lenny Longo made the score closer than the game really was. Their pitcher had a mean curve that our guys never did figure out. I was terrible, went 0-fer with two men left on, one in scoring position. In my first at bat I watched a ball low and then swung at the second pitch, a curve over the outside of the plate, hitting a dribbler that the second baseman could have fielded in his sleep. In my second at bat I did something I almost never do: I swung at the first pitch, popping it up in foul territory behind third base. In my last at bat, with a guy on third, I hit a one-hopper back to the mound on a 1-0 delivery. That ended the inning and when I walked back to the dugout to get my glove, Assenmacher said, "Standen, Wilson's going in. You're done for the day." I had played the first six and a half; he probably had planned on taking me out after our at bats anyway—but still it felt like retribution.

I played error-free ball, made four putouts and was a rock-solid anchor on the left side of our defense for over two hours today. But my hitting streak is done, I got benched in the middle of an inning, and the old doubts are creeping back, all after five pitches and three swings of the bat.

A good swing is like a good Swiss watch; there are a thousand parts that all need to move in sync to be effective. The problem is, everything you do to make your swing more effective has an equal and opposite

94

reaction that makes your success more unlikely. To get the bat quickly through the strike zone with force, you have to stand square to the plate, even though standing that way makes seeing the pitch all the way in with both eyes more difficult. You need to step toward the pitcher with a large enough stride to generate momentum for the bat, but your stride must be compact enough that when you hit the ball you're still balanced enough to take off for first base immediately. At the beginning of your stride, you need to start your hands forward because you only have a half second between when the pitcher releases the ball and when it hits the catcher's mitt. But you can't start them too soon, because only when the pitch is halfway to the plate can you accurately judge if it's high or low, fast or slow, and you need to gauge height and speed to know where and when to swing. You need both hands on the bat to hit the ball as hard as you can, but you should finish one-handed or you'll wind up off balance for the sprint to first. You want to hit the ball with as much power as you can generate, but if your swing isn't under control, you'll miss the ball completely.

All of which leads hitters and hitting instructors to say the most contradictory things. The pitcher throws a round ball and you swing a cylinder of wood, yet you're supposed to hit it "square." They talk about being patient at the plate while being aggressive with the swing. I've been told more times than I can count that you should beat the pitcher with your strength—fastball hitters hold out for a fastball; if you hit curves, wait for the curve—though the best pure hitters of this generation, guys like Wade Boggs, Tony Gwynn and Kirby Puckett, all talk about going with the pitch and using what the pitcher gives you. At least once a broadcast you'll hear a commentator say the best pitch most hitters are likely to see is the first pitch of an at bat. But those same analysts save their highest praise for a batter who works the pitcher to a full count, maybe even fouls off two or three more before they get a hit or earn a base on balls. And of course once batters get in a groove they all describe their success the same way: "I'm seeing the ball well." Hell, I see every pitch of every at bat just fine. What does that have to do with hitting it?

I double-checked my numbers last night and discovered that I'd goofed my calculations. While it's true that we open against the Mariners Monday, April 3, the regular season officially begins the night before, when Florida hosts New York at 7:05 on Sunday, April 2. If I'm reading the copy of my contract correctly, we'll all be "a member of the team on the active roster at the beginning of the regular season" as soon as the Marlins' starter brings his first delivery to the Mets' leadoff batter, in which case we'll not only get the Opening Day roster bonus but also qualify for the last conditional clause—the termination buyout of our contracts—as soon as that first pitch crosses the plate Sunday night. I expected the guys to razz me when I explained my goof during our clubhouse ceremony before we took the bus to Port Charlotte, but instead they all let out a cheer. And why not? In the past twenty-four hours, we each got forty-eight hours closer (on my sign, anyway) to being $25,000 richer.

Seventeen days—I mean it this time—till we're legit.

It was probably just as well that my streak at the plate stopped when it did. I wasn't sure what I'd done to start it or what had caused it to end, but I was getting a little tired of Chinese food, and there was no way my neck would survive a second trip to the obsessive-compulsive barber boy.

The bus ride back from the Texas game was quiet but as we pulled into the hotel parking lot, Folgers walked past Tall Boy and me in our seats. "Poker in my room tonight, gents," he said.

If you had gone searching for one, you probably could have found a card game in someone's room most every night of the week. Usually Tall Boy preferred to run, or one of us had something else planned, but after our lackluster loss and a quiet ride back to Dunedin, a spirited session of cards with Folgers and the boys sounded like just the thing.

We puttered around our hotel room for a while. Tall Boy called Karen while I surfed the TV channels for something to watch. When he got off the phone, he said, "There's a message on there for you," and went off to the bathroom. I hadn't even noticed the light was flashing.

It was Sadie of course, saying that she didn't realize we had an away game that afternoon but I should give her a call around seven if I got the chance. From Tall Boy's bed only the hour digit on the TV clock was visible. It was after five.

As Tall Boy walked back out from the bathroom, there was a knock on the door. Folgers's voice boomed from the hallway: "Game on!"

We followed him down the hall to the room he shared with Speedboat, where they were already setting things up. Speedboat sat at the kitchenette table while Hack Hennessey arranged chairs so that we all would have space. Their room was a carbon copy of ours—same double beds separated by a nightstand, same dark corner beside the window.

Folgers had stopped by the ice machine on his way down the hall and when he opened the bathroom door, we saw why: a dozen beers were icing in the sink. Another six-pack sat on the counter waiting for a place in the ice. I'm sure it's a result of all the road trips I took with the team while I was still underage at Ohio State, but few things in life cheer me as quick as the sight of a sink full of beers on ice. There's just something about it, most of the promise with none of the hassle of going out to a bar. It's about the most pleasant surprise I can imagine seeing in a hotel bathroom sink.

We ordered out for subs and then cranked up the card game, trying at various points over the next hour to figure out how to make "who goes on the next beer run" a chit you could win or lose as part of the pot. Eventually it occurred to me that for nearly every 5-4-3 double play I had turned that spring I had thrown the ball to Hack at second, but I had no idea how he wound up in Dunedin with the rest of us. When I asked, he laughed and told me it was mostly his brother's fault.

"Back home I do subcontracting work as a carpenter," Hack said. "I try to keep the rust off playing weekends in the local leagues around Albuquerque, so when they announced the Blue Jays' tryouts I went, figuring what the hell. The next thing I know they're sending me a plane ticket for spring training. I hardly expected to get signed, so to be honest, once they made me the offer, I wasn't sure I wanted to go through with it. Around now is when most of the housing construction starts for the summer, ya know? But my kid brother and I are pretty tight, and he was all psyched about me playing again, so I didn't want to flat out refuse either.

"Then one night I'm out at a club listening to the band he plays with—they got kind of a jazz combo; they're young but they're pretty good—and between songs the lead guitarist says, 'Ladies and gentlemen, please give a hand for our drummer's brother, who's headed to Florida next week to play with the replacement Blue Jays!'

"I could have killed 'em, doggin' me out in front of all those people." Hack smiled at the memory. "But when I stood up, everybody started clapping. It was the most amazing thing. There I was in the middle of all these strangers, and everybody's raising glasses, calling out, 'Good luck!' I don't think I'll ever forget the look on my brother's face. After that you couldn't have kept me from coming. I would've come down here and played naked, for free."

Hack snapped his fingers. "Almost forgot. I brought a little something to make this a full-fledged boys' night out."

With a flourish and a "Ta-da!" he pulled several video cassettes from a brown paper bag lying at the foot of the nearest bed and popped one in the VCR above the TV. The cheesy techno *bonka-chicka* music that accompanied the opening credits was enough to tip me off as to what cinematic treasures were in store for us. So Hack Hennessey was our keeper of the porn collection. Every team has one.

After roughly forty-five seconds of film we were looking at our first set of bare hooters, and by the two-minute mark Speedboat had his chair completely turned around from the card table. He apparently had never seen a porno before.

"What movie es these?" Speedboat asked.

"It's, um—" Hack checked the cassette box on the bed. "*Hard, Harder and Harriett*. We're also featuring *I Come from the Land Down Under* and *Free My Willie*. Preferences?"

Speedboat leaned to see around Hack, who was blocking his view. "These es good."

When Folgers stood up to take a restroom break, I noticed from the clock above the TV that it was past seven. I asked if I could borrow their phone.

"Calling in the party girls?" Folgers asked. "Boys' night out indeed."

Tall Boy answered for me: "Jake's working on his Florida harem."

"Already? Good man," Folgers said at the restroom door. "We'll get you married off yet, Golden Jake."

As I reached for the phone, Tall Boy made a broad gesture of plucking a few dollars from each person's pile on the table; he was volunteering to go on the beer run during our TV time-out.

For some reason that only a hotel could explain, the phone base was bolted to the nightstand and the cord reached just to the far side of the bed. It was obvious I wasn't going to get much privacy for this conversation. Sadie answered on the second ring.

98

"Hey there," she said. "How did your game go this afternoon?"

"We've played better. How was your day off?"

"Margaritas poolside, coconut oil rubdowns from my cabana boy. You know—the usual."

When Folgers returned from the bathroom he sat on the bed between me and the set, but from the sounds of it our gal Harriett was either practicing her scales or in mid–flagrante delicto. I wondered if the TV was loud enough to be heard over the phone.

"So is cabana boy still there, or are you free for the evening?"

"I am flying solo at the moment," Sadie answered. "But it sounds like you have some company on your end. What's going on?"

Just then Folgers decided to share his critique of the film. "That's right, darlin'. Put those ankles up around your ears."

"Nothing special," I told Sadie. "Hanging out with the boys."

"Oh, let me guess," Sadie said. "You're all sitting around playing poker with the Playboy Channel on."

For the first time it occurred to me, the downside of dating a Psychic Soulmate.

"That's a good idea," I replied. "Do you think they get the Playboy Channel in this fleabag hotel?"

"Back up!" Folgers called out. "I'll decide if I want to stare at her earrings. Back the friggin' camera up!"

"I'm sure they have pay-per-view," Sadie reasoned. "Call the front desk and ask for a group discount special."

"Don't give me close-ups, moron," Folgers yelled. "I don't care about her expression!"

"Anyway," I said to Sadie. "Do you want to get together and do something?"

"Oh, for God's sake," Folgers bellowed. "I really don't give a damn about *his* expression. Back up!"

Sadie laughed. "It sounds like you guys are in the middle of something. We can go out tomorrow instead."

"No, it's not a problem," I assured her. "We're just sitting around. Let's get together."

"Now you're showing me his ass?" Folgers moaned. "I bet the director of this movie is a fag."

"That's all right," Sadie told me. "I'll be off work by four tomorrow. Give me a call when you get free, and we'll catch a show or something, okay?"

"Okay," I replied, not because it was but because I didn't have a better answer.

Before I could think of something better, she said, "See you tomorrow," and hung up.

Just then Tall Boy burst through the half-open door, a twelve-pack in each hand.

"What did I miss?" Brian asked.

"Hack was showing us his gay porn," Folgers said.

"I just rent 'em. I don't make 'em," Hack said.

"I like it," Speedboat said.

"Let's play some cards," I said.

FRIDAY, MARCH 17

We lost 7–2 to the Cards in St. Petersburg. I went zero for one but raised my on-base percentage with an impressive .500 day. In my second at bat, top of the fifth, I took two heaters for balls, fouled off a low slider that I shouldn't have swung at, and then watched a changeup hit the dirt to make the count 3–1. Three balls and one strike is a hitter's dream. Unlike 3–0, when the coach is likely to give you the "take" sign, with 3–1 you can look for a specific pitch and swing for the fences if it comes, or let it go by and even if it's a strike you're still alive with a full count. On the mound was a right-hander whose best pitch was a slider. I hit sliders, and he needed a strike. I was amped for a cookie in my kitchen all the way.

As he released the ball it started inside and letter high, exactly where it should be if it was going to break across the plate at belt level. I took a big step and tensed my forearms, waiting till the last possible instant to bring my bat through the strike zone. The ball began to break down and over the plate just as I expected, but then the strangest thing happened. About halfway to me it must have caught a gust of wind, because suddenly it broke in. I'd never seen a pitch start to break away and then come back in. With all my momentum moving forward I had no chance to get out of the way, and the ball drilled me two inches above my left elbow. It made a fleshy *spack* noise against my arm, like the face-slap sound effect in a kung fu movie. Just after it hit me the ball dribbled toward first base in fair territory and I wondered if I should start running, in case the umpire thought it had gone off the end of my bat.

And then the pain came.

It felt like someone had speared me with a blunt syringe and injected lava into my elbow. I dropped the bat, or maybe it just flew out of my hands as scorching bolts of fire jabbed up and down my arm. My fingers went numb. For several seconds the only sensation I could focus on—the only thought there was room for in my head—was the pure, liquid fury racing through my left side. I swear even my left leg started to throb in sympathy for my arm. I danced a little jig at the plate, holding my elbow and clenching my teeth, trying to keep from yelling out the stream of obscenities I was ready to hurl at the pitcher and the catcher, the ump, their mothers, everyone.

"Dead ball!" the umpire shouted. "Batter, take your base." Then he bent down beside me, placing a hand on my back as I stood doubled over at the plate. "You all right, son?"

"Peachy," I whispered back.

The catcher quick-stepped out from behind the plate, ostensibly to get the ball but also to get between me and the mound in case I made an angry dash for his pitcher.

I know in recent years batters have gotten a bad rap for charging the mound after getting beaned, but there's no other way to describe being drilled on the elbow by an eighty-five-mile-an-hour pitch but to say it hurts like a son of a bitch. You overdose on pain. It's the same temporary insanity as when you're listening to music with headphones on and someone cranks up the volume to full blast. Your brain gives your body two immediate commands: stop the madness, and kill the bastard who started it—not necessarily in that order.

By the time the trainer jogged out to the plate I had my temper under control, so the best he could do was spray some Liqui-Freeze on my arm and make sure nothing was broken. I hadn't even left the batter's box yet and already an evil-looking purple moon had risen above my elbow. As I walked to first base I tried to stare the pitcher down, but gave that up when I realized I didn't look too menacing with tears clouding my eyes. Besides, it was the fifth pitch of my at bat. I had hit into a fielder's choice my first time up. Our pitchers hadn't beaned any of their players that afternoon. There was no reason to have done it on purpose. The pitch just got away from him.

The first-base coach let me stay in the game to prove my mettle, and for that I was thankful. I was equally thankful when our next man up hit into a 1-6-3 double play on the first pitch he saw. There was no shame in getting taken out before the next half inning; it was perfectly possible they were going to do that anyway. I watched the rest of the game with an ice pack taped to my elbow. As I sat on the bench feeling sorry for myself, I remembered being jealous of Lenny Longo the day he got nailed on the knee. Be careful what you wish for.

To anyone who thinks professional baseball isn't a macho sport played by the macho-est of men, consider this: despite all the inherent danger in the game, when was the last time you heard one of the union players talk about fear—just good old-fashioned being afraid? There are pitchers in The Show who throw one-hundred miles per hour, which gives a batter roughly four-tenths of a second to decide if the pitch is a strike, a ball, or headed for your head. And there are other pitchers who can throw 89 mph curves that start out head high, only to drop down over the strike zone in the last forty feet before the plate. And the best of the best pitchers, the Nolan Ryans who can throw both 100 mph fastballs and 89 mph curves, can throw either pitch with an almost identical delivery so that both pitches look exactly the same until they're halfway to you. Yet no player has ever been quoted in the paper saying the obvious: "I hated stepping in the batter's box today because if I made one simple mistake, just once misjudged the heater for the deuce, in one-half of one second Nolan Ryan's fastball could have ended my career." But the fear of God is always in you. In fact it's the pitcher's best friend. If it wasn't, what would be the point of Nolan Ryan ever having learned to throw a curve?

I wouldn't have said so out loud, but Sadie had been on my mind for three days straight, ever since she'd kissed me and then left me in the hotel parking lot the night of our last date. I wasn't about to let anything keep me from seeing her after Friday's game. The forty bucks I'd lost the previous night would be why I wasn't up for another card game, and my sore elbow would have been enough to get me out of running if Tall Boy had offered. As it turned out, no excuses were needed.

"You know what I haven't done in forever?" Sadie asked when I called. "Bowl."

I was hopeful, but I doubted I'd heard her right. "Ball?"

"Bowl. You know—pins, lanes, bowling ball."

"Bowl," I echoed. "Sure, right. Me neither."

The last time I'd gone bowling was in ninth grade. I hadn't missed it.

Sadie caught my hesitation. "C'mon. It'll be fun, except for the part where I mop the floor with your sorry butt."

I'm certain that was the first time I'd heard anyone talk smack about a game of bowling. She had gone too far.

"I'm in."

She picked me up at the hotel and we drove to a place called the Gator Bowl in Tampa. The bowling industry clearly hadn't missed me much either; the parking lot was packed with cars. I was confused at first because when we parked and then started walking toward the entrance the interior lights appeared to be off. My confusion continued all the way to the front desk. Instead of the usual blast of white fluorescence, the alley was lit almost entirely with black lights and flashing mirror balls. A Rolling Stones song blared from the overhead speaker system.

"It's Rock-n-Bowl," the guy at the counter shouted in response to my question. "Every Friday and Saturday till midnight. The kids love it. You want a lane?"

I doubted the lighting or the music would impair my meager bowling skills, so I shrugged and shouted back, "Set us up."

We got shoes and a score sheet, then wandered up the alley until we spotted the lane we'd been assigned. I was a little concerned that this might be a noisy repeat of our night at the pizza place but once we walked down the stairs to the seats behind our lane, the music wasn't directly overhead anymore and we could hear each other talk, at least from close range.

Sadie leaned into me as we put on our shoes. "Look at all these babies!"

She was right. The place was swarming with teens barely old enough to have a driver's permit, and some who didn't look even that old. There was no way to hear what any of them were saying over the music, but their body language and facial expressions suggested very little had changed since the last time I went bowling, when I was one of them. They formed small, same-sex huddles around the scoring tables and on the raised walkway behind the lanes where snack tables were set at intervals. To the girls and boys alike, the actual game seemed a complete afterthought. The girls were all jittery energy and wide-eyed gossip, touching and giggling in their tight cliques. The boys stood farther apart, usually in clumps of twos. One boy would talk while the other struck a pose, craning his head to check out the girls in the closest pack as he listened. After a time the second boy would respond while the first struck a pose of listening and gawking. I would have guessed that for every three lanes in the alley there was at least one couple who had agreed to meet here on a date, but I could see no boy-girl pair together in the place. Teen peer pressure and bowling alley protocol seemed to forbid it.

Being a grown-up had its advantages. I looked at Sadie and smiled.

Sadie's dark hair was loose around her shoulders, a little windblown from the drive over with the windows down. She wore white shorts and a yellow golf shirt with the collar slightly flared in back, and under the black lights her skin, usually an even tan, appeared a deep chocolate. The whites of her eyes shone as if lit from within. She looked fabulous, completely exotic, like an island girl from some unnamed place in the tropics. It almost startled me to hear English come out when she spoke.

"What in the world did you do to your arm?"

I looked down. My skin was unusually dark too, and just below my left sleeve the bruise from where I took the pitch that afternoon was clearly visible. After an hour with the ice pack it had turned a strange brownish blue, but under the lights in the alley it looked defiantly black, a patch of wet asphalt glaring out from a layer of dirty snow. I told her about the beanball and how I'd never seen a slider move the way it had.

"You poor thing," she said sweetly. "Does it hurt?"

"Did at the time. It's just a bruise now."

When she reached over and touched it, I realized I'd been mistaken; it was still damn tender. Sadie lightly poked the spot, pulling back to see if it changed the color of the mark. The dark bruise remained.

"When they stay the same color, they still hurt," she said. "You're just being a tough guy, aren't you?"

Her smile proved she wasn't accusing me of anything. Her teeth were radiantly white in the black lighting.

Just as I thought of it, the idea forming as a joke in my mind, Sadie leaned down and kissed my bruise. I could feel the cool texture of her mouth on my arm, and though it was impossible over the music, I thought I could even hear the moist whisper of her lips as they met and then left my skin. The image of her hair tumbling down her back as she leaned in so close let loose a tingle that raced up my elbow and down my side, not stopping till it had reached my legs.

We ordered a pitcher of beer and two burgers with fries from the snack bar, then got serious about our showdown. I quickly discovered my bowling skills weren't just rusty; they were rusted out. Sadie was actually pretty good, taking care to line up her feet and ball in the same way at the start of each throw. Her game, like her bowling stance, was sure and steady. She only hit two or three strikes, but she picked up the spare almost every time. She spanked me in the first game, scoring in the one-fifties to my one-twenty-something.

I went to refill our pitcher and get our food before the second game. When I made it back Sadie was seated, watching the kids on the lane next to ours, her foot tapping the air in time with the music. Both lanes shared a long, slanted scoring table, with armless plastic seats forming a semicircle behind that. I set our burger baskets down and doled out the napkins and condiment packets before I followed her gaze to the overhead projection of the scores for our lanes. I was happy to see that my score would have been competitive on the other side of the ball return carousel. For some reason the boys had used their last names on the score sheet. Henderson got the first game victory with a clutch strike in the final frame.

"I understand all those names ending in *son* just fine," Sadie said in my ear, "but I've never understood that name. It makes sense that Williamson was first given to a guy whose father was named William; Johnson was the son of John; Jackson was Jack's son. But that means there was once a guy named Hender. What kind of name is that?"

As a show of solidarity I rephrased her question. "Who the hell is Hender?"

"Exactly." She nodded. "Who the hell is Hender?"

One of the reasons I liked the way she talked was because I had been laughing at this kind of joke my whole life; Sadie and Tall Boy shared much the same sense of humor. She picked my left arm up and strung it along the top of the plastic seat behind her, then leaned back to lay her head on my shoulder.

"Well, I failed to get the conversation going," Sadie said. "Your turn. Tell me something."

"Like what?"

"Like anything. What were you thinking just now?"

Actually, one of the things I had been mulling over the last three days was the man who had given her the ring she no longer wore. Her husband was one of the first things Sadie had told me about herself, told me on our very first date in fact, but I didn't even know the guy's name.

I picked up her left hand with mine, rubbing my thumb over the tan line around her ring finger. "This was from?"

"Don," Sadie offered.

"That's what I was thinking just now. What happened between you and Don?"

Sadie didn't respond right away. Instead, she pulled my arm down from the seat back so it cradled her neck, running across her chest and down to her right side. She gently ran her fingers above my left elbow, circling my bruise. I had to lean in close to hear her reply.

"I'm not sure what happened between us," she said finally. "Everything. Nothing. The usual. Why do you ask?"

I didn't think I'd had a grand design behind the question, but when she asked me I realized exactly why I wanted the information.

"So I don't make the same mistake."

Sadie made a soft murmur. "Good answer," she said, low like a conspiracy.

Sadie slid down and across my legs so that she was facing me. This time when we kissed it wasn't just a peck on the lips. She wrapped her arms around my neck and pulled down hard, keeping a firm hold as I leaned to her. I could feel her body rise as we kissed, leaving her almost suspended above my lap, and we stayed that way—me leaning down, Sadie with her arms crossed behind my neck—for as long as our breath allowed.

"Don't worry," she said when she loosened her hold. "I won't let you."

As we were untangling, I looked up and caught one of the kids from the next lane staring at us. In the split second our eyes met before he looked away, I knew exactly what he was thinking, and I was ready with an unspoken reply: *That's right, boy-o. While you've spent the whole evening too cool for school, pretending to ignore that pack of little pretties behind our lane, I myself have a belly full of beer. A gorgeous island girl is draped across my lap. This is the life of a Major League ballplayer. Eat your heart out, son of Hender.*

We finished the beer in our cups and agreed to a rematch, but by the middle of the second game I had given up all hope of catching Sadie and her relentless seven/spare blitzkrieg. Just for laughs I switched to a twelve-pound ball with huge finger holes and discovered that if I bowled with my thumb out, giving my wrist a slight twist as I released, I could make the ball dive in at the end of the lane like a pro on the PBA tour. The new strategy didn't improve my chances much, but it was far more entertaining to watch. By the tenth frame the kids in the lane beside us were calling out, "Curve it! Curve it!" as I made my approach. True to my calling as a crowd-pleasing sportsman, I nailed two strikes in a row and almost finished with the turkey, but the ten pin wobbled without falling on my last ball. My big final frame gave me 119 for the game. Sadie beat me by an even fifty pins.

She had earned the right to gloat but I doubt the prospect even crossed her mind. When I turned to walk back after my last throw, Sadie stood at the end of the lane, smiling and clapping.

"That was an awesome finish," she said, throwing her arms around my waist. "Please tell me you're tired so I don't have to go up against your cheering section for an entire game."

I agreed that I should quit on that high note, so we collected our stuff and walked to the front desk to settle up. By the time we'd driven back to the hotel it was past midnight. I felt obligated to offer a drink in the hotel lounge, but I could tell before she answered that she was almost out of gas for the night.

"I better not," Sadie said through a yawn. "I have another early wake-up tomorrow. What does your schedule look like?"

"We're at home tomorrow and Kissimmee on Sunday."

"I doubt I can make it tomorrow," she said, "but we don't have to wait till Sunday for the other part."

It was maybe one o'clock when she put her car in gear and pulled out of the hotel parking lot, headed home.

SATURDAY, MARCH 18

Our pitching coach has been battling allergies all week and he phoned in sick this morning with a migraine. If he didn't have one before the game, he certainly would have had one after. We got shelled by the Cardinals, 15–5. I went one for three, got a single in the fourth. It wasn't exactly the kind of base knock that builds confidence, though. I hit a rainbow chopper off the plate, which the first baseman fielded twenty feet behind the bag. They would have had me easy, but no one covered first.

The closer we get to the start of the season, the more reporters have started hanging around before and after games. Maybe for that reason, or maybe because some of those reporters are women, Coach Assenmacher told us as we got ready to take the field today that he wanted us to clean up our language in the clubhouse and on the bench. At first we thought he was kidding; Assenmacher has the sharpest tongue of anyone on the team. "I mean it," he said when a few guys laughed. "I'll fine you five dollars if I hear any more of that shit. Now quit all the cussing."

"How about you, Coach?" somebody asked. "What if you cuss from now on?"

"I'm stopping too," he promised. "The next time you hear me cuss is when I lift the ban."

Most of the guys are like me—doing all right for money by living off the food per diem—but it would only take one spicy tirade to eat right through those seventy-eight dollars per day, so we took his fine threat seriously. Still, it's no fun when you're down eight runs after four innings, and we had to work pretty hard to keep our language in check. Nobody made any fucking errors this afternoon, but several guys flocked some plays. When someone did something stupid, he wasn't deemed a dipshit; he was a Damascus. If an umpire made a bad call, we said it was Bolshevik.

Speedboat started for us on the mound, and it seemed like every inning he was behind in the count before he'd even finished his warm-ups. When he began the fifth in trouble again, it was Assenmacher, acting as substitute pitching coach, who called from the bench for time. As long as he's not mad at you personally, it's always worthwhile to hear Coach rip into someone, so we infielders converged on the mound for the conference. We all wanted to hear how he would handle Speedboat, who had just walked the first two batters on nine pitches.

Assenmacher marched from the bench to the mound and asked Speedboat for the ball. Speedboat started to walk off, assuming he was being removed, but Coach held up a hand to stop him. Assenmacher rubbed the ball between his palms in silence a good five seconds before he finally imparted his wisdom.

"You know what separates the winners from the losers in this game?" He looked at each of us in turn, his gaze finally landing on Speedboat before he answered his own question: "The score. Now throw some motherfucking strikes, goddammit."

With that he planted the ball in Speedboat's glove, turned and marched back to the dugout. The Cards' rally continued—they plated two more runs before we got out of the fifth—but our team ban on cussing had ended as suddenly as it had begun.

In the sixth inning I got fooled by a slow curve and grounded a weak dribbler to the right side. After I jogged back to the bench, Assenmacher came and stood beside me in the dugout.

"You're still thinking about that backup slider, aren't you?"

I had no clue what he was talking about.

"From yesterday," he continued. When I still didn't catch on, he said, "Appleby was going in for you anyway. Grab a bat and meet me at Midget Field."

Midget Field was part of the practice facility surrounding the stadium. Sitting just beyond foul territory down the left field line, it featured a plate, a mound and three bases set at the regulation distances, but the back edge of the infield dirt apron was ringed by a four-foot chain-link fence. The team mostly used it for pitcher/infield drills, like pickoff moves and plays where the pitcher covers first base, but occasionally we would run through our regular infield practice there. I liked practicing on Midget Field because if you missed one of Assenmacher's scorching fungo line drives, you didn't have to jog all the way out to the 330 sign to bring it back.

Assenmacher followed me out of the dugout carrying a bat of his own, a bag of balls and a batting helmet. I wasn't sure just what he had in mind—an image of him putting on the helmet and challenging me to a duel kept popping up in my head—but when we got to Midget Field's home plate, he had me stand toward the backstop with the helmet on the ground in front of me. Assenmacher went down on a knee across the plate from where I stood and placed the bag of balls on the ground beside him.

"Get in your batting stance, but put your left foot on the helmet," he instructed.

It was easier said than done. I almost fell over before I found my balance.

"I can tell you're still thinking about getting beaned yesterday because your stance is a train wreck today," Assenmacher said. "Try to hit one without moving your foot off the helmet."

He pulled a ball out of the bag and tossed it over the plate. I swung as best I could, hitting a sorry little grounder into the backstop to my right.

"Feels ridiculous, doesn't it?" Assenmacher asked. "But where did your hits go today—grounder to second, chopped one off the plate, grounder to first, right? And where did you just hit that one? Know why? You were standing at the plate about as aggressively as you're standing right now. Do it again but this time step off the helmet as you swing."

He tossed another ball, and I missed completely.

"Hands, dammit," Assenmacher growled. "We talked about the hands already."

I was so focused on keeping my balance that I was holding the bat at my shoulder instead of at my ribs like we had worked on. I adjusted my grip, bent my knees, and nodded. When he flipped me a third ball, I was ready. Balancing on my back leg, I stepped smoothly off the helmet and smacked a liner into the backstop straight ahead, a good ten feet off the ground.

"That's what I'm talking about," Assenmacher said, pulling himself up from his knees.

We worked another fifteen minutes on my stance and swing, sometimes with me taking cuts at balls he tossed up, sometimes with me watching while he took the swings. Though I'd felt like a dunce the first time we worked on my batting, this time I wasn't bothered so much by the handful of people who watched as we stood at the plate talking. The old fart really did know a shitload about hitting, and I was impressed by how quick he was able to figure out what I was doing wrong. I liked that he wasn't trying to impose some perfect-hitter's stance on me but was trying instead to work small changes into the swing I already felt comfortable with. And he wasn't just telling me what to do; we worked it out together. When we were finished, we agreed that I should start with my weight back and take a slightly exaggerated step as I began my swing, not unlike I was stepping off a helmet.

Despite the lopsided score, Saturday's game wasn't a total loss. At one point in the middle innings, Tall Boy and I got to enjoy another song from the Player to Be Named Later. Lenny Longo was blessed with the same voice God probably used to sing baby Jesus to sleep. What's more, because he was so quiet off the field, the songs Lenny sang during our games were my best chance to get to know him. Based on the tune he broke out that day, I realized it was just as demoralizing to witness the Jays losing another game from left field as it was from third base.

The Rainout Song

A few more clouds, a touch more gray,
Just a little bitty—where's the pity?—rain delay,
Cause I'm dragging along.
Playing just feels wrong
When you got your hide a bona-fide date today.

If you have a fear the game right here
May never reach the end,
And you hope your nine comes out just fine—
Oh please don't make the last out mine.
I'll strand the runner, run for cover,
Give up my chance at fame and glory,
But let's get through here. Tonight my true dear
In my back seat, now there's the story.

Roll out the tarp, call off the game,
Pick it up tomorrow—where's the sorrow?—score's the same.
We'll play like heck.
Cash in that rain check.
Just let us go. This eve I know is my real shot at lasting fame.

Folgers gave a seminar today on a pitcher being both his own worst enemy and his own best friend. He walked three, gave up five hits and only struck out two, but he stranded runners in each of his six innings of work and left with a 3–2 lead and a good chance for us to get the win. In the seventh our bullpen removed all doubt: we lost 8–3 to Houston in Kissimmee.

Coach Didier told a reporter after yesterday's game, and I quote: "The first few weeks, everyone gets at bats. Now we will focus on winning." I thought for certain that meant I would be riding the pine, but I started at third today like usual. They even bumped me back to seventh in the lineup and I thanked them by going one for three, doubled in a run over the center fielder's head in the fourth. I thought he misplayed the ball by starting in when he should have been backing up, but when I got to the bench the guys all told me—no, straight shot over his head, he played the bounce clean off the wall, and I was already pulling in at second as the shortstop gloved the cutoff throw: a clean double in any man's league.

There was an article in the paper today saying that several service industry unions in Major League cities have agreed to honor the union players' strike by not delivering to stadiums that employ "strike breakers in the sports or entertainment fields." That sounded like a general pronouncement, but of course they meant us. If people come out to see our games during the regular season, I guess they'll have to BYOB. A union in which the median salary is over $125,000 a year has won the support of the Teamsters, and they won't be delivering any beer or hot dogs to scab baseball fans.

Two weeks till we're legit.

There were men on base almost every inning for the Astros that game, but the third inning was the worst of Folgers's troubles. The first two guys up hit singles, and then Hack fumbled a sure double-play grounder at second to load the bases. When Folgers began stomping around behind the pitching rubber before the next batter, Tall Boy and I saw it was time for a meeting.

"Shake it off," I said as we neared the mound.

"We'll get this next guy," Tall Boy said.

For all of his locker room modesty to the contrary, Folgers was still a fierce competitor on the days it was his turn to take the mound.

"Hennessey! That stupid shit," Folgers hissed. "How can he boot that goddamn ball?"

Behind Folgers we could see Hack starting to walk toward the mound to join our discussion. Tall Boy and I held our hands up in unison to keep him where he was.

"This next guy is a lefty," I pointed out. "Pitch 'em outside, and me or Tall Boy can get the runner at the plate. We get another double-play ball after that and we're out of this inning, no harm done."

"Another double-play ball?" Folgers exclaimed. "I just threw a tailor-made DP ball, and look where it got us. Fucking Hack turns my double-play dreams into bases-loaded nightmares."

Tall Boy suddenly busted out laughing.

"'Fucking Hack turns my double-play dreams into bases-loaded nightmares,'" Brian repeated, which made him laugh even harder. "What are the odds anybody has ever said those words in one sentence before?"

When Folgers glared at him, Tall Boy held his glove up to hide his grin.

"Think about it," Brian continued. "You just made a sentence that no one in the history of talking has ever said. That's pretty cool."

Folgers looked at me. I just shrugged. Tall Boy couldn't stop laughing behind his glove.

"Get the fuck away from me," Folgers spat. "Both y'all."

He did a nice job pitching out of trouble, surrendering one run on a sac fly to left and then inducing an inning-ending 6-4-3 double play. Tall Boy got his giggles under control enough to turn the DP, but he must have spent the rest of our half-inning on the field thinking about sentences that no one ever said before. When we took our seats on the bench at the start of the fourth, he declared, "Here's the deal. First person to say something original buys dinner."

"What's the time limit?"

"No limit," he said. "No limit and no repetition. Nothing but baseball clichés for the rest of the game."

"A platitude contest?"

"For dinner," Tall Boy said.

"For dinner," I agreed, and we touched gloves to make it official.

Tall Boy started: "All right, Jays. Let's get that run back now."

"One run at a time," I replied. "No such thing as a five-run dinger."

The Player to Be Named Later, our best hope for a five-run home run, was the first batter of the inning.

"C'mon LL, pick your pitch."

"Look for yours, Longo."

Lenny took the first offering for a ball.

"Way to go. Keep him honest, big shooter. At's my boy."

"Make him come to you, bay-bee."

In a business where men spend all day in close company with other men, even taking showers together, players can be understandably touchy on the subject of sexual orientation. But there's a double standard to the homophobia of baseball. It might sound faggy for a guy to call another guy "baby" or "my boy" or even "big shooter," but within the context of a game in progress, if you say it with a cliché, you're fine. That and the butt slap—you can pat teammates on the ass all day without having your manhood called into question as long as you remember the golden rule: always use a flat hand, never cup or squeeze.

Lenny took a big swing and fouled the next pitch back into the screen.

"Straighten it out!" Tall Boy yelled.

"Give us a poke," I added. "Just need a single—a little bingle is all."

Folgers came over from the Gatorade cooler and sat down next to me. He was clearly feeling much better after getting out of the bases-loaded jam.

"What's the story, gentlemen?"

"Can't talk," I said, nodding toward the game. "Must cliché."

The third pitch to Lenny bounced just in front of the plate.

"Good eye!" Folgers called out.

"Oh, he's a natural," I said to Brian, meaning Folgers and platitudes.

"Absolute ringer," Tall Boy agreed.

"What the hell are you boys talking about?" Folgers asked.

Lenny took another pitch for a ball, making the count three and one.

"Walk's as good as a hit!" Tall Boy yelled.

"I was gonna use that."

"You snooze you lose."

Folgers must have caught on, at least a little, to Brian's and my contest. Before the next pitch he turned to me and said, "That is a pretty stupid thing to say, isn't it? 'Good eye.' What does that mean, anyway?"

Lenny took ball four on the next pitch and trotted down to first.

"Way to look," I called.

"Keep it rolling," Tall Boy said as GQ stepped to the plate. "Bring him in, Voorhees!"

"Maybe the phrase 'good eye' started in Pittsburgh," Folgers mused. "You know—that pirate mascot with the eye patch? *Aye, me hearties, I seen it wid me one good eye.*"

Tall Boy leaned around me to look at Folgers. "What the hell are you talking about?"

"He already asked that," I pointed out. "You said no repetition."

"He's not playing so that doesn't count," Tall Boy said, and then added as GQ took his first pitch for a strike: "Just takes one, big man!"

Speedboat, who had been sitting in the bullpen with the relievers at the start of the game, walked down the dugout steps and took a seat beside Tall Boy.

"Guys," Speedboat said with a grin. "Did you see the red-hair woman up there?"

He made cups of his hands and held them in front of his chest. We had, in fact, seen the redhead with the big knockers sitting behind the dugout. Spotting hot women in the crowd was a player pastime as old as the game itself.

"These es third time I walk to the dugout," Speedboat admitted. "Just so I can see her again."

"Oh yeah," Folgers agreed. "She's definitely doable."

Speedboat looked confused. "Tall Boy Sloan," he asked quietly. "What is *dooble*?"

"Doable," Brian said. "It's the nice way of saying, you know—you want to screw her. She's fuckable."

"Ah!" Speedboat nodded. "Fuckable. Sí."

On the next pitch Voorhees grounded to the right side, getting thrown out but moving the runner to second.

"That's it, GQ," I called. "Small ball wins 'em all. We'll bring him in from there."

"Ducks on the pond," Tall Boy yelled. "Bring him around. We need the run."

I nudged Folgers and nodded toward the Boston second baseman, who was conferring with the pitcher before the next man up. Folgers had knocked him down the previous inning with a pitch too far inside.

"Did you see this guy glaring after you gave him that chin music? For a second I thought he was going to charge the mound."

"Yeah, the little pussy." Folgers laughed. "That guy's a size-four jock-strap with a size-two schlong."

The Red Sox infielders were having a full-blown conference on the mound now, and the home plate umpire went out to get the game moving again. From the corner of my eye I saw Speedboat tap Tall Boy on the arm.

"Sorry," Speedboat said sheepishly. "I don't know, what is *schlong*?"

"A schlong is a—you know." Tall Boy pointed toward his lap.

"Your pee-pee?"

"Exactly."

Speedboat nodded in silence a moment.

"I don't know if I can use that word *schlong*," he said. "It sounds bad."

"It's just a different word for the same thing," Tall Boy told him. "But you're right. You might only want to say it around the guys."

I had forgotten that they'd moved me in the batting order, which meant I was up man after next. As I went to grab a bat and take my place beside the on-deck circle, I realized I could give Speedboat an easy way to remember not just the meanings but also the proper context for both of the new words he had just learned on the bench. With one foot on the dugout step, I turned and said, "Just think of it like one of those word-association questions on an English test, Speedboat: doable is to fuck-able as pee-pee is to schlong."

That got a chuckle all around, but there was an added note of satisfaction in Tall Boy's laugh. "Doable is to fuckable," he repeated, "as pee-pee is to schlong."

He didn't even need to say it. Dinner was on me.

Tall Boy declared halfway home on the bus ride from Kissimmee that it was a meat-and-potatoes evening, so when we got back we hopped in my car and drove around Clearwater until we found a steakhouse that looked promising. Our instincts proved solid: inside, a big-screen TV and several video game machines offered distraction if we ran out of conversation. A cute but tired-looking blonde brought waters and then took our order. Instead of asking how we wanted our steaks cooked, she asked, "Rare or ruined?"

Tall Boy picked absently at the foil label on his beer as we watched a March Madness tournament game on the TV. During a round of commercials, he turned to me.

"I've been meaning to ask. What would you say to us looking for an apartment?"

Rumor had been heating up the past few days about us not being allowed to play our home games in the SkyDome. A pro-union law in Toronto declared strikebreakers illegal if workers and management were in the process of negotiating a new contract. Any day now an Ontario province judge was expected to hand down his ruling on a case brought to see if the law would apply to us as well.

"Do you mean it?" I asked. "Are we a couple?"

"Couple of scabs. I just figured, if we wind up playing here for any length of time, assuming you don't get cut for being such an easy out..."

"And you don't get cut for being such a jag off."

"Right. It would save us some money, is all. I'd forgotten how much I hate living out of a hotel room. Too many ghosts of minor league seasons past, I guess."

I was surprised to hear he had been thinking about us getting a place together, if only because Karen was so close to delivering. From all reports on that end though, it sounded like she was doing fine. If she needed anything in an emergency, my mom or his folks were twenty minutes away. The more I thought about it, the more Brian's planning ahead made good sense.

Although we hadn't yet finished the ones in our hands, our waitress appeared with two more beers.

"Your steaks will be out in a minute," she promised. "These are compliments of the guy over there."

117

I had to twist in my seat to look in the direction she nodded. At first I thought she meant the bartender, a barrel-chested black guy with wire-rimmed glasses reading a paper behind the bar. Then I saw a middle-aged white guy on the corner stool look our way and raise his glass.

"Our adoring public," Tall Boy said, raising his beer in return.

"Do we know that guy?"

"I was about to ask you the same."

Our benefactor turned back to catch the end of the game on TV, and the waitress brought our orders before we could decide if we should invite him over. My T-bone seemed a tad pink to be considered officially ruined, but it was nothing a little steak sauce couldn't overcome. I was down to my last few bites of baked potato when I heard a voice over my shoulder.

"How'd it go today in Kissimmee?"

I recognized his face but couldn't pinpoint from where.

"We were great for six innings," Tall Boy answered. "But those damn Astros insisted we play the full nine. We lost, eight to three."

"Prince was starting, right?" the guy asked, and that's when I finally placed him. He was one of the reporters who covered our team's home games. I'd seen him on and off for the last two weeks in camp.

Tall Boy nodded. "He left in the seventh with a run lead. Solid outing."

"Your bullpen's been weak from the beginning." He pulled up a chair from another table and extended a hand. "Bob Hawkey, *Tampa Trib*. Mind if I join you?"

Since the beers he'd bought cost money and chairs were free, we shook his hand and said no problem. We started to introduce ourselves but he already knew our names.

"So what do you guys think of the competition so far?"

"Saint Louis beat us up pretty good a couple days back," I offered.

"I saw." Hawkey laughed. "Twenty-two to seven in two games. That'd make a lopsided football score. No, I meant, what do you think of the players you've been up against? The pitching and so forth, is it what you expected?"

I thought my answer covered his question just fine—the pitching we'd seen so far was better than the pitching we had—but Tall Boy didn't seem bothered by the inquisition.

"I played against several guys on their way up while I was in the Twins' system, and some of those pitchers could bring the cheese. Mostly though, what we've seen so far this spring is about what I expected."

"That's right," Hawkey said. "You played some in the bushes. Was it single-A?"

"I played double-A my last season and a half."

"Cut or quit?"

That struck me as a callous way to ask a man how he gave up his chosen profession and livelihood. Maybe Tall Boy thought so, too.

"I had to give it up," he answered, looking toward the game on the big screen. "Personal reasons."

Hawkey let out a snort. "There's a sure sign I need to change the subject. How 'bout you, Standen? You play in the bushes any?"

"Some college ball, that's about it."

"Is what you've seen so far different than what you played against in school?"

"The game's a little faster." I shrugged. "Some of the pitchers have better stuff."

"I've watched that College World Series on TV," Hawkey said. "Ping! I can't get over the sound of those bats. Did that take some getting used to when you got here?"

"It took about a day to get used to," I told him. "I always bring a wood bat when I go to a batting cage."

"I'll bet. You guys using that ashtray?" Hawkey pulled a smoke from his shirt pocket and lit up without waiting for a response. "Say, how'd you wind up here anyway? I mean, how did you get signed?"

I told him about attending the tryout in Cleveland, how strange it was to see five hundred guys all milling around an indoor practice facility.

"And they signed five of you to contracts?" Hawkey asked. "Doesn't that seem a bit high for a local tryout?"

"They've cut the squad down to thirty-six, and four of us five signed in Cleveland are still on the roster," I pointed out. "It sounds to me like the scouts did a good job."

"Well, I dunno." Hawkey let out a billowing plume of smoke that rolled across the table between Brian and me. "According to you guys the talent level falls somewhere between college and double-A ball. You tell me they found over ten percent of the roster in one tryout. I'm not sure the scouts who signed you had that hard a job to start with."

He could have been drunk or trying to provoke us. Either way, there was something about him—maybe his laugh, or how he kept asking questions without paying much attention to our answers—that just rubbed me the wrong way. When Tall Boy spoke up I knew I wasn't alone in thinking Hawkey was a dick.

"Buddy, look. Alex Gonzalez is the only guy in the Jays' organization who has earned the right to play shortstop for Toronto this year, and as far as that goes, Bernie Williams is the only guy good enough to play center field for the Yankees. But they walked away from the gig. Am I supposed to apologize for that?"

"Don't get your panties in a bunch," Hawkey said, stubbing out his cigarette in the ashtray. "I'm not asking you to apologize for anything."

"So what exactly are you asking, paperboy?"

"I'm just trying to figure out how you two justify being here. I mean sure, getting signed in Cleveland proves you have one-in-a-hundred talent, but you'd need to add about five zeros to that equation before I'll believe you belong in a Major League jersey."

Suddenly Brian was more animated than I'd seen him since the day I got the phone call and we knew that we'd be coming down to Dunedin together.

"Mo-ther-fuck-er." He spit out each syllable in a way far more menacing than a shout. "I don't have to justify shit to you, all right? I've got people back home who are supporting me on this—people whose opinions I actually value—and if they're behind me, then I don't give a flying fuck what you think, or what you say, and no free beer is gonna change that."

Brian slid his bottle across the table, more of a push than a fling, and it tipped over the edge, spilling beer on Hawkey on its way down. The glass shattered when it hit the floor. When Hawkey jumped up, his chair flipped over backward, making a crunching noise as it landed in the broken glass. He looked down at his shirt as if it might be on fire.

"You're crazy!" Hawkey nearly screamed. "You throwing bottles at me? Are you gonna take a swing at me now, huh? C'mon, take your best shot. Come on!"

He feinted toward Brian and then made a grab across the table. I had piled my silverware on the empty plate in front of me, the heavy wooden handle of my steak knife in full view. When Hawkey pulled back, his fists were clenched, arms cocked at the elbows in a cross between a boxer's crouch and a Tae Kwon Do stance. Something silver flashed in his hand.

Once I got past my surprise at the sudden call to arms, it was all I could do to keep from laughing. Combined, Tall Boy and I had probably ten inches of height, thirty years of youth and eighty pounds of muscle over Hawkey. In a fight we would make a formidable combination of strength, quickness and agility. If this mushy, middle-aged sports hack was planning to make a stand, he would need something more dangerous in his fist than a coffee spoon.

"Careful, Jake," Tall Boy warned. "He's got the scoop on us."

We placed our arms on the tabletop simultaneously—nothing threatening, just enough to prevent him from getting another free grab at the cutlery. It took a few seconds for Hawkey to register our blatant disregard to his challenge. When he looked down and saw what he held, Hawkey dropped the spoon like it had scalded him, and bolted for the exit.

I twisted in my seat again to watch his retreat. Based on how quickly he snagged his jacket, threw money on the bar, and made it to the door, Hawkey might've put up a decent fight after all. When I turned back to the table, Brian was pouring half of my beer into his empty water glass.

"You really need to work on your interview skills."

"If you had to choose one or the other," Tall Boy asked, "would you rather have your panties in a bunch or go play in the bushes?"

"You know that old phrase," I reminded him. "Opinions are like assholes."

Brian nodded toward the door Hawkey had just run out. "And so is he."

MONDAY, MARCH 20

Lost 5–3 to the White Sox in Sarasota, which was a nice comeback of sorts. Chicago's starter had us no-hit through five and two-thirds. I played my usual six, 0-fer my usual two at bats. Pete Rose Jr. played for the Sox wearing 14, his dad's old number. It's funny how you can get used to even the most extraordinary things. At the start of the exhibition season I was aware of every detail, noticed every nuance of our games and opponents. After three weeks all the crowds are starting to sound the same, all the stadiums starting to look the same, all our losses feel the same. Since our win against the Marlins last Tuesday, we've lost six in a row. A three-game stand starts in Dunedin tomorrow. We could use some home field advantage about now.

You hear a lot of strange things coming from the crowd when you're standing on a ball diamond. Snippets of conversation, shrill whistles and half-discernable shouts, cries that would sound like somebody was being mugged if they came from an alleyway instead of a grandstand, all come spilling down onto the field during a game. In the bottom of the fifth against the Chi Sox, as we were taking warm-ups before the first batter, I kept hearing a woman call out, "Eighty-three! Hey, eighty-three!" I ignored it as just another part of the usual crowd babble until I heard a second, familiar voice join in the call.

"How you doin', Third Base?"

When I looked up it was like seeing a long-lost relative in a nonsense dream: you know it's not logical for this person to be here now, but how can you deny what your eyes are taking in? At the walkway railing between the sections above third base stood Sadie and a young blonde woman I'd never seen before. I waved hello but could do little else because the first batter was about to step to the plate. Sadie waved back and I held up three fingers, pointing toward our bench—in three outs meet me by the visitors' dugout. She nodded, and the two walked up the stairs together.

"What are you doing in Sarasota?" I asked when we rendezvoused after the fifth.

"We met up in town to do the lunch thing." Sadie locked an arm with the blonde beside her. "And we decided to come out and ogle all the good-looking players at the ballpark. Jake Standen, meet my favorite sister-in-law, Melinda Holder. Lynn, this is Jake."

"I'm her only sister-in-law." Melinda smiled, stepping up to the rail to shake hands.

Sister-in-law was short, but she looked way more grown up from three feet than she had from third base. My guess would have put Melinda somewhere in the middle of her undergrad years. If she had worn a halter top instead of a loose-fitting blouse to the stadium, I'm certain the good-looking players would have been ogling right back.

"So how's the guy watch coming along?" I asked. "Spotted any finalists?"

They exchanged a quick glance and conspiratorial grins.

"We've narrowed the field down to several favorites," Sadie answered. "Oh, speaking of which, here—take our picture."

She pulled a disposable camera from her purse and handed it over the railing.

"Are you here for the whole game?" I fumbled with the camera a moment, trying to figure out the viewfinder and shutter release. "They usually sit me down after the sixth."

Sadie put her arm around Melinda's shoulders. "No, this one has to be in class in an hour. We need to get going pretty soon."

When they leaned their heads together and smiled, I took the shot. Though they were only a few years apart in age, their disparity in height made it look almost like a mother-daughter pose. I handed the camera back.

"Don't go anywhere." Sadie pushed Melinda toward me and moved back a few steps. After she snapped the picture she said, "One more," and the two exchanged positions.

While Melinda tested one step, then moved up another trying to frame us in the viewfinder, Sadie leaned in close at the rail. "You free tonight?"

"Should be home by six," I murmured back.

Just as Melinda said, "Okay, smile!" from behind the camera, Sadie whispered, "Call me."

Canned organ music over the PA system indicated the next inning was about to start. I was due up second.

"You probably have to go," Sadie said. "Don't let us get you in trouble."

"I should get back," I agreed. Then a thought occurred to me. "Do you have any pictures left on that roll?"

"I've got a couple."

"Wait here," I said. "Nice to meet you, Melinda."

They both waved as I descended the dugout steps.

I was a little perplexed about the whole idea of meeting sister-in-law. Was I supposed to take this as a reminder that Sadie was still married? Then again, the two of them looked and acted like regular girlfriends, and it's not unheard of for a woman to remain close with her ex-husband's family after a divorce. Maybe they were close enough outside of Sadie's marriage that she wanted to show me off to Melinda. Why else would Sadie have brought a camera? But then, what was all that whispering for at the end?

Fuck it. I had an at bat to focus on now, a date to look forward to later, and one quick promise to fulfill.

"GQ!" I called to Voorhees, who was talking with Hack near the Gatorade cooler. "There's a cute blonde up there who wants a picture with you at the railing."

Though news like that directed toward me would have put a stupid grin of surprise on my face, GQ only nodded. I suppose being the female fan favorite on every team you've joined since junior high would do that to a guy. As we passed each other along the bench, headed in opposite directions, I gave his arm a quick squeeze.

"She's a friend of a friend. Behave yourself."

GQ just laughed, climbing the dugout steps to claim his rightful prize in Sadie and Melinda's beefcake contest.

Sadie had a way of looking at me when I talked—her head tilted and nodding; a sly smile parting her lips; her eyes watching not just my eyes but my entire face—that made me never want to stop talking. I found myself saving up things to tell her when I saw her next; anything would do. She loved to hear stories about the team and our games, and during even the most mundane tale of a play on the field or a joke in the clubhouse, she would ask just the right questions to make sure she caught all the details. Sometimes she even noticed things about the games she watched that never occurred to me down on the diamond. Over dinner that night she asked me what I spent so much time talking to Brian about when we played the left side together. At first I had no clue what she meant.

"You do," she insisted. "When you're on the field, you talk his ear off the whole time."

"I'm not talking his ear off. We're having business-related conversations, just like any coworkers."

She asked me for an example.

In the game that afternoon against the White Sox, a guy hit a rainmaker pop-up between the two of us. In the six or eight seconds it took for that ball to land, Tall Boy and I held the following discussion:

ME: Mine! Mine! Mine!
BRIAN: I go! I go!
ME: No, I got it.
BRIAN: I said I got it.
ME: It's mine, I got it.
BRIAN: Shut up, I got it.
ME: You got it?
BRIAN: I got it! I got it!
ME: Don't miss.

He didn't.

Tall Boy and I did carry on lengthy exchanges during games, but many of the things we conversed about, I wasn't sure I could translate for Sadie. That's not to say I thought she was dumb or we were too raunchy; it was just that our conversations were so laden with baseball jargon they wouldn't make much sense to someone who hadn't spent a large portion of her life on a ball field.

One reason I talked to Brian so much is that a third baseman has to be the shortstop's eyes on any play coming in from the outfield when the shortstop is the cutoff man. The same inning as the pop-up, on a single hit to the left-center gap with a runner on first, Tall Boy went out to take the relay throw. Because his back was turned to the infield, he needed me to tell him (1) that he was standing too far toward second and he should move more in line between the center fielder and third base; (2) that the runner had reached second, was coming around hard and headed for third; but (3) because the center fielder didn't get to the ball in time, we had no chance to get the runner; so (4) he should catch the relay throw and run it back to the infield to prevent the batter from getting to second base. How could Sadie make sense of the conversation we had on that play?

"Cut's you Brian—left, left! Second base—man two. Round two, look three, look three. Coming three, Bri. Shoot three. Shoot three! No man! Cut! Cut and hold. Carry it two, Bri. Bring it yourself."

"And that's what you're calling a work-related conversation?" Sadie asked.

"Of course it is. I said something; he answered. I added to my original statement and he responded to my response."

"How do you know if he hears you or if he's even paying attention?"

"I know because he answers me by doing what I'm telling him to do."

"But his back is turned. What if he doesn't understand what you're telling him to do?"

"He holds his hands out, palms up, like he's testing for rain. If that happens, I just keep it simple: *cut* means catch the ball, *three* means throw it to me, stuff like that."

Sadie thought it over, then shook her head. "I still don't see how even your half of the conversation is conversation. It's barely English."

I shrugged. "It's baseball talk."

Sadie leaned back in the seat across from me and cradled her drink in her hands.

"Tell me all about baseball talk."

Baseball talk is one of the great things about baseball. It's like a language all its own. Baseballese, you might call it. Because the game is measured only in successes and failures—balls, strikes, outs, runs—and is not built around a clock or a finish line, language is an integral part of baseball. Put another way, seasons (and games, for that matter) take time, a lot of time. And what do you do with all that time? Well, you talk. And what do you talk about? Anything and everything. Sometimes even the words we use to talk the talk have a story to tell.

Examine some of the oldest words and phrases in Baseballese and it's like you're taking a history lesson on the growth of our nation. Before there were trains, planes and automobiles, the fastest way to get around in America was by water. It's no surprise then that a lot of Baseballese comes from the shipyard. A batter has a wheelhouse and maybe a hitch in his swing. Guys on base are men aboard. The hitter up next is the man on deck. The guy up after him is in the hold. When infielders get an out with the bases empty, they throw the ball around the horn. There's even a Major League team called the Mariners and a couple more named after fish. Of course plenty of Baseballese came from people who worked the land, too. The game is played on a field, on a yard or in a park. The grounds crew tends to the mounds, fences, and bullpens, and the farm systems are stocked with farmhands.

Since one of a ballplayer's favorite things to talk about is eating, food, drink, and dinner references are everywhere in Baseballese. You might do well in the Grapefruit League and earn a cup of coffee with the big club. When you get there you'll want to warm up by playing pepper. You go to bat not at a base but at the plate. The pitcher might offer you a fork ball, throw a curve that drops off the table, fire some cheese that will probably look like an aspirin, or if you're lucky he'll serve you up a fat pitch right where you want it—a.k.a., a cookie in your kitchen. If he gets three outs in a row, they'll say he put up a bagel, a doughnut or a goose egg, but if he's off his game, you can lay down a good bunt and they'll say you planted a seed. Hit an easy fly ball? It was a can of corn. Smacked one over the fence? You hit a tater. If you get a big red welt from sliding into a base, you have yourself a strawberry. If you get called out the fans might salute you with a raspberry. If you dispute the call, the old Brooklyn Dodgers' announcer Red Barber would say you were in a rhubarb. Hard throws have some mustard on 'em, good fielders can make a honey of a play, and really bad fielders are said to make vitamins instead of errors. (One-a-days, get it?)

Do you think Yogi Berra would have been as famous for his quotes if he had played football? Only in baseball is so much of the game built around talking. And since it has been a part of our country for so long, the language of the game has become part of the language of our country. People who don't even pay attention to baseball use Baseballese all the time. Horny teenagers measure their success on a date by what base they reached. Those at the forefront of their chosen profession are said to achieve Ruthian heights. You can pitch an idea, have a banner day, step up to the plate, go to bat for someone, hit a home run, have a grand slam of an idea, be on the A team or in the minor leagues, be a bench warmer or have a deep bench, offer figures that are or are not in the ballpark, bat a thousand, choke, get a charley horse, go back-to-back, get doubled up or have a double header, touch base with someone, touch all the bases with everyone, get caught off base, go over the ground rules, play hard ball or make a heads-up play, show some hustle, enjoy a ladies' day, be on deck or on the ball, take a swing, get your licks in, be out in left field or even out of your league. You can play ball or play the field, offer play-by-play accounts, or take a rain check. Some people are rookies, showboats, strikeouts, or screwballs; others are smash hits, safe by a mile, playing out the string or just waiting for the seventh inning stretch. You might be a southpaw, in your strike zone, just getting to your windup, or have two strikes against you. Even if you're the swing man your side might get whitewashed, which means you'll just have to wait till next year. Every one of those phrases is courtesy of the great American pastime and if you don't believe me, as Casey Stengel used to say, "You kin look it up." In fact, for my senior thesis in American studies at OSU, I did just that.

Sadie and I got together the next three nights in a row—nothing special, just dinner and drinks. By that point I had long since stopped counting dates. I never felt pressure to say or do anything to keep her from losing interest, and I never once made a remark or a move that Sadie didn't welcome and respond to in kind. She even switched her schedule around so she could make Wednesday's game. That night we had a late dinner, and after I drove her home we sat in my car in her driveway until one in the morning, just talking. I don't know if it was the questions she asked or the way she looked at me when I answered, but with Sadie I always had the feeling that she would listen to me all night long, hear every story I had to tell, if I could just keep talking. And I wanted that, too. To be the center of her attention, the focal point for those brown eyes, it felt like home.

TUESDAY, MARCH 21

Won a wild one today in Dunedin, 14–1 against the Tribe. They went through five pitchers in eight innings with so little success even the bottom half of our order batted .400. I went two for four, singled in a run in the second, then doubled and scored on my last at bat in the fifth. Tall Boy hit a towering dinger over the center field wall to cap a four-run seventh inning. I don't know where our bats have been hiding the past week but we found them all this afternoon. We scored just one fewer run today than we had in the last five games combined.

As we were driving to the stadium, a woman with Illinois tags on her car motioned for Tall Boy to roll down his window at a traffic light. She had missed a sign and wanted to know how to get back to Route 19A. When we asked where she was headed, she named a medical center in Sweetwater that just happened to be across the intersection from the Trey Yuen / Piggly Wiggly strip mall. Not only did we tell her how to find the road but in about four steps we told her exactly how to find the address. Pretty funny, considering we only got to town ourselves less than a month ago. I bet if she had seen my Ohio plates she wouldn't have even bothered asking.

I read in the paper that during a game over the weekend Pittsburgh used Jimmy Boudreau, a pitcher who was making his first start since he played with the union guys in 1986. After the game, the Pirates' radio announcer Steve Blass was asked what he thought of Boudreau's performance. Blass answered, "He should have been better, pitching on 3,195 days of rest."

Twelve days till we're legit.

When we arrived at the stadium Tuesday morning and walked into the clubhouse, the first thing I noticed, couldn't miss it really, was that someone had been messing around in my locker. I never had much stuff in there to begin with, but now it was nearly empty and what was still there had obviously been moved around and rummaged through. My first thought was that somebody—maybe one of the clubhouse guys or someone who had snuck in with the reporters—had been looking for a wallet and went rooting through my locker trying to find one. But that would have had to happen early in the morning for someone to get away with it, since guys on the team were likely to wander into the clubhouse at any point two or three hours before home games. Besides, mine was the only stall that appeared disheveled, and nobody else in the locker room seemed surprised at the mess or at my reaction to seeing it.

"What the hell happened here?" I asked to no one in particular.

Tall Boy leaned over from his locker three doors down and peered into mine. My hat, jersey and practice glove were all conspicuous in their absence, and several playing cards were scattered along the bottom of the locker. That was especially odd since I didn't keep a deck of cards with my stuff to begin with.

"Maybe it's a clue to a mystery," Brian suggested, "like in Scooby-Doo."

I gathered up the cards from the floor of my locker: a four, five, and seven of spades, six and eight of clubs. That seemed to suggest something beyond random flinging. Maybe Tall Boy was right. It was a straight, in black cards. I started doing word association: a black straight, straight black, safe black, safe back. Straight back. That sounded about right. I turned around. If you went straight back from my locker, you would walk into the shower room. I don't know how I'd missed it when we came in, but someone had taken three-inch-long stretches of black tape and made a dashed line from the middle of the clubhouse leading into the showers. As I peered in that direction I was looking right along the line of the tape. That definitely seemed like a clue to a mystery. I headed for the showers.

Hanging on the showerhead farthest from the entryway was my cap. Even from across the room I could see there was something stuck to the wall behind, so as I pulled my hat from its perch, I examined my next clue. Someone had pilfered several used numbers from my "Days Till We're Legit" sign. The number three had been torn from my "23" card and taped beside "15" on the wall—315. That could be several things, but the most prominent 315 at Dunedin Stadium was the short-porch distance to the wall down the right field line. It appeared I was about to go on a scavenger hunt. I put my hat on my head and walked back through the locker room.

If the perpetrator was in the room, I couldn't tell by looking around. All the usual suspects were there. It couldn't have been Tall Boy; he and I were together almost every moment from waking up that morning till arriving at the stadium. Hack and Lenny Longo were paying me no attention, talking by their lockers. Folgers was leaning through the manager's office doorway, chatting with one of the coaches. GQ was at the black-and-white TV in search of a sports broadcast to narrate. From the sounds of it, he had come across a horse race about to start. "They're just now lining up at the gate," GQ called. "The favorite seems a little skittish entering the chute, but this looks to be the beginning of an exciting steeplechase." They might not have been giving anything away, but I was sure at least one of them knew something about it. I could feel their smiles at my back as I headed for the tunnel leading to the field. The bastards.

The sun had already burned the dew off the grass as I climbed the dugout steps and started across the infield. Two guys from the grounds crew were running a lime roller along the first-base line in preparation for the afternoon's game. They nodded as I passed. Were they in on it as well? It felt like there were several sets of eyes on me as I walked toward the fence but when I looked around I could see no one in the stands. Halfway across the outfield grass I spotted my practice glove sitting on the warning track, propped up against the right field wall below the 315 sign. I didn't realize until I got close that another playing card had been stuck in the webbing of my mitt: the queen of hearts. That stumped me for a moment.

If there had been several face cards I would have guessed it had something to do with the Kansas City Royals, but we didn't even play them on our spring training schedule so it's just as well that wasn't the case. The queen of hearts is a lady, of course, so that could be something. She's a big card in the playing deck and she's red. A big red lady, big red. Then I remembered that two days ago when we played Houston there had been a redhead in the stands whom several of the guys commented on. She had gotten so much attention primarily because she was sitting in plain view along the first row of seats above our dugout and she had a great rack. Big red indeed.

I started to walk back toward our bench, looking close at the seats in the section directly above our dugout. When I was halfway across the infield and still couldn't see anything, I figured some more of my stuff was probably there, just stuck on or under a seat, out of view. Then it occurred to me that we had been the visitors that game against the Astros and our dugout was along the first-base side. I did a ninety-degree turn at the pitcher's mound and, sure enough, there on a seat two rows above the visitors' dugout was my shirt. I had to pull myself up to get over the railing and reach the stands.

My jersey had been stretched over the back of the seat, and two baseballs had been stuffed under the first and last *Os* on the Toronto logo, approximating two tits. One of my batting gloves was stuck on the end of the armrest and the other was bent over the back of the seat, waving hello. Since there were no more card clues, I figured I had found everything. I pulled my shirt off the seat back, put my batting gloves and the ball-boobs in my pockets, and hurdled the railing onto the field again.

My footfalls echoed down the tunnel as I descended to the clubhouse entrance, and I could hear GQ's running commentary from his corner of the locker room. "Here's the favorite rounding the clubhouse turn and heading toward the stretch. There's nobody even close as he makes his final strides. Does he have enough gas? He's almost to the finish line, and here comes the moment of truth!"

I walked through the locker room archway and everyone let out a cheer. Tall Boy stood leaning against my stall, where it appeared the mess had been put back to normal. Hack and Lenny Longo were laughing and clapping, waving T-shirts in the air to egg me on across a stretch of black tape repositioned in the middle of the room, the final lengths to a faux finish line. Folgers stood beside the line, bent over a stopwatch, waiting expectantly with his finger on the button to record my official time. I noticed the TV wasn't even on; GQ had been calling play-by-play on me and my one-man steeplechase all along. The only person in the room who wasn't actively enjoying a laugh at my expense was Speedboat, who had his back to me, trying hard to look busy with something in his locker. I hadn't realized it, but I should have: if Folgers was already at the stadium, then of course Speedboat was there too, since they always drove together in Folgers's car. It had been Speedboat the whole time, the little Cuban imp. That's why he wasn't around when the prank started; he had been a step ahead of me from the beginning.

When he turned from his locker, a huge smile creased Speedboat's face. "You snipe hunt good, Golden Jake!"

I hustled across the finish line and took a long bow, ending with my middle fingers in the air, shooting the bird to all those present. Another guy might have gotten pissed at having his chain yanked for public consumption like that, but I couldn't get too upset. I realized this wasn't the sort of crap you dumped on someone nobody likes. No, going to that much trouble and having everyone in on it was the kind of prank you only pulled on somebody you already knew would enjoy the joke, too. Just like giving the Illinois lady perfect directions, this seemed a sure sign that

I was starting to find a place in my new home away from home. Amid the laughs and the bullshit, I was where I was meant to be.

WEDNESDAY, MARCH 22

Played Chicago again this afternoon in Dunedin. It was my best game in a Blue Jays uniform so far, and I started it on the bench. The guy Didier put at third was nursing a tender back, and when he got into a collision with one of the White Sox on a close play in the first inning, he asked to be taken out. I had known since about an hour before game time that I wasn't starting, so I'd mostly just stood around during warm-ups and I was tight as hell. When I trotted out there the bases were loaded and I had my game face on, but I was stretching between pitches, trying to get loose. I still wasn't 100 percent when the next batter hit a one-hopper down the line. I had to backhand the ball, step on the bag, then twist as I threw across my body to turn the 5–3 to end the inning. Damn near wrenched my back onto the PUP list as well.

Then in the fifth inning the weirdest thing happened. In yesterday's game the webbing in the pocket of my glove had broken near where my thumb and forefinger join, and though the equipment manager fixed it before today's game, I could tell that the restitching had caused me to lose some sensitivity in the fingers. Didn't seem like a big deal until a guy in the fifth hit a screaming liner about ten feet off the ground, right at me. I jumped as high as I could and was sure I was going to pull it down, but I didn't feel the ball stick in my glove like I expected. It felt like I'd only gotten a piece of it. I landed on my feet and spun around, certain the ball was in the grass just behind me. Out of habit I brought my free hand into the palm of my glove as I made the turn. Only then did I realize I actually had caught the ball and it was stuck in the (I thought) fixed hole in my webbing. I felt like an idiot. Everyone in the stadium could tell that I hadn't known I made the play until I whipped around like a whirligig and discovered the thing in my mitt. "That's all right," Tall Boy said, touching his glove with mine as we jogged to the dugout. "I'd rather catch it and not know it than not make the catch and think I had."

I was still feeling a little sheepish when I stepped into the warm-up circle to start off the home half of the fifth. A fan sitting behind the screen even yelled out, "Look what I found!" as I walked toward the plate. I thought about a snide comeback, but I just turned and smiled at the guy, nodding as if to say, *Yep, that's about the way it happened*. I've always thought you should let your game do the talking and let the fans say what they will. Wouldn't you know it, the very first pitch was a slider that didn't slide, and I smacked the living shit out of the thing. It was almost like it happened against my will since I so rarely swing at first pitches. The ball just hung there in the air though, like it was daring me to take a rip. I gave it a whack and lunged out of the batter's box, sure it would hit halfway up the left field wall and come back, but the ball just kept sailing and sailing. I'd already reached first base before I saw the infield umpire making circles in the air with his finger, and only then did I downshift into the home run trot. Assenmacher gave me a low five from the third-base coach's box, and of course all the guys were lined up at the dugout steps to give me bumps and pats. You bet I tipped my cap to that loud-mouth fan behind the screen as I touched the plate. How many times do you see that on the highlight shows—a guy makes a solid play to end the half inning and then leads off the next by hitting a dinger? In today's game, that guy was me.

I know I was never meant to be a power hitter. On the rare occasion when I do go yard, nobody in the park is more surprised than I am. It's not that I can't hit the ball hard; at least three or four of every ten times I connect is a line drive somewhere. But to get the distance and the trajectory and everything needed to make the ball fly over the wall just right, that's a kind of alchemy I never seem to have at the plate. It is a magic feeling to get all of a pitch though, to smack one as square as a round ball can be smacked. It's counterintuitive really, because you don't feel a thing. When the ball jumps off the bat so quickly that there is no resistance, it feels like you've missed completely. But there's no mistaking the sudden lift and the white streak, the way it seems to shoot out over the infield and rise and rise. How many outs did Pete Rose make while collecting the all-time hits record of 4,256—nine, maybe ten thousand? I couldn't guess the number of outs I've made in the years I've played ball, but despite all that failure I still can recognize the success, just as you swing and the ball begins to climb and you think it might sail for days without end. Flies only become outs when the ball comes back to earth. But when you hit one that isn't going to land—at least not inside the park—there's no other feeling like it. To hit a ball so far that they stop the game, just stand there with all eyes on you and wait, the fans on their feet as you round third and head for the plate, it makes you think anything is possible. You believe you might still get everything you've ever wished for. It feels like you could stay young forever.

I figured up in the clubhouse afterward that, between all the ground outs, catches and double plays, I'd had a hand in ten of the twenty-seven outs on defense. In addition to the dinger, I got a single and a walk, scored our only run, and was on deck with two men on when the guy ahead of me made the last out. I could have been the tying run. We went down, 5–1.

That's the story of my life: I always perform my best in support of a lost cause.

I'd never had a problem with my glove like I had that game against the White Sox, and I've used the same glove since high school—or rather, I've kept three gloves, all the same make and model, in various stages of use, every year since tenth grade. The first season I bought one I liked it so much that I bought another the following year, and I bought a new one every three years after. One glove I use only for games, another is just for practice, and a third—always the newest—I work with linseed and mold the pocket an entire season before I'll consider using it as my new practice glove. I can't fathom how some guys just grab a mitt off the rack and start playing with it the next day. Using a brand-new glove in a game is the last thing you want to do. Your glove is literally an extension of your hand, and it needs to *feel* like your hand if you harbor any hope of using it properly. That's why you want the oldest glove for games; only the old glove has been worked in enough to fit and feel just right, like how a pair of comfortable sneakers eventually takes on the shape of your feet. If I were ever to change gloves I'd pick a smaller one over one that's huge. If you can't feel the ball in your glove, you can't field the ball with your glove.

The one I use is a Spalding T3000, Ted Williams's signature series. Why they have a signature-series glove signed by a man who billed himself as the best hitter ever is beyond me, but it's a good glove all the same. They say Williams was so familiar with his bats that he once returned a batch to the manufacturer because he thought the handles were too thick. When the bat makers at Louisville Slugger received the rejects, they double-checked and discovered that Williams was right: the handles were five-thousandths of an inch thicker than what the Splendid Splinter had ordered. I'll never be as familiar with the bats I use as Teddy Ballgame—I spent too many years in aluminum-bat leagues to understand how wood is supposed to feel in the way he grew up understanding it—but I know exactly how my glove should feel when a ball lands in the pocket. When my game glove stops feeling like I think it should is when my practice glove gets a promotion.

My father was the one who taught me how to take care of a baseball glove. I didn't realize till years later that he passed this knowledge on not so much to improve my defensive skill on the diamond but because it's the best way to get the most life out of a mitt, thereby saving himself the expense of buying me a new one every few seasons.

The spring before I turned eight, he showed me how to work the leather with linseed oil, how to mold the pocket by sticking two baseballs in the webbing and then wrapping the whole thing up tight with string. You have to let it sit like that, stinking from the oil and wrapped up like a present, for weeks at a time to get the best results. It was probably the first lesson in delayed gratification that I ever understood. I remember how excited I was, like a second Christmas, that warm April evening when we finally untied the strings from my mitt and headed out back to test it. We threw for a good five minutes before either of us said a word.

"How's it feel?" my father finally asked. "Right with Eversharp?"

"Feels good."

"Need more work with the oil? We can wrap it another week if it needs it."

I had waited over three weeks to get a chance to try out my new glove. I wasn't about to let on that the fingers still felt a little stiff, the pocket still too loose.

"No. It feels good, Dad."

We threw another minute before he asked, "So how are things over at the Sloans'?"

Mrs. Sloan had returned from the hospital two weeks earlier, after delivering Ricky, Tall Boy's brother. Brian and I were under strict instructions from both our sets of parents to play outside when we were at his house, starting now until further notice. I had only seen the baby once, when we snuck inside to get some Kool-Aid.

"Good, I guess," I answered my father. "We have to be quiet all the time, but Brian likes being a big brother."

"Have you seen the baby?"

"No," I said out of instinct, but then I reconsidered. I had my new glove on. My father was playing catch with me for the first time in ages. It seemed like a good time for honesty. "Well, once. Real quick when we were getting a drink. He looks like a blanket with a face."

My father laughed, catching my throw in his bare hands. He held the ball a moment, looking at it as if he was staring into the future.

"How would you like to be a big brother?"

"Sure, I suppose. As long as it was a boy. Girls don't play baseball."

My father walked toward me, a smile on his face. "Well, then you'd better hurry and tell your mother so she doesn't get it wrong."

As far as babies were concerned, about the only thing I knew when I was seven was that you got what you got no matter what you wanted. I wasn't following his point at all.

"What does Mom have to do with it?"

"The rest is up to her." My father knelt down in front of me so close I could almost feel his five o'clock shadow. "I'm trying to tell you that your mom is pregnant. You're gonna be a big brother, Johnny."

Ever since Brian first told me that his mom was expecting, I had been thinking about what it would be like to be a big brother, but now that I was hearing the news for real, I wasn't sure what to think. Would I have to share my room, start sleeping in a bunk bed? Would I only get half my allowance from now on? Would I be banished to playing outside for the rest of my life?

"I can't promise it won't be a sister," my father said. "But your mother and I are one for one at having boys. There's at least a fifty percent chance you'll have a little brother in the fall."

I started to consider the possibilities of having a brother. It might not be so bad. He could be best friends with little Ricky, and we could play all kinds of games that Brian and I couldn't play with just the two of us. First bounce or fly would be a real competition with four players instead of just one hitting to the other like we did now. We could get up games of hotbox with two boys at the bases, another as the runner caught in the middle, and when one of us got tired we could just switch to the boy who had been sitting out. We could play Wiffle ball, big kids vs. the little kids, or even the Standens vs. the Sloans. The more I thought of it, the more excited I got.

"So what do you say, Johnny?" my father asked. "You like the idea?"

I thought I'd been happy just moments before when we were breaking in my glove, but this news put my previous happiness to shame. This was a real second Christmas, right in the middle of a late-April evening. I threw my arms around my father's neck.

"It's the best idea I ever heard."

Now that I think about it, that may well have been the last time I embraced my father. I'm certain it was the last time I ever wanted to.

THURSDAY, MARCH 23

We suck.

Lost to Brian's old team the Twins at home this afternoon, 5–4. We've dropped two in a row, eight of our last nine, and at four and sixteen so far this spring our winning percentage is worse than the '62 Mets. No wonder Toronto doesn't want us. We just received word that the judge in the Ontario labor case ruled against us and we won't be allowed to play at the SkyDome when the regular season starts. There was talk that we might move down to St. Petersburg to use the ThunderDome as our home field, but maybe the thought of all those empty seats as backdrop to our games scared the front office away from that idea. Just before we showered and headed back to the hotel, it was announced that they will hold all of Toronto's regular season replacement games right there on Grant Field at Dunedin Stadium, home of the single-A Dunedin Jays, seating capacity 6,201.

I don't know why I took the news so hard. We'll still get to play in Yankee Stadium, still get to bang balls off the Green Monster in Fenway, still take the field at the new ballpark going up in Cleveland. But finding out that we aren't welcome in the city whose name is stitched across our jerseys—it feels like we've been shunned somehow, like we were all set to move into a great new house but at the last minute the loan fell through.

Maybe that's the thing about this game, the feeling I've never been able to shake. Baseball has always felt like a second home. It's a place full of friends, people you care about who care about the same shit you do. They know what you're thinking and feeling, can sense what you need without having to ask or be told. When I graduated from OSU three years ago and thought I was finished with organized ball, no one outside the game ever told me, maybe never even realized the one thing I needed to hear most: it's okay.

It's okay that you wasted your childhood playing a game you would never be good at. It's okay that you stood your date up two years in a row because your team played an invitational the same weekend as junior-senior prom. It's okay that you weren't drafted after high school or out of college. It's okay that no one ever thought more of your skill set than a one-line scouting report: *Good glove, no hit.* People guess wrong all the time Jake, and you just guessed wrong, buddy. It's okay that you were never meant to take third base on the same fields as the greatest players who ever put on a uniform.

It's okay.

I remember hearing the news about us staying in Dunedin for the regular season, and I remember feeling down the rest of the day, but the Ontario court ruling wasn't what was really bothering me that Wednesday. Before the Twins game, our equipment manager once again restitched my glove, and though I planned on using it as long as it would hold out, by the third inning paranoia was starting to eat my brain. What if another line drive came my way but this time it went through the webbing instead of sticking in it? What if I lost a grounder because I couldn't feel the ball at the tips of my glove fingers? What if this, what if that, what if some other damn thing? Finally I couldn't stand it anymore. Enough game-time events can ruin your concentration on a ball field any given day. You can't have doubts about your equipment too and expect to play your best. Besides, I'd had no reason to rotate my gloves after I played my last game at Ohio State, so my practice glove had been a bridesmaid for three years now. When we retired the side in the third, I knew I was a three-run rally away from batting next, so I jogged down the tunnel to the locker room to officially put my practice glove in the starting lineup.

As I neared the clubhouse entrance at the bottom of the tunnel I could hear water running from one of the sinks by the showers. That was odd, since players were expected to stay near the field during games and even the clubhouse guys tended to sit on the bench or out in the bullpen when the weather was nice. I never expected to find Speedboat, head under a stream of water, hiding out in the locker room while a game was on.

Thanks to the noise from the faucet, I didn't even have to be quiet to sneak up on him. I had been trying to think up a prank to repay the snipe hunt he pulled on me the other day, and though this seemed boringly low key and unwitnessed, I figured it would have to do until I could create a better opportunity. I stood behind him for what seemed a long time, waiting for maximum effect to jab him in the ribs right as he turned off the water, but he just let it run and run over the back of his head. After a moment it occurred to me that our 7-8-9 hitters were batting this inning so there was a strong possibility we could go three up and three down pretty quick. Speedboat may have had the starting-pitcher luxury of hiding out on days he wasn't in the lineup, but Assenmacher would definitely rip me a new one if they had to hold up the game because I was down in the locker room when I should have been watching from the bench. Finally I gave up on surprising him and just rapped my knuckles on the porcelain sink by his ear.

"Speedboat," I called. "How you doin' under there?"

Speedboat didn't flinch when I knocked on the sink and called his name. He didn't even seem surprised that someone was standing next to him. When he lifted his head and saw my reflection behind his in the mirror, he just nodded, slowly turning the sink handle to stop the flow. His kinky mop-top was matted down over his forehead. Rivulets of water spilled down from his hair, running over his eyes and cheeks, but he made no move to wipe them away. He looked like a dog that had been left out in the rain.

"Hola," he said quietly.

Speedboat was one of the most naturally ebullient people I have ever met. In the month since spring camp opened, I could count on one hand the number of times I'd seen him without a smile on his face, and every one of those times had been either during or immediately after a bad outing. He had taken his turn on the mound the previous day, giving up five runs to the White Sox in five and a third.

"What are you doing?" I asked, turning to walk to my locker. "Coach is gonna chew your ass if he finds you down here during a game."

I stopped short when I saw it: Speedboat's duffel on the chair in front of his locker, full to the zipper with his belongings. His cleats hung down, one on each side of the bench, laces joined under the handles of his bag.

"Mostly I am sad for my parents. They want so much for me to come and play baseball. They risk their lives for me and my brothers. They risk everything for us to come and have a chance to live out our dreams."

Between the two rows of hanging shirts, pants and equipment that diverged from Speedboat's corner locker, his stall stood glaringly empty, like a missing front tooth. A sticky gleam from the tape adhesive was visible against the flat wall paint above his cubicle; the tape that read "Martinez" had been pulled down.

"My dream was to be a Blue Jay," Speedboat continued, almost to himself. "But my other dream was to make my parents proud. Now I have no dreams." He turned and patted my shoulder, as if I was the one needing consolation. "Ees just you now. You dream for me too, Golden Jake."

Speedboat walked to his empty locker, picked up his duffel and headed for the clubhouse exit that led to the parking lot. I tried to think of something to say, anything to help ease his heavy heart, but I couldn't find any words.

As dumb as it sounds, while I watched Speedboat cross the empty locker room, I couldn't help thinking of a hamster I had when I was a kid. I went to check on him one night and found him struggling in the bottom of his cage. It seemed like his back legs weren't working, so I pulled him out and tossed him several times in the air. Each time, he landed and bounced helpless on my bed. I just wanted to wake him up. He was stiff in the bottom of the cage when I woke up the next morning. My mom didn't understand why I was so mopey about a stupid little hamster, but I couldn't bring myself to tell her how I'd treated him his last night on earth, how I could have been kind and understanding but instead I'd tossed him around trying to get him to liven up.

Now here was Speedboat, his dream of playing pro ball receding with each step toward the door. How could I have wished it was him instead of me the day Assenmacher called out from the coach's office, the afternoon I thought I was being let go? How could I have laughed at his English during one of GQ's broadcasts in front of the clubhouse TV? How could I have plotted my practical-joke revenge on the very day Speedboat got his walking papers? I could have been kind and understanding, but instead I acted just like me.

Speedboat pushed the exit bar on the clubhouse door and recoiled at the bright light that washed across the threshold. He paused to adjust to the sun and, blinking, turned toward me.

"I am proud to have been your teammate. Be a good Blue Jay, my friend."

When I fished my practice glove out of my locker and jogged back up the tunnel to the dugout, the guys were all grabbing their equipment to take the field for the next inning.

"The little son of a bitch didn't even say good-bye," Folgers groused into his beer.

Tall Boy and I went out for dinner after the game, and when we got back I walked down to Folgers's room to see if he had heard anything from Speedboat. There was no answer to my knock on the door. Eventually I found him sitting alone at the bar in the hotel lounge.

"He was probably angry, or embarrassed, or both," I told him. "Maybe Speedboat just didn't want to talk to anyone until he'd gotten a chance to get his head together."

"Don't make excuses for him," Folgers said. "I know why he disappeared. I'd have done the same damn thing."

With the bar otherwise empty, the bartender had little else to do but watch the news on the lounge TV and keep Folgers's glass full. I had no way to gauge how many beers he'd had, but based on the ashtray, Folgers had been sitting there for at least half a pack of cigarettes.

"It was all on account'a his mechanics," Folgers continued. "I tried to get him to change his delivery. You saw him. When he was pitching from the windup he got a good push, but every time he was in the stretch he took this dinky little step, like he was afraid he was gonna fall into a pile of dog shit. Why the fuck didn't he just listen to me?"

For some reason I didn't want to let on that I'd seen Speedboat in the locker room after he was released. Nobody had noticed that I'd gone down to switch out my glove, and it just didn't feel right to tell Folgers that I had been the last one to speak with Speedboat before he left. If anyone had been the last to see him, it should have been Folgers. You could hardly picture one without the other. They were a natural mental pairing, much like Tall Boy and I probably were to the rest of the guys on the team.

I said the only thing I could think to say: "I'll miss him."

"The fuck you will," Folgers replied. "You won't miss him and neither will anyone else. He lost every game he pitched and he wore out our bullpen in the bargain. Plus he was a slob. There was hair in our bathtub drain every time he got out of the shower. We're better off without him. Maybe now we can win some games."

I had sat down at the bar intending to be company to Folgers's misery, but I couldn't in good conscience sit quiet while he bad-mouthed Speedboat. He probably didn't mean a word of what he was saying, but I was at least four beers behind Folgers in the fog that passes for drunken logic. I wasn't sure I could catch up before closing time and doubted I wanted to even if I could. Instead, I used his shoulder as a brace to help me stand up.

"Bus leaves for Winter Haven at eleven," I told him. "Don't forget you've got the start."

Folgers nodded without looking up. As I walked out the lounge door he was still sitting where I'd left him, lighting a new cigarette from the smoldering stub of the one he'd just finished.

FRIDAY, MARCH 24

I think the Indians gave the Reds the wrong five players in their deal three weeks ago. This afternoon Folgers bounced the first pitch he threw two feet in front of the plate, but eventually both he and the team got our collective shit together as we beat the Tribe 12–5 in Winter Haven. I played five innings, one for three, a single, a walk, an RBI, and a run scored. In our home and away vs. Cleveland this week I have a combined .500 OBP with two RBI and two runs scored. If we played these guys every day for the rest of the season I'd be in the hunt for the Silver Slugger Award.

The Maryland state legislature passed a bill this week banning replacement games from being played in Camden Yards. That just put into law what was obvious already, as the Orioles' owner, Peter Angelos, is the only suit who has refused to field a replacement team during the strike. They say Angelos made his money as a labor lawyer, so I guess it goes to follow. The newspaper article also quoted some Orioles players saying what a stand-up bunch the Maryland legislature was, but you just know those same players were howling this past winter when Congress tried to revoke the MLB's antitrust exemption so they could impose a settlement between the union and owners to end the stalemate.

It's tough to say who is most at fault in this strike. For the bulk of the twentieth century the owners treated players like rented mules, but in my lifetime the players' union has grown so strong that they clearly call the shots now. There's certainly enough blame for both sides.

On the one hand, the suits' biggest complaint is that the players won't help save the owners from themselves: the large-market teams with all the money outbid the small-market teams for all the best players, creating a disparity they claim can only be solved if the union guys agree to a salary cap so that every team has the same chance at landing the big talent. The owners all bitch that without a salary cap, the effort to compete is driving every team into bankruptcy. In order to buy this argument, of course, you have to willfully forget that the owners are the ones paying the player salaries to start with. It would make for better theater if ownership groups in Arizona and Tampa Bay hadn't just this month ponied up $130 million each—during a strike, no less—to get the next two expansion teams expected to begin play with the '98 season. One hundred thirty million dollars each. Baseball is so expensive now, only corporations and the super-rich can afford to own a club. How many corporations or billionaires would be willing to pay a $130 million cover charge to enter a club that is burning down as fast as the MLB owners say theirs is? Either the suits are actually super-rich buffoons and only under the klieg light of public scrutiny is their business incompetence showing through, or every owner in baseball is lying through his teeth to the fans, and not very convincingly at that.

On the other hand, the union guys want our sympathy because the owners are trying to shove a salary cap down their throats, even though the players walked away from what most people in America would consider the ultimate job. I love it when a player shows up on TV dressed in a coat and tie, talking all in legal-speak because he's his team's union rep, trying to get across the idea that "the public doesn't understand the socioeconomics of the modern game." Maybe we don't, but the union guys seem to have forgotten the socioeconomics of modern life.

I'm one of those people who plunk down a couple bucks a week for a lotto ticket even though I full well know that the chances of my numbers hitting are roughly the same as a meteor knocking the bat out of my hands as I try to check my swing on a curveball low and away. What my money buys me is not a realistic shot at the lotto jackpot but simply the *dream* of winning those millions—a dream so entertaining I'm willing to pay $5 a week to have it renewed. Why? Because at $77.50 per U-Haul workday, I know exactly how long it will take me to reach my first million the old-fashioned way: a lifetime. In 1994 when this strike started, minimum wage for the lowliest bench warmer in Major League Baseball was over $100,000, the average salary was over $1 million, and more than a hundred players had contracts worth over $3 million a year. In other words, the union guys don't just make a lot of money; they make lotto money. Yet they want us to commiserate in the fact that they get so little off the MLB money tree that they'd rather strike than let the current system continue to make them one of the highest-paid groups of unionized labor in the world.

During his failed attempt to help broker a settlement last winter, even President Clinton described the strike as, and I quote, "just a few hundred folks trying to figure out how to divide nearly two billion dollars."

Nine days till we're legit.

In the third inning of the Cleveland game, as our leadoff man took his warm-up swings before stepping into the box, Folgers motioned Tall Boy and me over to the corner of the dugout.

145

"Gents," he said, looking around as if someone might be eavesdropping. "Remember that curveball I bounced to the first batter? Wanna know why? Feast your eyes—far side of the plate, eight rows up, yellow tank top."

Tall Boy and I scanned the crowd. The subject of Folgers's objectification was obvious immediately. Dressed in Daisy Dukes and a bright-yellow tank top, a black-haired beauty leaned across several seats to hand money to a popcorn vendor. It was clear with just a glance that gravity had not yet been informed of her existence. Tall Boy let out a soft whistle. I actually said the word *yowza* before I could stop myself. She couldn't have been a day over nineteen.

"She was leanin' over for the Coke man when I let that curveball go," Folgers said.

"God loves teenage girls," Tall Boy said.

"Me too," I said.

When she received her popcorn and sat back down, the best parts of her disappeared into the sea of heads in her section. We followed suit, taking seats on the bench behind us.

"Why do you think that is?" Folgers pondered.

"Because Jake's a walking hormone."

"No, I mean about God making teenage girls look like a million dollars."

"Actually," Tall Boy said, "I have a theory about that."

You learn to hate hearing those words from Brian Sloan. I let out a groan.

Folgers waved away my protest. "Lay it on me."

"Let's say you're God, right? And you want to make this new species, call 'em humans. You've already got prototypes all figured out. Maybe that's Adam and Eve, who knows?"

Folgers nodded. "With ya so far."

"You want your new species to have a fighting chance in the wild kingdom, of course, so you have to give them some kind of advantage, something so they can compete. Now compared to lions and tigers and bears, oh my, your new species isn't very big or strong, they don't have especially sharp teeth or claws, they aren't very scary looking, and they can't run very fast. At this rate they won't last a week, right?"

"It is a jungle out there," Folgers agreed.

"Right. So what do you do? You give humans big, fast, smart brains—the best brains of any animal on the market. And that's our main advantage, our big brains."

"Still with ya," Folgers said.

"But—and this is a big but—because there are so many drawbacks to your new species, simply giving them the best brains in the jungle isn't gonna be enough. First, it takes nine months before they're ready to come out of the oven, and when they are born they're so wimpy for the first ten or fifteen years that they die for a thousand different reasons above and beyond getting eaten by another animal. And unless you make major changes to the size and plumbing of the female, she's only gonna be able to have one, maybe two at a time. So you'll have to adjust some things, tweak the details to give your new species a chance at having enough babies to make it."

Our leadoff batter had drawn a walk on five pitches, and the next hitter was stepping up to the plate.

"The first thing you tweak," Tall Boy continued, "is how often women can get knocked up. As God, you already gave most animals a special time for them to get pregnant so that they'll have their babies when the weather is warm and there's the most food around—meaning the spring-going-into-summer time."

"Like dogs and cats going into heat," Folgers said.

"Exactly. With humans though, you're gonna need more babies than that because they have so few at a time and they die so easy. So you make them constantly in heat: women can get pregnant any month of the year, and men are horny every minute of the day. But that's not gonna be enough, because these big brains need to learn a lot to survive in the jungle with such wimpy bodies. It takes a kid years before he can fend for himself without winding up as some boa constrictor's lunch. So you make them want to live in groups, since they're so worthless on their own and because there's safety in numbers. But even that's not gonna be enough. You still need to crank out more babies.

"Oh shit," Tall Boy said when he looked out at the game. "I'm on deck."

He grabbed a bat out of the rack and I threw him his batting gloves as our second batter hit a slow roller to the right side. Their pitcher covered first in time for the out. Tall Boy jogged up the dugout steps and headed straight for the batter's box.

With one out and a runner on second, Brian lined the first pitch he saw to the right-center-field gap. The run scored easily, but the Indians' right fielder made a nice play to grab the ball on a hop and fire a strike to second base. The throw surprised Tall Boy, beating him to the bag by a foot as he tried to stretch his hit into a double. When he jogged back to the dugout, Brian waded through a forest of high fives and pats on the back, finally taking his seat again between Folgers and me.

"Anyway, your new species still needs work," he started in again. "You got them living in groups, and they're always in heat, but they still die too easily. You're gonna need more babies that have a fighting chance to make it into adulthood. So now you tweak each of the two sexes to make them specialists within each mated pair. You make men the stronger and faster of the two so they can do the hunting and gathering. And you make the women specialists at having and taking care of the babies while the men are out hunting and gathering."

"How do you do that with the women?" Folgers asked.

"Three things," Tall Boy answered. "You give women a higher pain threshold because the birthing process hurts so much and you'll want them to have more than one kid each before they say 'enough.' You give them big boobs so they can still feed the kiddies even if the men have a bad day at the hunting-gathering office. And finally—this is the best part—you make the women as attractive as possible, as young as possible, so the men will want to have sex with them as soon as the women are old enough to start caring for the kids."

Lenny Longo's long, lazy fly ball to center field ended the inning. We all grabbed gloves and headed up the dugout steps to take the field.

"So why isn't the opposite true?" I asked. "Why don't adult women look at sixteen-year-old guys and say 'yowza'?"

"Because you want your humans to pick mates who are in the best shape to do the job they need to do within the family. For women, their job is to make and care for the babies, and they can do that job starting in their late teens. But men need to be wise enough to outsmart the next meal and strong enough to kill it and drag it back to the cave."

Tall Boy stopped a few feet from me at third and fielded a warm-up grounder, tossing it back to the first baseman before continuing.

"Men don't reach their physical peak until their twenties, and they keep maturing mentally for years after that. So adult women don't say 'yowza' about most sixteen-year-old guys for the simple reason that most sixteen year olds aren't men yet."

"But wait," I protested. "If we already made the men horny enough to screw anything that moves any hour of the day, why bother making teenage women so attractive?"

"Because it's a jungle out there," Folgers called over his shoulder from the mound.

Tall Boy nodded. "You make the men constantly horny because you want as many babies coming down the pike as the species can produce. More babies overall means more are likely to survive to their teen years, when they can take care of themselves." Tall Boy paused while I took a grounder and fired it back to first. "But the babies most likely to survive will be the biggest and the strongest. And which women are likely to have the most, biggest, and strongest babies?"

Our catcher threw the last warm-up pitch down to Hack Hennessey at second.

"The youngest, most fertile women," Folgers answered from the mound.

"Meaning teenage women," Tall Boy said, gloving Hack's throw from second. "So you make teenage women their most attractive, horny men will want to have sex with them as soon and as often as possible, and they're the most likely to have babies with the best chance to survive."

"And that's your theory?" I asked as the game ball came around the horn to me. "That's why Yellow Tank Top up there looks like a million dollars?"

"You tell me," Brian answered. "Would you like to go make a big strong baby with her right now?"

"Or pass out from tryin'," Folgers agreed.

Tall Boy followed me and the game ball to the mound. "See? It works. That's exactly why Yellow Tank Top looks like a million dollars. It's all part of the master plan."

Folgers was laughing as he took the ball from my glove. "Makes sense to me."

"You're only encouraging him," I scolded, but it did no good. Even after Brian and I jogged back to our positions I could still see Folgers's shoulders bouncing in full chortle as he toed the rubber, looking in for the catcher's first sign of the inning.

Played Detroit in Lakeland this afternoon. They hold their spring games in a great old park called Joker Marchant Stadium, on Al Kaline Drive. No clue who or what Joker Marchant is, but the ten-time Gold Glover Kaline, an outfielder for the Tigers some twenty years back, needed no introductions for me. I played the first five and a half, went zero for two. Tall Boy had a good game: hit a triple and scored our first run, then hit a single and scored again when Lenny Longo smacked a homer in the seventh. We lost, 4–3.

We heard the news today that a replacement player for Atlanta, a pitcher with the sadly appropriate name of Dave Shotkoski, was gunned down last night in West Palm Beach during an apparent robbery attempt. They got him to a hospital but it was too late. To make matters worse, the guy had a wife and kid back home. Maybe I've reached the point where I can't watch sports shows anymore without jaded glasses on, but I swear the TV talking heads reported the story with this expression of total surprise, like they didn't realize we replacements could have families, or be victims of violent crime, or get murdered over the fifty bucks in our wallets. It all reminded me of J. R. Richard, the huge, hard-throwing ace of the Houston Astros back in the late '70s. Richard had a reputation as a showboat and a mouth, so when he started complaining of fatigue and a sore arm in the middle of the 1980 season, all the reporters got on him as if Richard was just trying to make excuses for a bad season, or get more press attention, or maybe he was on dope. Then one day Richard was working out in the Astrodome, started feeling nauseous and decided to lie down for a minute. If they hadn't called an ambulance he would've died from a stroke right there on the Astroturf. I can still see those broadcasters—the same guys who'd been ripping Richard just a few days earlier—trying to report the story with all that egg on their faces. It took J. R. Richard suffering a stroke on the plastic grass of the Astrodome to remind the sports talking heads that even guys who throw 99 mph fastballs are mortal, and maybe it took Dave Shotkoski dying over a handful of dollars last night to remind them that we replacements are flesh and blood, too.

Eight days till we're legit.

After I popped out to end the top of the sixth, I grabbed my glove and started out to my position, only to hear Assenmacher calling me back to the dugout. "Standen," he said. "Where you going?" I did a U-turn and flipped my glove back down the dugout stairs.

"Come here," he said, crooking a finger my direction. "I don't blame you for being pissed off. That piece of crap you just hit? I'd be fucking embarrassed, too. Tell me what you did wrong that at bat."

I had gotten comfortable with keeping my hands at my ribs and I knew I had taken a short, sharp step at the start of my swing like we had worked on. I didn't know what he wanted to hear, but usually when Coach asked you a question, he didn't expect you to have a reply. He just wanted you to shut up while he told you the answer.

"I think hitting that home run last week was the worst thing that could've happened to you. Your swing has been a piece of crap ever since. Are you trying to pull every pitch out of the park? It looks like it. Now, out of your two at bats today, which was your best?"

I'd hit a liner to short in the third and then popped out with two guys on to end the sixth.

"Exactly," he continued, "and what was the count when you hit that line drive? It was two and two, right? Now think about this at bat. You swung at a tits-high fastball. What was different in that first at bat that you didn't do this last time up?"

As mad as I was about my at bats and about getting pulled from the game, I still wasn't ready to risk the wrath that spouting off to Assenmacher would surely bring.

"Two strikes," I told him. "I was protecting the plate that first time because I had two strikes."

"The best hits you've gotten this spring have all come when you simply put the bat on the ball. You ain't a slugger. You know that as well as I do. The next time you hit a home run, I'll have you running wind sprints after the game."

151

I would've assumed he was joking but I couldn't remember hearing Assenmacher make a joke about anything.

"I mean it," he said. "When you're protecting the plate, you choke up on the bat, you take a compact swing and you hit the ball on a line. From now on I want you to do the same thing every time you step into the box: Approach each pitch like you're down to your last strike."

He could be a serious prick sometimes but I didn't think Assenmacher would really go drill sergeant on me if I put an occasional hanging slider over the fence. Still, the help he'd given me on hitting so far had been simple and mostly effective. I took a seat on the bench and filed this latest piece of advice away for future reference.

Sadie and I hadn't gotten together since Wednesday, and when I called Friday night she already had plans, but she promised to make up for it by keeping her whole evening free the following night. So once we got back from Lakeland Saturday I went straight into the bathroom to prep for our night out. Since Tall Boy usually waited till after dinner to call Karen, he had nothing better to do but lie back on his bed, flip through the TV channels, and spy on me as I shaved and got dressed. Finally curiosity got the better of him.

"What are you getting all dolled up for?"

"Girls get dolled up," I corrected him. "Guys get gussied up."

"Is this that same woman you went out with last week?"

"Her name is Sadie, and yes, if you must know, we're going out again."

"So we've reached the she's-got-a-name stage of the relationship, have we?"

"We're already up to the impress-her-quick-before-she-changes-her-mind stage."

Tall Boy sat up on an elbow. "Well that sounds serious—for you anyway. So go on, bust my chops. Tell me everything."

"A gentleman doesn't kiss and tell."

"That's okay. You can kiss and write me the details. I'll even start the letter for you. 'Dear Penthouse Forum: I never thought I'd be writing to you. . . .'"

"Dear Penthouse Forum," I cut in. "All's quiet on the western front."

Tall Boy tilted his head and wiggled a finger in his ear like a swimmer trying to get water out.

"Am I hearing you right? This from the original ooze-'em-and-lose-'em lover? C'mon, Standen. You've never been with a woman longer than three dates without having some lurid details you can't wait to tell me."

"It isn't like that, Tall Boy. Sadie's getting a divorce. She's still trying to find her feet. And I may be wrong about this but I think she's actually a lady."

"Oh, puke." Brian waved me off like he was shooing a fly. "Get back to me when you've got something worth reporting."

I had details to report, but I knew he wouldn't believe them.

I would've been lying if I said some cheesy crap like every moment away from Sadie felt like an eternity. Between the team and the coaches and the fans and the games, I was never at a loss for people or things to think about. But if I stopped at a traffic light and a woman in a jean skirt walked across my field of vision, I would instantly search my memory to see if I knew where Sadie was at that moment. Even when I knew she was miles away at work or running errands, a glimpse of her would suddenly appear in the crowd at a game, in line at the grocery, in the lobby of the team hotel. Though in one sense she stood out like a Playboy bunny at a Teamsters rally, in another very real sense she was everywhere, under every pretty hat, holding every bundle of flowers, behind every woman's soft laugh.

One night when Tall Boy and I went out for dinner, we walked past a booth in the restaurant and I caught a scent like cherry blossoms and baby powder. I stopped dead in my tracks, certain that Sadie was at the table beside me. When I looked down it was obvious the woman seated there was only wearing the same perfume, but until that moment it hadn't even occurred to me that Sadie wore perfume. I just thought that that was how she smelled.

By now I was beyond simply saving up things to tell her; I'd started having conversations with Sadie even when she wasn't there. I could hear her voice and anticipate her reactions. When Sadie agreed with something you said, instead of responding with "I know what you mean," she would say, "Right?" If you said something she didn't quite catch, she would ask you to repeat it by saying, "Sorry?" If you asked, "Do you want more bread?" I would just say "sure" or "okay." Sadie always answered,

"Please." And every now and again, during the most casual conversation, she would say something that let you see right down into her soul.

After dinner Saturday night, Sadie and I decided to walk the beach in Clearwater. We had been talking about one of the clients she spoke with at work that afternoon when Sadie asked me, "If you were a woman and you didn't like your body, would you consider breast augmentation?"

"This lady called the Psychic Soulmates number to ask about getting a boob job?"

"No. She was talking about feeling inadequate around her boyfriend, but she didn't ask me that. I'm just asking you. Would you do it?"

Had I given her a reason to feel inadequate when we were together? Did I say or do something to make her think that I thought her breasts were too small? At least twice during our last evening out I'd had to remind myself to stop touching Sadie, if only because the weather had been warm and I didn't want her to start equating "Jake" with "feeling clammy hands on my ass." Did I touch her enough to make her feel wanted? Had I been groping her entirely too much? It sure seemed like there was a right answer here somewhere, but I was too busy avoiding all the obvious wrong ones to say anything for a moment.

"Well, not being a woman, I'm not sure I can say one way or the other," I finally stammered out. "But I do know that the, um—appendage enlargement options available to men pretty much never cross my mind."

"Sure, but nobody can just look at you in a tight sweater and see that your appendage is undersized."

"Now you're on to me," I admitted. "It's all about clothing choices. This is why you have yet to see me in a Speedo."

Sadie had a wonderful laugh, warm and inviting.

"So you're saying a woman shouldn't?"

"I'm saying it depends on the woman. As potential mates though, I don't think small-breasted women get the positive reinforcement they deserve."

"For example?"

"For example, they make frugal wives, since they can exercise all they want without wasting your hard-earned money on sports bras."

Sadie's groan told me my argument wasn't yet convincing. I took that as encouragement.

"And you can buy small-breasted women those beach T-shirts with the funny phrases printed across the front, and rest assured the words won't get distorted and ruin the punch line."

Sadie just shook her head, refusing to dignify my joke with a response.

"But the best part—" I stopped in the sand and waited for her to turn toward me. "The best part is that, when one of those double-D women hits forty, where do her double-Ds wind up? Down around her belly button. But you marry a B cup and when she hits forty, hers will still be as perky as the year she grew 'em."

When she laughed again, I knew I was in the clear. I pulled Sadie to me and cupped her breast in my hand as we kissed.

"I wouldn't change a thing," I told her.

We walked along the shore for several minutes without speaking. It occurred to me that there might be three inches of snow still on the ground back home while we were here with sand between our toes and surf lapping at our ankles. I would've been happy just to stroll the beach all night, but I didn't want Sadie to think I was a boring date, so I searched my brain for one of Tall Boy's hypothetical questions to break the silence.

"If you could have any superhero power, what would you choose? On top of being psychic, I mean."

"Would I have to fight crime?"

I liked that her first impulse was to ask a clarifying question.

"Nope, just wake up tomorrow and your new power is switched on."

"I think I'd go for invisibility. Well, sometimes everyone ignores me and I feel invisible already, but that would be a cool superhero power to have."

After years of fielding Would You Rathers from Brian, I've come to realize that the point of the question is not in hearing the answer but in finding out the rhyme and reason behind the answer.

"Be specific," I pressed. "Are you all there when you're invisible or is it more like an out of body experience, just your mind cruising around while the rest of you is home on the couch?"

"I think you'd have to have your body with you or else you wouldn't be invisible; you'd just be a ghost."

"Why invisibility?"

Sadie was quiet a moment, as if trying to decide how to word her answer.

"You know those times when you're in a situation where you really don't want to be there, but you can't leave without offending the person you really don't want to be there with? I think if you could just become invisible and sneak away, that would be the perfect solution."

It sounded to me as if she was picking invisibility out of politeness.

"Wouldn't it be just as rude to disappear and sneak off as to get up and walk away in full view?"

"Of course not," Sadie insisted. "Nobody can just become invisible. So if you could, you'd have the perfect excuse: 'What happened to you last night?' 'I don't know. One minute I was there, and *poof*, next thing I knew I was home in bed.'"

Without even thinking, I reached out and took her hand as we laughed. When we caught our breath, Sadie looked down and back up at me.

"Don't worry," she said. "I won't disappear on you tonight. What would your power be?"

Naturally I had known my answer when I asked the question, but I pretended to mull it over a minute anyway to make it seem like I was being spontaneously thoughtful.

"I think I'd like to fly. That would be great to just take off for Jamaica or somewhere. You wouldn't have to worry about airline reservations or any of that. You could just call your friends up and say, 'Let's go! Trip's on me.'"

"Oh, you can carry people when you're flying. Won't you get tired?"

"Sure I can carry people. Or maybe they can just hang on to my arms as we fly along."

"So now you can fly and you never get tired? Isn't that two superhero powers?"

There was something in the way she questioned the logic of my superhero power that cracked me up.

"No, it's not two powers," I pointed out. "The never-get-tired-while-flying power comes with the flying power. It's a set, like you controlling when you become invisible. Or would your invisibility just go on and off without you having any say about it?"

"Oh God, no," she said. "That's the way it works for me now."

We walked a little farther down the beach, holding on to our shoes with one hand and each other with the other. I guess Sadie picked up on the hypothetical question theme and decided it was her turn to ask one.

"If you could relive any moment from your life, what moment would you pick?"

I had never before thought about it, never heard Tall Boy ask anything of the sort with one of his questions, but I knew my answer immediately.

"Babe Ruth League, the summer between junior high and high school," I said. "I usually played third base even back then, but for some reason they had me playing in left that day.

"In the middle of the game, right before we took the field for the next inning, one of our assistant coaches—he was just some high school guy whose little brother played on our team—he asked me, 'Do you think you can make varsity next year?' I didn't know what to say. I was just a scrawny eighth grader, after all. So I said, 'Sure, I guess so. What do you think?' And he gives me this condescending smirk, like—'Yeah, right.'

"So in the next inning they get runners on first and second with one out, and the guy up at bat hits a hard shot between shortstop and third, rolling right out to me in left. I remember charging the ball, and in my peripheral vision I see the runner from second busting around third, trying to score. So as soon as I got the ball, I popped up and fired it home. My throw takes one hop, hits the catcher smack in the mitt; he puts down the tag and nails the runner sliding in. Pretty good, right? But wait; there's more.

"The runner from first, seeing that I was throwing home, figured he could keep going, so here he comes flying around second and heading for third. I'm out in left field patting myself on the back for my play at the plate when suddenly I realize I'm the only backup if there's a throw to third base. So I start running toward the left field line just as our catcher sees the runner trying to take the extra base. He hops up and whips the ball down there. Sure enough, the ball goes sailing over the third base-man's head and out toward me. The runner slides in, sees the ball go into left, jumps up and heads for home. I race to the foul line, bare-hand the ball and fire it back in. The catcher grabs it on a hop, lays down the tag—bang. A two-assist double play, from left field, at home plate, to end the inning. Even the other team's third-base coach gave me a high five as I was running back to our bench."

Sadie let out a soft cheer there on the beach for the fourteen-year-old me.

"And you know the coolest part? When I got back to the bench, that high school kid ran over to me and he goes, 'Hell yes, you're gonna make varsity next year!'

"If I could relive any moment," I said, "that would be it."

When I finished, I half expected Sadie to laugh at me because it had taken longer to describe my moment than to live it, but she just squeezed my hand.

"How about you? What moment would you go back to?"

"I don't know if the moment I'm thinking of counts, really," Sadie said. "It wasn't anything special. No big event happened or anything, but one time when I was little my parents and I were going to Orlando on vacation. I was sitting up in the front seat between them, and we were just talking. I'd hardly gotten any sleep the night before—I was way too excited about going to see Mickey and Cinderella and all the rest—but as we were driving up the interstate, chitchatting away, the sun felt good coming in through the windshield and I was getting sleepy, so I leaned my head into my mom's lap, and she reached down and started to circle the little bumps on my spine with her fingers. I'm not sure how long we stayed like that but I just remember feeling so warm and, I don't know—wanted, I guess. Sitting between my folks while my mom rubbed my back. It's not much of a moment, is it? I guess I'd just like to go back to any moment before the accident, before my mother turned into whoever she is now."

For an instant I felt my knees go soft. All this time I'd believed Sadie despised her mother. The only times she had ever spoken about her mom were when Sadie was telling me what a bitch she'd become. But to hear her saying now that one of the best moments of her life had been with her mother—I swear for a second I almost choked up. I'd just spent five minutes describing some obscure play from a game I was in ten years before, and Sadie only needed twenty seconds to show me how shallow and easy my childhood had been. If anyone else had done that, I probably would have resented it. With Sadie it only made me want her more.

158

Beat the Pirates at home today, 5–2. I went in after the fifth, grounded out my only time up. Nobody said it in so many words but I think we all wanted the win to shut up our newest critic. This morning the Tampa paper carried a feature article by whom else but our old drinking buddy, Bob "Spoons" Hawkey, in the Sunday sports section. Beneath the headline "Blue Jay Subs Out of Their Depth in Replacement Sea," Hawkey gave *Tribune* readers a position-by-position breakdown of our team's chances at the start of the regular season. According to Hawkey, we have none. Most of his write-up was just a rehash of what the local papers and TV guys have been harping about all spring so far—our lack of clutch hitting and bullpen depth.

Of course he had an opinion about the hot corner. If only the jerk had gotten my name right. "Third base is currently run by committee, but it seems starting duties will go to Jack Standen by defensive default. While rudimentary hitting skills should banish Standen to a permanent spot in the bottom third of the lineup, an adequate range, decent arm and solid glove could come in handy bolstering an otherwise shaky infield unit."

Hawkey offered similar one- or two-line opinions for seven of our starting eight on defense. I wouldn't have thought one spilled beer could buy Tall Boy so much animosity, but Hawkey outdid himself when he finished his piece by describing our team's prospects at the six hole: "A castoff from the Minnesota Twins' farm system fills in at short. Brian Sloan's bat is his only asset, which reveals as much about the team's poor hitting as it does about Sloan's talent. Though shortstop is widely considered the most crucial position along the base paths and is arguably the most important defender after a team's catcher, Sloan's weak arm, minimal range and suspect glove all call into question how serious the Blue Jays are about fielding a competitive team during the upcoming season. Expect a replacement for this replacement if Toronto hopes to contend. Until they find one, expect opponents' hits up the middle to be as frequent as Jays' losses have been of late."

As condescending as Hawkey's article was, he wouldn't have written it and the paper wouldn't have run it if there weren't some indisputable facts on the table right now: (1) the owners' and players' union reps haven't so much as met in the same room to discuss a compromise since March 4, over three weeks ago; (2) despite the fact that President Clinton's own mediator, Bill Usery, requested last week that the owners put their "best offer" on the table in the hopes of restarting negotiations, Red Sox CEO John Harrington—the chairman of the owners' negotiating committee—said on Friday, and I quote: "We are not in the process of preparing a revised proposal or a best proposal or a final proposal or anything like that"; and (3) even if the union guys' latest legal ploy works and they get the National Labor Relations Board to file an injunction against the owners in US district court to declare that the suits bargained in bad faith, at best that sets up a daisy chain of ifs to keep us replacements from taking the field next week. IF an injunction is filed, then a judge will have to agree to rule on it—and then rule in the players' favor—almost immediately; and even IF the judge rules that both sides must return to the old labor agreement until a new one is struck, then the players will have to make good on their promise to end the strike outright; but even IF the players do, then the owners would still have to agree not to lock the players out of camp until a new agreement is reached; and even IF all those other ifs happen, then both sides will have to agree to postpone the start of the regular season, thereby losing more money and more games in a shortened '95 season, until the union guys have had a few weeks to get themselves in shape to play. For better or worse, the only reason Hawkey wrote that article is because we replacements are here till further notice and it's time to start looking at the "replacement baseball experiment" for what it is about to become: the regular Major League season.

One week.

"That fat cocksucker." Tall Boy was livid about the article. "I should have broken his typing finger when I had the chance."

We had picked up the morning paper for something to read over breakfast. Tall Boy was bringing the sports section with us so he could tape the article on the clubhouse message board.

"I don't know if breaking his finger would have helped," I told Brian. "How do you think a guy winds up with a name like Hawkey, anyway?

You saw his beak. He could pound out a story without ever lifting a hand."

I tried to illustrate my point with an imitation of Hawkey at the keyboard, but stopped when I caught a glimpse of myself in the rearview and realized I looked more like a bobblehead doll than a man typing with his nose.

"Do you think the son of a bitch ever watched a spring game when the union guys were here?" Tall Boy kept picking up the paper and slapping it back down on the seat between us. "The starters don't play but four or five innings. Predicting a team's season based on how they look in spring training is like guessing if a woman is beautiful after only seeing her elbow."

I thought about Hawkey's review of our club, the things he had to say about Hack and GQ, Lenny Longo and the rest of the guys. It seemed to me he could have written the entire article without doing more than cribbing other pieces that had appeared in print over the last several weeks.

"You'd think if a paper was going to print news," I finally decided out loud, "they'd make sure what they were printing was actually new."

Tall Boy turned to me. "What's that supposed to mean?"

"I just mean that he's not saying anything we haven't already heard ten times before. Everything in there is common knowledge."

"Common knowledge?" Tall Boy picked up the sports section and held it up again. "So you're saying you agree with this moron?"

"I'm not saying that. Of course I don't agree with him. He's just not saying anything new, is all."

Tall Boy slapped the paper down. "So it's old news that I'm the weak link up the middle? It's common knowledge I'm the reason we've lost so many games this spring?"

"Stop it," I told him. "You know exactly why Hawkey wrote those things about you. It's Fat Boy's revenge for the other night at the restaurant."

I had to slow and check my mirrors as we approached the turn off of 19A that would take us to the stadium.

"And what about that?" Tall Boy asked, a little too loud. "Why was I the only dog in that fight? Where were you when he was saying we have the talent level of a single-A team?"

"You know where I was—same table as you, telling Hawkey to go screw himself. Do you think I got off easy in there? Is he being kind when he says I'll never bat higher than ninth the rest of the season?"

"At least you're still on the team." Tall Boy picked the paper off the seat again. "He's got me on the next bus to Palookaville. 'Expect a replacement for this replacement if Toronto—'"

"I read the article," I cut in. "I don't need you to read it for me again."

We got through the stoplight on Douglas Avenue and I turned into the stadium parking lot. We had a good two hours before game time, and I was willing to sit in the car for as long as Brian needed to vent about Hawkey and whatever it was that seemed to be pissing him off about me. When I pulled into our usual spot, I put the car in park and cut the engine.

"Look," I said, turning to face him. "All I'm saying is—"

But Tall Boy didn't let me finish. Casting me a glance that fell somewhere between disgust and resignation, he collared the paper with one hand, pulled his duffel up from the floorboard with his other, and pushed open the passenger door.

"Where the fuck are you going? Will you wait a minute? Brian—"

Tall Boy got out of the car, swung the door shut, and walked toward the stadium without looking back.

As I watched him make his way across the parking lot I ticked through the things I had planned to tell him. The stuff Hawkey had written was obviously bullshit because he overlooked a bunch of positives about our defense and the fact that our batting order wasn't set yet. I was even willing to admit that Hawkey seemed surer of my position on the team than I was. But then it struck me that Tall Boy wasn't all that mad about what Hawkey had written about the club; he only seemed pissed by what Hawkey had written about him.

I knew that feeling. I'd lost count of the number of articles written in the weekly High School Roundup section of the Columbus papers during our run at the state title senior year, how many times I read glowing praise for our "star shortstop" who "led the team in every way." If those articles mentioned me it was always as an afterthought, just another role player who fit the bill on this team but had no real shot to move on to the next level. The *Dispatch* had a full paragraph write-up in the Local Player

News column when Tall Boy signed with the Twins. The fact that I got offered a scholarship to play at OSU didn't even warrant a mention two weeks later.

Now you get it, I thought as Brian reached the locker room entrance and disappeared inside. *Now you know how it feels when the shoe is on the other foot.*

Tall Boy and I had argued countless times over the years, just like any friends who grew up close as brothers. Punches were thrown back in the day, genuine knock-down, roll-around-in-the-dirt tussles between two take-no-shit ten-year-olds. Then, when we got big and strong enough to actually hurt one another, the fistfights gave way to aggravated verbal assaults—the raised voice, the cutting word, the cruel put-down that only each knew how to use for maximum effect against the other. But the same intimate knowledge that gave us both the secrets of how to inflict greatest damage also gave us a conciliatory key, a mutually understood set of shortcuts that made the act of apologizing into the simple exchange of a glance, a smile, a quiet "How's it going?" and all was forgotten.

But this time it was different, and I knew it was more than what Hawkey had written in his article. There was something else the matter, some nagging fear or offense raging in Tall Boy that I was clueless to understand and powerless to breach. Maybe it was that powerlessness that kept Tall Boy from confiding in me what was really the problem. Honestly I wasn't that upset over our fight in the car, but the residue of it hung between us like smog, clouding every discussion, choking off any attempt to bridge the distance.

To an outsider it probably didn't appear as if anything had changed. The guys on the team still saw us sitting together on the bench, still throwing to each other during warm-ups, still performing in tandem all our usual game-day habits. I don't even remember how our most public ritual got started, but before the first pitch of our first inning on defense every game, we always converged between his spot at shortstop and mine at third. The words we traded as we high-fived gloves were a prayer of sorts, the thing we each hoped for from our afternoon in the field. "Easy hops," Tall Boy always said. "No holes," I always answered. For the game against the Pirates that day, we still danced our ritual steps, but it felt more like a shared obligation than a private pact. We were just going through the motions.

Thanks to our victory the mood was pretty light in the clubhouse after the game, but at some point once I'd showered and changed, I looked up to realize that Tall Boy was no longer in the room. I walked the tunnel all the way to the dugout, then to make sure, I even checked to see that the weight room was empty, but still no Sloan. Finally I asked Hack, who said he thought Brian had hitched a ride with Folgers back to the hotel. GQ overheard me ask and added that he'd seen the two of them heading out the locker room door toward the parking lot together.

I was glad to hear it, on several fronts. It never would have occurred to me to strand Tall Boy without a ride no matter how much we were feuding, but I wasn't looking forward to the trip back with him today for fear he might want to restart the argument. Plus it might be good for him to talk with Folgers since talking, or more precisely not talking, to me hadn't solved anything. If needed I could even touch base with Folgers later and see if he had any insights into what burr had gotten stuck up Tall Boy's butt.

I knew just where to find Folgers later if it came to that. For the past several evenings, pretty much since Speedboat got released, Folgers had been spending more and more time in the hotel lounge. One night Tall Boy and I had come in late from dinner and seen him sitting alone at the bar when we passed by heading for our room. We joined him for a beer, and while the conversation was lively enough, it didn't seem as if Folgers really cared whether we were there or not, so we left him to his own vices after that. Though the lounge closed by eleven thirty most nights, more than once Folgers had shown up in the locker room the next day with pronounced bags under his eyes, and I couldn't help but wonder how strictly he was obeying the midnight curfew players were expected to follow during spring camp.

With no taxi duties to perform, and not eager to head back to the hotel to discover what conflict might await my arrival, I decided that tonight I would be a lover instead of a fighter.

"Of course I'd like to see you," Sadie said when I called from a pay phone outside the stadium. "But I am flat broke until Friday. Do you have any low-cost ideas?"

Her being between paychecks seemed a weak excuse not to go out, if that's how she meant it, as I had treated on every date but the dinner she bought to celebrate my game-ending play that one night. She must have meant it as an invitation to stay in.

"How about a race?" I proposed. "If you call the pizza delivery people and I pick up a bottle of something on the way, I should just beat them to your house in about a half hour."

"On your mark," Sadie answered. "Get set. Go."

I started for the store intending to grab some beers but then I remembered her saying something once about drinking margaritas at home, so for a change I bought tequila and a bottle of mixer instead. Sadie lit some candles while I whipped up a batch of drinks in her blender, then we ate at her kitchen table with the open pizza box as our only plate. On our second slice she caught me eyeing her copy of the Sunday *Tribune* sitting in sections on a counter by the sink.

"I'd guess by the look on your face that you saw the piece about your team in today's paper."

"Good news travels fast." I nodded. "Bad travels faster."

"What did your teammates say?"

Even though it was the reason I had come over, I didn't feel up to recounting Tall Boy's and my fight just yet. It felt like a fresh sunburn where your skin is radiating heat. The nerves were still too raw.

"Nobody was real happy with the article," I told her. "But to be honest, we're kind of used to it by now. Well, most of us anyway."

"That guy really raked your friend Brian over the coals, didn't he?"

What is it about having an argument with one person that makes you so suspicious of talking on the same subject with someone new? I had never told Sadie about our confrontation with Hawkey at the bar two weeks earlier. Since there was no way she could have known about the exchange between Tall Boy and me that afternoon, I needed a second to confirm in my mind that she wasn't taking sides here. She assumed that Hawkey's article was based solely on his observations of our team, and this was simply her honest opinion of what she had read.

"You think so?"

"He practically blames Brian for all of your losses this spring. I always thought he was a pretty good shortstop, at least in the games I've seen. And he is the best—well, one of the best hitters on the team, isn't he?"

I could tell she corrected herself midsentence to guard against offending me, in case I had delusions of grandeur concerning my own ability. In all my years I swear I never met a female baseball fan more observant than Sadie.

"He's our best pure hitter, hands down."

"Anyway," she concluded. "If Brian thought that guy was way out of line, tell him I did, too. The whole article was just mean spirited, about everybody on the team—including you, Jack."

Sadie finished her drink and made a conspicuous effort to set the empty glass on my side of the table.

"Does that mean you'd like another?"

"Please," she said, rising. "But I need to powder my nose first. We can move to the living room if you want."

I refilled our glasses, then checked to make sure she had enough ice in the freezer for another batch before I put the pizza leftovers in her fridge. With margaritas in hand, I set out to reconnoiter the rest of the main floor.

I was glad for a quick chance to nose around. Though I refused to read too much into it, before tonight I'd never been invited inside Sadie's house. For several dates in a row I had done the driving, but each time she was just coming out as I was pulling up. The lack of a previous offer couldn't have been for fear that I might look down on her lowly state; she lived in a beautiful split level, roomy without being ostentatious, middle class with an eye toward upward mobility. At U-Haul we measured houses in terms of how much truck you'd need to load all the belongings for a one-trip move. It wasn't as precise a yardstick as you might get from a realtor, but if you told me the neighborhood and the size of the truck the estimator requested for a job, I could probably guess the cost of any house in Columbus within ten grand of the sale price, sight unseen. Since I didn't know neighborhoods or land prices in Tampa, I wouldn't have ventured a guess on Sadie's place, but I knew you'd need at least a TH—the biggest truck U-Haul rented for DIY moves—if not a TH with an RV, meaning the truck would need a trailer as well. It was really a very nice house.

All traces of the sun were gone from the square of sky visible through the living room picture window, and a few stars were just starting to peek through the city-lit haze above. It was almost too dark to navigate through the rooms without turning on more lights, but I figured Sadie should know her way around her own place at night, and I was perfectly content to settle into the comfortable trough of her couch until a better offer came along.

When Sadie returned from the restroom, she sat in the overstuffed chair across from me, the coffee table as footrest between us.

"Let me ask you something," she said.

Just for the sake of being a smart-ass, I replied, "Not for free."

"I have to pay to get you to answer a question? I told you I'm broke till payday."

"Well then, what have you got?"

"Just the clothes on my back."

I liked the way that came out.

"That'll work," I said.

"Okay," Sadie said. She took a drink from the glass I'd set on the table in front of her. "I feel like I've bored you silly with all my stories about my folks, but you're an only child too. Why haven't you told me about your parents?"

"My mom's great. But since you don't get along too well with yours, I didn't want to seem like I was bragging, so I figured—discretion equals valor, that whole thing."

"So how is—" Sadie started, but I cut her off.

"Wait, wait, wait. You have to pay for that one before you get to ask another."

My words hung in the air for a long second, and if she had balked I wouldn't have pushed it further. Though I couldn't see her clearly in the dim light I could sense her smile, feel it growing almost, in the dark. She knew exactly what I meant. Just when I thought she was about to back down, she put the heel of her left shoe on the toe of her right and flexed. The room was silent except for the sound of her sneaker hitting the carpet.

"Tell me about Mom," Sadie continued. "What's she like?"

"She's the best. Worked two jobs to cover the bills while I was in school, even took night classes to earn a promotion so she could quit the crappy job and keep the good one, and still I bet I could count the number of games she missed my senior year on one hand. A ball-playing son couldn't buy a more supportive mom than the one I got through sheer luck."

A shadow from the window curtain cast Sadie in near darkness, but when she leaned forward I could see her nodding. She slipped off her right shoe and paired it with the other beside her chair.

"And your father?"

I felt my face go flush. Since I hadn't yet worked up the energy to tell her about Brian's and my tiff, I knew I wasn't ready to launch into that epic.

"Pass," I said.

"Oh, no," Sadie protested, soft but firm. "If I have to pay for the question, then you have to answer."

"You don't have to pay if I don't answer."

"If you don't answer," she corrected me, "then you have to pay."

I thought it over. That seemed fair. "Okay."

"Okay," she repeated. "And your father?"

I pulled off a shoe and dropped it over the padded arm of the couch.

"Touchy subjects are good," Sadie murmured happily. "How about this: if you could change one thing about me, what would it be?"

Oh, brother.

"Just to clarify," I said. "You're allowed to ask any question that you're willing to pay for, but let's say for the sake of argument you ask one I have no answer to."

"Either you give me an honest answer or I get the other shoe. Name one thing you'd change about me."

I'd been in enough heart-to-heart conversations before with girl-friends asking what would I change about them to learn this simple rule: do not answer that question.

"I mean this as a high compliment," I said, my other shoe in hand and headed for the floor.

"You're very sweet."

For a game that started out with such promise, things were getting tricky in a hurry. I realized I needed to go on the offensive. I even had a few toughies I thought would be worth my socks to get answered, though I figured I should start off with a slow-pitch question first to hide my ulterior motives.

"My turn. If you could change one thing about yourself, what would it be?"

"I would change the fact that I'm in the middle of a separation." Sadie took another drink from her glass. "Growing up, I had a lot of dreams about who I would be when I got older, what I would be doing—just like every kid does, I guess. But now I look at myself and I think: I'm halfway through my twenties; I only took a couple classes, so I'm still about a thousand credits away from a college degree; I don't have a career or even a job I want to make into a career. What do I have that proves I haven't just been wasting my time since I got out on my own? My marriage was my only thing, and now that's a question mark, too. I just always thought I'd have done something more—I don't know—permanent, by now."

It was hardly the answer I'd hoped for, but since she went there voluntarily it made my next question seem a natural follow-up. "So why did you marry what's-his-name?"

"Why did I marry Don? Well, he proposed. That was a good start. And he already had a career, so I knew he could support us and provide a nice home. He was generous and had a good sense of humor, which I liked, of course, and the things I wasn't sure I liked about him I assumed I could fix. It was just like that old saying: a woman marries a man hoping she can change him into the husband she wants, and a man marries a woman hoping she'll never change. Turns out both of those are dumb hopes to have at the beginning of a marriage."

I took off my socks to pay the bill so far and started to undo my watch in anticipation of the next question.

"What made you decide to separate?"

There was a long pause. I could barely see her outline among the shadows but it sounded as if Sadie was adjusting her position in the chair. I waited a moment and then, careful to word my question as a statement, said, "I take it you're thinking."

Something flew across the table and landed in my lap. It was the shirt she'd had on during dinner.

"I'm passing," she said. "My turn again. Do you squeeze the toothpaste from the middle or the end?"

"And this is an answer worth paying for because . . ."

"Because there are just some boundaries that need to be established, some envelopes you need to know the edges of before you can feel comfortable letting someone—" Sadie paused for a delicious second. "Before letting them see your bathroom, for instance. Besides, I just remembered I'm wearing earrings, so I have more wiggle room than I thought."

That level of honesty deserved an honest reply. "I squeeze from the middle. I hope we can still be friends."

"So far so good," she assured me. "Okay. You're buying a new house. Which is more important: acreage or square feet?"

"Acreage, definitely. As long as you have an extra room with a spare couch so friends have somewhere to crash for the night, that's enough square feet for me. This place, your house, is just about right. I never understood the allure of the Big House any more than I understand the allure of the Big City. Buy a house too big and you spend all your time chasing dust bunnies. Move to a city too big and you live in a place that has more people than trees. Between college dorms and a couple of apartments since I graduated, I've lived next to a lot of people over the years. On the whole, trees make better neighbors."

Sadie leaned in from out of the shadows, turning a hand as if she was rolling tiny dice on the coffee table. Her earrings made a soft clatter along the wooden surface.

"And so you play a sport that involves thousands of people all cramming into one place at the same time."

"I play a sport that involves dirt and grass and wearing comfortable clothes. The people who come to watch mostly matter to the guy who owns the team."

"I always thought you athletic types were motivated by the roar of the crowd."

Sadie leaned in toward the coffee table for another sip of her drink. Her bra straps, shining in the window light as they creased her bare shoulders, were slashes of hypnotic white against all that shadow.

"What?" I asked before catching her point. "Oh. No, it's not about that for me. I was happy to play in front of a few dozen people for most of my career, so a couple hundred more in the stands now doesn't really change the equation."

Sadie looked up, and for the first time since we'd moved from the kitchen, I could see her face clearly.

"Then what is the equation? Why come all the way from Ohio to Dunedin to play baseball like this?"

I could tell she wasn't talking about the game specifically. She was asking why I was willing to put up with all the crap, like Hawkey's sports page article and the talking heads on TV constantly putting us down. I'd never even asked myself that before. I needed a second to decide how to start my answer.

"When I first got to college I remember the coaches asking what I planned to study. That just struck me as such a huge question. How do I know what I'll want to do thirty years from now? What if I picked a major that I ended up hating or that I sucked at? There was only one thing I never had a doubt about, and that was playing baseball. And this season, today, right now—this is my time. I don't need another degree; I don't need more money before I can afford the down payment. I know there are lots of old-timers who were better at third base than I am, lots of kids growing up now who will be better than I could ever dream of being, but right at this moment there are just a handful of guys who can play better than I can, and they're not here. It's just me.

"When I see things like that article in today's paper—it's as if people think the strike is our fault. But I didn't chase the union guys off. I didn't walk away from the job. I'm here because I love to play and I play better than most. If you think you play better than me, come talk to the coaches and see if you can take my job. But if you love the game and just want to see it played well by people who love it too, then come on down and buy a ticket. I can't promise I'll hit three homers in consecutive at bats, but I'll play as hard as I can, as well as I'm able, for as long as they let me. I don't see how that makes me the bad guy. I'm not the bad guy. I just play third base."

When I finished I felt a little foolish. I hadn't meant to get up on my soapbox like that, and considering how many of our spring games Sadie had come to watch, I was obviously preaching to the choir.

She didn't seem to hear my answer, though. For a second Sadie remained still. Her gaze seemed fixed on a spot somewhere above me.

"I just remembered. He called last night. I was half-asleep when the phone rang."

"'He' being your husband," I guessed.

"Don called, right. I can't believe I forgot that. He said he had work in Tampa later this week and wanted to know if we could get together. Sounded like he wants to talk things over, though I don't know what there is to say. What do you think? Should I have lunch with him?"

Under different circumstances I'm sure the news would have bothered me more. Under these circumstances though, with Sadie maybe four questions away from full frontal, it just seemed an odd choice to make this one of the four she had left to ask. And the way the subject just popped into her head, I really had no reason to believe she was asking to hurt or upset me. It sounded like she simply wanted a second opinion, the same way you'd ask a friend for their thoughts on any personal matter that you hadn't yet decided. In a weird way I was flattered that she was asking for my input.

"I guess it couldn't hurt to see what he has to say," her friend suggested.

Sadie let out a sigh, as if to put the question away in her mind. "So what one thing would you change about yourself?"

"I'd change the fact that I'm such a sucker for a curveball."

"It's your chin," she said. "You move your chin on high pitches, and it throws your timing off."

"Are you serious?"

"Absolutely. You did the same thing when I threw you my shirt."

"I thought it might be a brick or something."

"That shouldn't matter," she said, and then laughed. "Well, it might matter in my living room but it shouldn't in the batter's box. If you need to raise your chin to see the pitch, then it's too high to drop down for a strike. So, keep your chin steady, and if the pitch gets to the top of your sight line, you already know not to swing when it gets to the plate."

Her suggestion seemed both sensible in practice and senseless in this context, like receiving sound financial advice from someone you just loaned twenty bucks.

"Have you been moonlighting as a hitting instructor for the Yanks?"

"I would never work for the Yankees," she insisted. "But that's the same advice my coach told me when I played varsity softball. Here we go. Chin steady. Try again."

More sounds of Sadie moving in her chair, and then another gray blur flew across the table, sailing over my head and landing somewhere behind the couch. Considering what she was down to, she must have used her shorts to make the pitch. That reminded me of something I'd been meaning to ask her for a few days.

"Did you notice I've changed my batting stance?"

"I noticed you've gotten a couple nice hits lately."

"I've been working with one of the coaches. He's been a big help, actually."

"Show me."

Sadie rose from her chair and came around to where I sat on the couch. I always knew she was thin, but somehow I'd never realized how fit she was until seeing her in just her underwear.

"C'mon, get off your lazy butt and show me."

"I'd need a bat."

"Excuses, excuses." She grabbed a magazine off the coffee table, rolled it into a tube, and pushed me to the open floor beside the couch once I'd gotten up.

"No jewelry in the box," she said, stopping me to take off my watch. "All right, let's see it."

I got in my old, straight-legged stance and put the magazine bat at my shoulder. "At the beginning of camp I was standing about like this, but my coach has been telling me that if I . . ."

Before I could show her my new stance, Sadie reached around from behind me to unbuckle my belt.

"You can't molest the batter," I protested. "Or is this another tip your softball coach shared with you?"

"Coach Bruce was not just a happy man; he was downright gay." Sadie moved around to face me. "So no, he didn't teach me this. I'm only collecting what you owe me."

"How do you figure?"

"First I told you about the chin thing, and you asked if I was serious. That was for the watch. Then you asked if I worked for the Yankees, and though you of all people should know that I'm a Blue Jays girl—and I should slug you for the insult—I'll settle for your belt instead." By now she had unbuttoned my jeans and was working on the zipper. "Then you asked if I noticed your new batting stance, which is why I get these pants."

Sadie kneeled slightly to pull my jeans from around my waist. The sight of her as she bent gave me a blood-rush flashback to the night she kissed my bruise in the bowling alley.

"Oh wait," she said, rising to take the magazine from my hands. "Then you asked if my softball coach was a pervert, so this shirt is mine, too. And didn't you just ask how do I figure? Unless you're wearing two pairs of Jockeys, by my count you should be butt naked right now."

"Something tells me you really weren't that interested in my new batting stance."

"Batting stance? No." Sadie pulled off my shirt, then reached around to unfasten her bra. "Interested? Hmm."

I was right about my theory that perky can be just as sexy as big. Sadie could have gotten all the breast augmentation she wanted and it wouldn't have made the slightest difference in my desire at that moment.

Just as I turned to see how close we were to the couch, I stepped on one of the shoes I'd set on the floor. When Sadie leaned in to wrap her arms around my neck, she caught me perfectly off balance. Together we fell over the padded arm and into the comfortable trough as if we'd planned it. Though we each had one piece of clothing still on, we skipped the formality of the game that got us here, since there was just one question left to ask and we both already knew the answer.

MONDAY, MARCH 27

I blew it. Bottom of the third against Pittsburgh, no outs, runner on second and us down 1–0, I booted a two-hop grounder. It wasn't even that hard a play. When a two-hopper comes off the bat, you have to judge the speed and spin immediately, as that's what tells you if you can be lazy and wait on the ball or need to charge it before it takes the second hop. The trick is, if you wait and the batter has good wheels, you'll have to make a quick throw to get him at first. When I saw that the ball had a lot of spin, my immediate reaction was to wait for the hop to come to me so the runner would have to hold at second base. But then I remembered this was the top of the Pirates' order and the man at the plate was their center fielder. Because he had speed to burn, I would need to charge the ball if we were going to get him at first. Despite my late break I still could have gotten him, but the ball hit a seam and took a flat bounce. When I reached down to make the bare-handed scoop, it skipped through my fingers and rolled behind me.

I could say I was a victim of my own success. Even during these spring training games, they have an official scorer to decide what's a hit and what's an error, and the guy scoring today's game was a reporter who sometimes covered the Jays for his paper. Since he'd seen me make plays like that during games in Dunedin, he assumed I should have made this one in Bradenton and when I didn't, he ruled it an error. You could even add that of the third basemen we've faced on other teams so far, few if any would have been able to make that play either. But if official scoring decisions are based on a relative scale, it shouldn't be one that scales down. If you want to be the best, you have to play like the best. The best third basemen among the union guys could have made that play, so I should have made it, too.

How is it possible to be so alone in front of two thousand people? How can you feel so exposed in full uniform, glove, and hat? If only we played soccer so I could have flopped on the ground and maybe gotten a referee's whistle, or football so I could have waved in the second-string guy a few downs while I licked my wounds on the sidelines. But two-strike foul balls are the only do-overs in baseball, and there are no built-in chances to hide till you're ready to try it all again. The best you can hope is that your pitcher gets back to work and the next batter hurries up to the plate, so you don't have to spend more than a few seconds standing naked and untethered in front of God and everyone.

It only takes one fuckup to remind me why I work so hard on my defense; making an error for a team that depends upon your glove is the worst feeling I know. It's worse than that moment when you got where you were going and just as the car door locked shut you realized the keys were still in there. It's worse than that morning after the one-night stand when you asked her to answer the phone just before you remembered your girlfriend was due in from out of town and she said she'd call the moment she got in. Pick any memory you have that makes you smack your head and wonder, *How could I be such a dumb-ass?* Then treble the embarrassment. That's what it feels like to make an error in front of people who paid to watch you play baseball at your best.

I had good reason to be pissed about my error. Because baseball is turn based and offers no opportunity for defensive scoring, every contest is an unfolding of the chances both teams have to score while it's their turn on offense. Each game can be examined through its individual innings, each inning broken down to the batters sent to the plate, and every pitch of every at bat adds to the narrative of that contest. In a game that turned into a 16–2 rout, my error in the third might have been easy to overlook, but instead of having one out and a man on second, my error allowed the batter to reach first and the runner to move to third. With no outs and runners on the corners, the Pirates were willing to push their luck, so they sent the runner to steal second on the very next pitch. Our catcher had to hurry his throw and it sailed into center field, allowing the runner who'd just stolen second to move to third and the guy on third to score. The next man up hit a pool-cue squib past the pitcher. Tall Boy gloved it but not in time to get the out at first or keep the runner from scoring. Facing a man on first, two men in, nobody out, and no confidence in his defense, our pitcher got rattled and walked the bases full without getting another out. Now we faced bases loaded and a pitcher with control problems, so Coach Didier brought in a reliever. The guy who had just been replaced was our third starter, meaning he wasn't the best pitcher on our staff but was certainly better than any middle reliever we had. For him to get pulled that early meant that our bullpen would have to get us through the rest of the game, which was just like saying the floodgates were about to swing open. By the time we retired the Pirates in the third, they'd built a 6–0 lead, and they scored five more before Lenny Longo put two on the board with a dinger in the seventh. We lost 16–2 because our starter got chased before he'd recorded seven outs, and my mistake was the beginning of the end. My error cost us the game.

I had an even bigger reason to worry about my miscue against the Pirates. Over the weekend the team cut a pitcher and an outfielder, but then signed a new guy to work out of the bullpen Monday afternoon.

It was obvious the coaches wanted to carry seventeen pitchers into the regular season, and we were still one player over the thirty-two they would keep for the season opener. With three catchers, five outfielders, and three guys interchangeable as DH-first basemen, that left four spots on the roster for second, short, and third. Tall Boy and Hack were shoo-ins at their positions, which basically meant the last cut would be either me or one of the two guys who played as utility infielders. It made sense that I should have the inside track as the sole specialist at third, but the first chance I got to prove that, I went zero for three and made my first error of the spring.

The only good news regarding my error was that, by the time we got back to the dugout after Pittsburgh's six-run outburst, everyone had forgotten I was the reason the rally had started. Tall Boy was the only one to say something about it. Right after the play on the field, as soon as I had possession and called time, Brian jogged over and held his glove out for me to give him the ball. "Shake it off," he said. "Yesterday's news. Next one's coming to you. Be ready." I think that was the longest conversation we had all day.

Tall Boy and Folgers must have gone out to dinner after the bus brought us back from Bradenton, because I didn't see either of them the rest of the evening. Since Sadie had told me as I was leaving her house that she had a full schedule all day, I just grabbed a burger at a drive-through near the hotel and watched some movie on TV while I ate at the kitchenette table in our room.

After a while I got to thinking about our talk in Sadie's living room the night before. Why had I felt so uncomfortable when she asked about my family? She had always been completely open about her issues with her mom. Why had I been so coy about my father? Maybe it was just a timing thing, a question I wasn't prepared to answer at the moment when she asked it. Or maybe I only had enough courage for one intimate act that night and I chose stripping down naked in front of a beautiful woman over describing to her what happened one day when I was seven, a day I would spend the next eighteen years trying to forget.

Because the Sloans lived just around the block and it was only a ten-minute walk to either of our houses from the elementary school, Brian and I had both been surprised to find his mom waiting in her car outside the school entrance one afternoon two weeks before the end of third grade.

"Why don't you come over for dinner?" Mrs. Sloan asked when we walked over.

"I'd have to check with my mom."

"Your dad called me. He said he would pick you up from our house later tonight."

When my father came to get me after dinner, we could hear him talking to Mr. and Mrs. Sloan in the kitchen a few minutes before he called me down from Brian's room. My father was never the talkative type, so right away I guessed something was out of the ordinary by how interested he seemed in my day.

"How was school?" he asked as we walked home. "Did you get something to eat? You look tired; are you feeling okay?"

"I'm fine." There was still a half hour of daylight left, and his sudden interest gave me an idea. "Can we go to the field? I want to get some batting practice."

"Sure. Whatever you want."

We stopped by the house to get my glove and bat, then walked to the ball field behind the elementary school. The summer teams had just been organized, and based on one Saturday morning practice my father declared that my defense needed work, so instead of helping me with my batting like I'd hoped, he positioned me near home plate while he stood at the mound, fifty Little League feet away, with my bat in his hand.

"You're too scared of the ball," he explained. "You need to work on staying in front of it."

He was right. I was still a month shy of my eighth birthday, and the ball scared the hell out of me. But I didn't like the look of this remedy, either.

"Shouldn't I stand at third base?"

"We just have the one ball here. You'll spend as much time chasing it down from the outfield as you will learning to stop it. This will be more help, anyways. If you get used to stopping grounders this close, when they come to you at third in a game they'll be no problem. Ready? Here comes."

He tossed the ball in the air and swung the bat limply with one hand. It was such a slow dribbler that I had plenty of time to position myself as it rolled to the plate.

"That's it. Move your feet," he said. "See? It doesn't bite. Keep your hands together when you reach for it."

My father caught my return throw in his bare hand and hit another roller. When I picked it up and turned to face him, I remembered the question I'd meant to ask coming out of the house.

"Where's Mom?"

"She's in—did you talk to her? Did she . . . ?" He seemed confused, and for the first time I saw a hardness in his eyes that I hadn't noticed walking to the field. "No, of course you didn't. Listen, Johnny. Your mother had an accident."

His next grounder had a little more speed. I kept my head up as I put my glove down, and even though it took a hop just before it got to me, I was pleased to find the ball stuck in the palm of my glove. It didn't hurt at all.

"What kind of accident?"

"She's all right," he said. "She's not hurt bad. But she's going to stay in the hospital for the night. I'll bring her home in the morning."

"What happened, Dad?"

After each of the first few swings, he had stepped back to his starting position on the pitching rubber, but this time when I returned the ball he didn't look down or move back.

"Keep your eye on the ball, John." He grabbed my throw and held it aloft. "If you're not watching close, this thing will smack you upside the head and put you in the hospital, too."

Another grounder, two hops, and then my glove. I was starting to feel more comfortable about getting in front of the ball. All these grounders and not one had hurt my hand yet.

"I don't understand, Dad. What happened?"

Another grounder, harder this time.

"She fell, all right?" He snared my throw with his left hand and slapped another grounder with the bat in his right. "She tripped, I think."

My father was well in front of the mound now. I backed up several steps behind home plate after I fielded the one-hopper to my left.

"How did she trip?"

He snagged my throw with a flick of his wrist. "How the hell should I know?"

179

His next stroke didn't touch the ground. I gloved it just above my shoe top.

"I picked up my toys last night like you said."

"Am I blaming you? Nobody's blaming you."

The dirt behind home plate sloped up to meet the metal rail that formed the bottom of the backstop, and as I retreated another step I could feel the ground rising under the heels of my sneakers. When my father swung this time, the ball came at me on a line. I got my glove up just before it hit me in the chest. Still no pain.

"What about Mike?"

"Who?"

I hadn't told him I'd been thinking up names for my baby brother. The previous night, before I nodded off to sleep, I decided that I liked the name Michael.

"What about Mom's baby?"

"Look, forget what I said about that, all right? Throw the ball back."

"What do you mean, Dad?"

He took another step toward the plate.

"I mean your mother's not gonna have any more babies. Will you throw the ball already?"

"Why not?"

"Grown-up reasons," he said. "Don't be so nosy. Gimme the ball."

He was halfway between the pitcher's mound and the plate, maybe ten yards away.

"Are you mad at me, Dad?"

"Throw the goddamn ball!"

As I twisted at my waist to return the ball, the sloped dirt beneath my right heel gave way. My father didn't see me slipping, and he didn't reach out to catch my throw either. He just swung the bat with both hands as hard as he could, as if I had pitched it.

It seemed as if I was falling forever, loose in a limbo of midair suspension and dread-anticipation for the white-hot pain sure to come. Instinctively my hands flew out in front of my face, elbows clenched in to protect my ribs. I shut my eyes tight and braced for impact. Just as I landed hard on my ass, the ball ricocheted off the backstop, not ten inches from my ear. The sound of it hitting the chain-link fence rattled off the bricks of the school and echoed back across the field.

For a moment afterward everything was still. My heart was pounding, but I was too scared to cry out. When I looked up, my father was standing on top of home plate, my bat jutting straight out from his clenched right fist. At first I thought he was out of breath from swinging the bat and that's why he was gasping.

"Don't you cry, Johnny. Goddamn it, don't let me catch you cry one fucking tear. Do you hear me? Crying is for sissies. God doesn't give us any burden we can't handle, and that which doesn't kill us makes us stronger. So you can either start crying or start getting a new plan. Right now. Decide!"

He looked like he had more to say, but he just dropped the bat, turned his back, and walked across the grass toward the gate in the corner of the right field fence. I assumed he was having trouble seeing in the fading light because every few steps he would stumble, look down, then continue on his way. The strangest part of it was, as I watched him go, it didn't seem like he was receding in the distance. He just shrank, getting smaller and smaller until he wasn't there at all.

Eventually I would find out more details about Mom's failed pregnancy. My father was correct; it had been nobody's fault. He was also right when he said Mom wouldn't have any more babies. It had something to do with bleeding and uterine damage. I didn't understand all the words but, even at seven and three-quarters, I knew enough to accept the short version and stop pressing when Mom frowned in that way that made the corners of her mouth go tight.

But the part of my father's lesson I took most to heart that night at the elementary school field was that crying is for quitters and losers, and the only time tears are appropriate from a man is when you've given up the fight and are ready to admit total defeat. I didn't cry from the shock and fear of that ball striking the backstop inches from my head. I didn't shed a tear when my hamster died in his cage late that summer, and I made damn sure not to cry when, the Saturday before my eighth birthday, Mom and I came home from the mall to find my father's note stuck under a magnet on the fridge, informing us that he could no longer stand living in, and I quote, "a house as broken and sterile as this." In fact, from that night forward, I never cried again.

This is what I was worried about: we're still one player over the roster limit, and Appleby, the utility infielder who tweaked his back in the game against the Chi Sox last week, started at third today. He didn't screw anything up in the field but he didn't have that many chances. Folgers threw six strong innings and left with a five-run lead. They put me in as part of a double switch in the seventh so I could get an at bat. Appleby got a double and a walk in four trips to the plate. I popped out to second base to end the eighth inning. We beat Cincinnati 7–3 in Plant City.

The Reds have made some changes since we met up the first week of exhibition season. Someone in the Cincy front office must have decided Davey Johnson could be more productive somewhere other than fishing the pond in back of their practice facility, since he's coaching a minor league camp and Ray Knight manages the replacement team now. They also released Pedro Borbon, the forty-eight-year-old pitcher from the Big Red Machine days, in the middle of last week. During his final outing as a replacement he'd fallen on his ass trying to field a slow roller in front of the mound. The Reds told the media they had released Borbon out of fear that he might hurt himself.

The National Labor Relations Board met over the weekend and on Monday filed for an injunction on the union guys' behalf in federal court. While the original complaint set May 22 as the hearing date, they're asking for a preliminary injunction sooner to restore the expired labor agreement from last year. The judge hearing the case asked the owners to file their paperwork by tomorrow evening and the players to do the same by Thursday at five. It's clear she's trying to honor the NLRB's request for an expedited ruling. The paper this morning also said that players' and owners' representatives met last night in NYC but that both sides reported, and I quote, "no substantial progress was made."

Five days till we're legit.

I was never quite sure how Sadie got her information. Even on days when she worked, she always seemed to know the outcome of our games before I'd talked to her. I had just walked into our hotel room after Tuesday's game when the phone rang.

"You won," she said when I answered.

"We won."

"So come over in an hour and I'll make you dinner to celebrate."

Since there was no reason for me to hang around—Tall Boy went with Folgers and Hack to catch a movie matinee right after we got back to the hotel—I decided to head out and pick up a few things on the way to Sadie's.

"Perfect timing," she said when I arrived, rising up on tiptoes to kiss me at the door.

While Sadie got dinner out of the oven I filled a vase with water for the flowers I'd brought. It occurred to me that, between the afternoon spread they served in camp and all the dinners out I'd eaten thanks to the per diem, I hadn't enjoyed a home-cooked meal in over a month. The smell of pasta mixing with the steam rising from the foil that covered the chicken made me suddenly famished.

"This is the best dish I know how to make," she said as we sat down. "So if you don't like it, you better be willing to lie to me."

On the drive over from the hotel, I realized I'd never told Sadie about the scavenger hunt the guys had sent me on last week, the day I had to walk the stadium to recover all the things they'd pilfered from my locker. Since she always enjoyed hearing stories about the team, I decided to share that one as dinner conversation. I had only gotten to the part where I found my hat hanging from the showerhead when she interrupted.

"Wait. You said they got the numbers three and fifteen from your sign. What sign?"

"I hung a sign in the locker room to count down the days until the season opener, and all the guys know about it because me updating the sign is part of our clubhouse routine before each home game. Well, we do it before we get on the bus for away games too, so I guess it's a routine we do every game."

"Your first regular season game is next Monday, right?"

"Right, but there's a game Sunday night, Mets verse the Marlins. That's the official start of the Major League season."

"I still don't understand. Why the emphasis on their first game instead of yours?"

"Our contracts are just conditional bonuses until the season starts, at which point we'll get paid the league minimum for as long as we're around. We earn one bonus if we're on the Opening Day roster, and they'll pay us a termination buyout if the union players come back after that."

"Am I allowed to ask how much?"

"Between the roster bonus and the buyout, it'll be twenty-five grand."

I wasn't surprised by Sadie's wide-eyed reaction when I told her the amount, but she surprised me with her follow-up question.

"Do all the players have that in their contracts—on the other teams, too?"

"I haven't exactly done a survey, but the few guys I have talked to, it sounds pretty standard."

"Oh, Jake." Sadie looked down at her plate and furrowed her brows in thought. "Twenty-five thousand, times all the players on all the teams? That has to be tens of millions of dollars. This strike started because the owners didn't want to give the players more money. There's no way they'll pay that kind of money to let you guys play."

When Sadie looked up, her expression changed immediately. "I'm so sorry. That was a terrible thing to say. I don't know a single thing about it. Just ignore me."

I couldn't decide if I was more embarrassed that Sadie had caught me pouting like a child or because I'd never thought about the strike in exactly those terms. I had always been so focused on what I would gain from making the Opening Day roster that it never occurred to me how much all of us replacements would cost the owners if the strike lasted into the regular season.

Sadie was quick to change the subject, reminding me that I'd only gotten partway through my story. She laughed when I told her the rest of my scavenger hunt adventure, but a weight seemed to drag on our conversation that evening and we ended up turning the TV off and going to bed before the eleven o'clock news had gotten to the sports segment.

After Sadie and I made love, I thought briefly about trying to make it back to the hotel before curfew, but I knew Tall Boy would cover for me if anyone bothered knocking on our door for a bed check. Besides, Folgers had clearly stopped caring about being in his room before midnight, and if that was the example our team captain was setting, I'd be a rookie fool not to follow his lead.

I must have dozed off but awoke when a clock somewhere in the house chimed twice. Sadie, one arm disappearing beneath a pillow, lay facing me, breathing softly. Moonlight slanted in through the blinds on the bedroom windows, casting a striped column of light across her bare shoulder, drawing a half circle along the side of her breast. In the light her skin was the color of talcum. I traced the contour of her body with my eyes, down past her waist to where the bedsheet draped over her hip. She looked sculpted, flawless, completely content—like a statue of a woman dreaming. I wanted to believe that her contentment was the result of my being there, that my presence allowed Sadie to lose herself in the vulnerability of deep slumber, but then I remembered we were in her house, lying on her bed. This was where she always retreated to feel the comfort of belonging. I was borrowing from her stockpile of serenity, not the other way around.

I've never liked the word most people would use to describe my occasional noctivagations because insomnia sounds like a thing you suffer from. I don't suffer from insomnia. There's just something in the still of the single-digit hours that speaks to me, and I enjoy being a part of that solitude, moving around in it, letting my mind wander without the noisy distractions of the day.

I found a pair of sweatpants in an open drawer and pulled them on. For the moment I felt fine but there was a chilly bass note in the air that suggested I would get cold if I went bare-chested, so I shrugged on a bathrobe hanging from the back of the bedroom door as I stepped out into the hallway. Both the pants and the robe were too big for Sadie but fit snug on me. They must have been his.

I had been focused on more important things than the details of decoration my last two evenings here, but now that I was free to look at my leisure, I couldn't help notice how many reminders of her husband Sadie kept around the house. There were still work commendations and a diploma hanging on a wall in the office, still vacation and wedding pictures displayed along the bookshelves in the living room. She looked happy in the photos. Don was younger than I'd imagined. He was skinny and had a thin nose. I've never understood how a woman could be attracted to a man who wasn't athletic. Based on those pictures, there was no way Don played sports. I thought he looked exactly like what he was: a twenty-something accountant one birthday shy of being middle-aged for the rest of his life.

A little wine was left in the bottle I'd brought for dinner, so I poured myself a glass and settled down in the overstuffed chair in the living room. For some reason I got to thinking about the fall of my senior year at Ohio State when my adviser, Dr. Huntley, went to a conference over Thanksgiving break and asked me to feed his cats while he was away. He and the wife had a beautiful house north of campus in Worthington Woods, complete with a stained deck that looked like a battleship when you looked up from the hot tub rising above a flagstone patio below. I remember lying in the hot tub one night, drinking a beer and watching the stars wheel overhead, trying to imagine myself living in a house like that, leading an existence like that. The creature comforts were easy, anyone could get used to those, but I couldn't shake the feeling that I was just a library patron who, instead of checking out books, had borrowed someone else's way of life. I could examine it, test the size and weight of it, read between the lines to see if I could understand what it was all about, but I would still have to return it when my time was up.

After I finished my drink, I felt tired enough to give sleep another try, so I cleaned up what little mess was scattered about in the kitchen, rinsed out the two wineglasses, and tiptoed back upstairs. Sadie was still asleep on her side but faced the other direction now, so I got out of the robe and sweatpants, climbed back in bed, and molded myself against her back. She murmured a quiet sigh and we spooned together, her back warming my chest, until I was able to drift off for the night.

WEDNESDAY, MARCH 29

We needed extra innings to beat the Phillies 3–2 in Dunedin. Appleby started again, went one for three with a single. I was in by the seventh, walked my only at bat. Our pitching seems to be coming around at long last. Our starter got us through six with a 2–1 lead. The usual fears started creeping in when our reliever gave up the tying run in the seventh, but then we held them until Hack Hennessey, of all people, sliced a double down the right field line, and three batters later Tall Boy singled in the winner in the bottom of the tenth. As recently as a week ago I wouldn't have believed it but our staff went thirty outs today and only gave up two runs, all without Folgers's help. Yesterday was his last preseason game; he'll be our Opening Day starter next Monday.

I noticed a group of teenagers today (Is it spring break already?) sitting a dozen rows up from the first-base dugout. They were in their seats by the end of pregame warm-ups and stayed all the way till Tall Boy's game winner in the tenth, and I doubt they stopped talking to each other for two minutes the entire game. I never saw them cheer a good defensive stop or a run scored by either team. I know exhibition game tickets are cheap and when you live ten minutes from the Gulf of Mexico a spring break trip to the beach is just like every other weekend in March, but why come to the ballpark at all if you couldn't care less about the game being played?

I do wonder if this strike has changed people's attitude toward baseball so dramatically that it doesn't mean as much to kids now as it did to me fifteen years ago. Do they still stay up after lights-out, risking a lecture or even getting grounded for the weekend by hiding a transistor radio under the covers because their favorite team is in a pennant race just heating up as the new school year starts in late August?

Some of my fondest childhood memories involve baseball during the mid-70s, when the Big Red Machine was the only team in the world to a kid growing up in central Ohio. I would lay my handheld radio beside my pillow, one ear listening to the play-by-play and one ear trained for the sound of my mom coming down the hall past my room. Marty Brennaman and his partner Joe Nuxhall painted me a picture in words, leisurely filling in the details as the game worked its way through the middle innings. Between Marty's soft southern drawl and Joe's deep baritone, their delivery was so familiar and soothing that I could never stay awake all the way to the end if the Reds went into extra innings. Even when it was Marty's turn to call an inning, you knew Joe was never far from the mike should anything exciting happen while the Reds were at bat.

"Hernandez looks in for the sign as Bench awaits the pitch. The two-one delivery. It's swung on and a deep drive to left—"

There was Joe in the background, shouting encouragement as the ball traced a parabolic arc toward the left field seats. "Get out," the Old Lefthander would yell. "Get outta here."

"The left fielder goes back, back, to the warning track—"

"Get out ball!"

"And it's GONE! A two-run blast courtesy of Johnny Bench here in the bottom of the seventh might just have put this one out of reach."

For home games during those Big Red Machine years, the guys knew to let the cheering crowd wear itself out before they even tried to continue. Listening to those six or eight seconds of static-filled roar it was all I could do to keep from cheering too, and giving myself away. There's no telling how often Marty's victory call was the last thing I heard before I dozed off to sleep: "And this one belongs to the Reds." Marty and Joe on Reds Radio were the soundtrack of my childhood dreams.

Four days till we're legit.

It's impossible to wake up in the same hotel room as someone, eat breakfast and lunch across from them, then play five or six innings of baseball beside them without talking, and Tall Boy and I had talked plenty since our argument. Still, we had managed to get through the past seventy-two hours without actually saying anything to each other. We could chat about the weather, debate the virtues of a Caesar salad over those of a chicken sandwich, compare notes to decide the best way to play the left side with one out and runners on the corners, but we couldn't manage to get past the barricade that had sprung up between us since our fight on Sunday. For three days he had remained quick to anger, slow to smile, and utterly unwilling to share with me anything more meaningful than the morning paper.

I had also noticed a certain disconnect in Tall Boy's game that whole week—no falloff you could point to directly, just an overall feeling that he wasn't fully in the moment while we were on the field. Whereas Brian's single in the tenth led the team to our second victory in a row and sent the fans home happy, he sort of owed a game winner to the team and fans alike. Tall Boy played a pivotal role in the miscue that forced us into extra innings in the first place.

With a one-run lead, one out and a runner on third in the seventh, our first objective was to keep the Phillies from scoring, so the infield was playing in. That should have put the runner on high alert, but when the next man up smashed a one-hopper to my left, I saw from the corner of my eye that the runner was too far up the line. He was hoping I would throw to first without looking him back, and as soon as I did he would scoot home and score. Instead I charged the ball, gloved it and made a dash for third. He was caught fifteen feet up the line in no man's land. His only hope was to take off for the plate and pray that we made a mistake during the rundown.

What should have happened next is this: everyone in our infield had to know that getting the runner at third out was the best thing possible in this situation, so except for Hack—who could defend against the batter advancing to second simply by staying at the base—everyone else should have immediately started running either to third or toward home to be backup in the rundown. On paper a runner's chances of being safe after getting caught in a rundown are roughly the same as you making big money at the roulette wheel in Vegas: as long as there's no cheating and nothing to ruin the natural odds, the house and the defense will almost always win. But since a successful rundown often takes several throws and requires the defenders to continually get closer to the runner as well as each other, we would need players to back up each end—someone behind the catcher at home and someone else behind me at third—in case one of us got too close and the runner dashed past us before we'd gotten the ball back and tagged him out. Being the closest defender to the plate, the pitcher should have been the first man to back up the catcher, and the same rule of proximity meant Tall Boy should have backed me up at third.

Now here's where the problem started, or at least it's what I could surmise based on where everyone was standing once the play ended: when the rundown began, the pitcher stood watching on the mound without ever making a move to back up home. Seeing that, our first baseman started for home but when he was halfway there decided he should get back to his base because by now the batter had reached first and was making advances toward second. When Hack saw the first baseman heading for home, he must have taken off to cover the runner at first. When Tall Boy saw Hack leave second base, he chose to stay to prevent the batter from advancing. Any of those things would have been fine in and of themselves, but again: getting an out by removing the runner on third was the best thing we could have hoped for. So regardless of those other events—our pitcher with his feet glued to the mound, our first baseman doing the shimmy along the first-base line, Hack going AWOL from second—it was still up to Tall Boy to realize that backing me up at third was more important than preventing the batter from advancing to second.

All of this led to one of the least effective, dumbest-looking rundowns in the history of baseball. When I caught the runner off of third base I did what I should have, which was to chase him toward home plate, and when he was halfway down the line I threw the ball to the catcher. The catcher then did what he should have, which was to grab my throw and start chasing the runner back toward me. At this point there were three possible outcomes: we tag the runner out (best case); the runner makes it safely back to third (bad but not a calamity); or the runner scores at home (major fuckup). By the time the catcher was chasing the runner back toward me, I could see that no one had shown up at home to back up the catcher, and assuming Tall Boy had arrived to back me up at third, I decided it was more important to get behind the catcher to prevent the runner from having a chance to score than it was for me to stand my ground fifteen feet up the line and wait for the catcher's return throw. So with the catcher and the runner both heading to third, I took off to back up at home plate.

How freaking stupid did that look to someone watching all this from the stands? I had no way of knowing if Tall Boy was behind me because I was too busy realizing that no one was backing up the catcher in front of me. So despite my good play on the grounder, and my quick thinking to trap the runner off the bag, and the fact that we had all but gotten the man tagged out—just as we were about to close the noose we'd put around the runner's neck, I went sprinting toward home as the runner and the catcher zipped by me heading the other direction. Of course the runner made it safely back to third because no one was there to take the throw and tag him out. But my first priority was to prevent the runner from scoring, so I made the correct adjustment based on the circumstances. In short, the play would still have resulted in us getting the runner out if Tall Boy had only backed me up, but my assumption that he would when he didn't led to us getting squat from the opportunity. No out recorded, the batter wound up at second anyway, and now they had two runners on with one out in the inning.

The next batter hit a long fly to left and the runner on third tagged up to score. The batter after that hit a dribbler to first base and we ended the inning, but not before we had lost the lead.

When we retired the side and headed for the bench, Assenmacher stood on the top step of the dugout, eyes closed, massaging the bridge of his nose between thumb and forefinger as if it was too painful to contemplate what he had just seen on the field.

"Torres!" Coach barked as each man filed past him. "Why the hell are you standing on the mound when there's a rundown going on right in front of you? Tomlinson! What the fuck are you dancing between first and home for when the play is between home and third? Hennessey! You're the second baseman. If I need another first baseman, I'll cut your sorry ass and sign another first baseman. Sloan! Remind me during warm-ups tomorrow to teach you how to play shortstop. For the love of God and all that's holy, use your fucking brains, you fucking brainless morons!"

The reason Assenmacher didn't bitch at the catcher or me was because we were the only ones who did our jobs during the rundown. The reason he saved his last bitch for Brian was because Assenmacher knew Tall Boy could have single-handedly made up for all the other infielders' mistakes simply by backing me up at third. Brian knew it too, but his head wasn't in the game today. We almost lost because of it.

When we got back to the hotel we ordered some takeout off a local restaurant menu we'd come across in the desk drawer, then Brian called Karen and they talked while he and I ate. During what sounded like a lull in their conversation, I called out, "Karen, your boy won the game today," loud enough for her to hear on the other end. Tall Boy gave me what was meant to pass for a stern look, but I also saw the shadow of a smile cross his lips. Bragging about a game winning hit wasn't his style, but Karen would want to hear about it all the same. When I was full from dinner, I started to watch TV, but they were still deep in conversation so I decided to clear out and give Brian some privacy.

Sadie had left a message on our phone saying a friend from work asked if she would take the friend's shift and since money had been tight the last month Sadie wanted to work as many overtime hours as she could get. With nothing else to do, I walked down to a convenience store not far from the hotel and bought the latest *Sporting News*. I spent the rest of the evening in a chair in the corner of the HoJo lobby, reading my *TSN* cover to cover. A couple times the lobby doors opened and I caught myself looking up expectantly, hoping that Sadie had finished work and driven over to see if I still wanted to get together. If she had, I would've suggested we grab a drink in the hotel lounge. I saw a couple guys from the team walk through the lobby to stop in at the bar, and I really wished Sadie was there so I could show her off to my teammates. It would only take a minute for them to see that Sadie was the kind of woman who could be with anyone she chose, and I wanted the boys to see that she chose me.

It's funny how guys react when you get into a serious relationship. No man wants his friends to hear him making goo-goo noises into a phone or catch him coming out of a flower shop with roses and heart-shaped balloons in tow, but there comes a certain moment, a tipping point in the story when it just doesn't matter what your friends think or say, and guys always take notice and ease up on you as a result. After that, you don't need to make excuses for begging off another beer and heading home while the night is still young. It's understood that spending time with your guy friends is what you do until you've found a lady friend worth spending time with instead. Whatever bonehead hookups or idealistic crushes you've chased in the past, no matter how many girls you missed with or years it took for you to reach this summit, ending up beside someone special can make it all seem like you had a plan from the start. The love of a beautiful woman can justify every idiot thing you've ever done in life.

THURSDAY, MARCH 30

We were scheduled to play Baltimore today but the Orioles' owner, Pete Angelos, has refused from the beginning to field a replacement team.

That refusal, and our canceled game this afternoon, were both under-scored when the owners announced today that they had voted 26–2 in favor of using replacement players to start the season—playing games that would count in the final standings—if the strike hasn't ended by next week. The two votes against came from the Orioles' Angelos and the beer company that owns the Blue Jays. In response to the owners' vote, the MLBPA sent Commissioner Bud Selig a letter promising that the players would end their strike immediately if the NLRB wins a ruling in the players' favor following a hearing in Manhattan tomorrow morning.

The coaches told us the stadium facilities would be open today if we wanted to work out or take some BP off the machines, but they didn't schedule an official practice or any team activities. Brian and I went in for a couple hours after lunch.

One of the TV sports shows ran a segment about the replacement teams tonight. They started with a clip of the Reds' recently released, forty-eight-year-old Pedro Borbon falling off the mound as a ball rolled past him, then followed it with a low-lights reel of replacement players' base-running gaffs, flubbed grounders, and dropped pop-ups. Every now and then they interspersed a clip of some famous play—Mays's World Series over-the-shoulder catch at the Polo Grounds; Ozzie's bare-handed, midair grab of a bad-hop grounder; Jackie Robinson's hook slide steal of home plate—to emphasize that we aren't them. If you took out the iconic plays by the Hall of Famers, the segment would have looked just like those blooper reels of the union guys Marv Albert always brings with him on Dave Letterman.

When I was in school I considered a career as a sports broadcaster, but the more I thought about it, the more I realized I felt sorry, rather than envy, for those already doing the job. In a sense it wouldn't be much dif-ferent from earning a paycheck critiquing new music or movies. Even if you became the best in the business, all you've managed to do is find a unique and interesting way of describing somebody else's accomplish-ments. On a ball diamond, to be the most influential player in the game means that one day others may look upon you as the second coming of Babe Ruth. For sportscasters and art critics though, the best they can hope for is one day to be considered the next Howard Cosell.

Three days till we're legit.

I got back to the room around five thirty to find a phone message from Sadie saying she'd forgotten she had an appointment with her hairdresser and since the lady only worked a couple days a week at the salon, Sadie didn't want to cancel for fear of not getting another appointment for weeks. Anyway, she hoped I wouldn't mind her bailing on me tonight and she would give me a call when she figured out her schedule for the weekend.

I made a mental note to tell her about a funny thing that happened before Wednesday's game. I knew Sadie would enjoy it, especially because she had already met GQ at the game in Sarasota, when I sent him up the dugout steps to have his picture taken with sister-in-law Melinda.

With just a few days to go before the start of the regular season, one of the local TV stations realized we replacements could be around awhile and sent out a camera crew to interview some of the coaches and players on our team. They arrived and began setting up a half hour before the game, just as we were taking the field to begin our warm-ups. The on-air talent, who must have been the weekend guy because I'd never seen him on any of the local channels before, was obviously not thrilled with the assignment.

"Gimme a break, Clarisse," he said to a sharp-dressed redhead standing next to him. "I've never even heard of any of these guys. What am I supposed to talk to them about?"

"Baseball stuff." Clarisse had the air of someone accustomed to giving orders. "This team is local news, and you're a local news man, Roger. Do your job."

"How about we get one of the players to conduct the interviews," the cameraman suggested, "like they do sometimes on *This Week in Baseball*."

Roger snapped his fingers. "That's a hell of an idea. I'm sure they all know each other by now. It'll give the piece an insider's perspective."

"Can we skip the perspective discussion for one day, please?" Clarisse asked.

But Roger the Weekend Local News Man was already on the move.

"Hey, buddy," he asked the nearest guy in a Blue Jays cap. "Do any of your teammates have a good speaking voice?"

He was talking to one of the veteran clubhouse hands, a kindly old-timer who was probably in his seventies. Three or four of us players standing nearby all answered in unison.

"Voorhees," Roger repeated. "Which one's Voorhees?"

Clarisse began tsking Roger as if she were calling a dog to heel, but when we pointed out GQ stretching against the railing in front of the dugout, she stopped in midhiss.

"Well, he certainly has the look for television," she said.

Roger, who probably tipped the scale around 230, hitched his pants up over his gut.

"All right," Clarisse said. "Bring him over here. Let's see what he sounds like on camera."

When they were introduced, GQ was the picture of charm. "It's my pleasure, ma'am."

Clarisse put a hand to her throat as if fighting to keep her heart in her chest.

"Do you have any broadcasting experience, Mr. Voorhees?"

"I have no professional experience to date, but I hope to enroll in the RTVC program at Santa Cruz this fall, assuming we're not still playing ball by then, of course."

"I'm sure you'll be wonderful," Clarisse gushed. "Listen, could we talk in private to go over some things before we start the interviews?"

Together they walked down the left field line, Roger and the cameraman trailing behind.

After a few minutes the team finished stretching and the starters headed to their positions to run through some warm-up drills. When I took a seat on the bench, I noticed they had set the camera up near the third-base coach's box. GQ had begun to gently perspire in the sun, and with microphone in hand he looked like a seasoned broadcast veteran, perfectly composed for yet another field report in a distinguished career of Johnny-on-the-spot coverage.

"Should we start with Coach Didier?" he asked Clarisse.

"Let's start with your introduction," she answered from behind the cameraman. "Then we'll talk to the players and coaches as we get a chance."

GQ nodded and closed his eyes, no doubt to concentrate on the remarks he and Clarisse had worked out for his intro. Roger stood off to the side, arms folded, a pained look of boredom on his face.

"Anytime you are," the cameraman said.

GQ opened his eyes. "Just start?"

Clarisse nodded, an encouraging smile on her lips.

GQ coughed emphatically to clear his throat. "Hello, everyone, I'm Clyde Voorhees, the starting right fielder for the replacement Toronto Blue Jays. I'm coming to you live from Dunedin Stadium in Dunedin, Florida, where my teammates and I have been holding spring training, and I'm here to introduce all of us to all of you—the viewers of Channel Fourteen News."

"Thirteen," Roger called out.

GQ paused. "What?"

"We're Channel Thirteen." The cameraman pointed to the side of his camera, where a large orange "13" was painted on a white background. "Also, we'll be airing this over the weekend, so don't say it's live."

"Oh," GQ said with a nervous laugh. "Right."

"Not a problem," Clarisse soothed. "Just take your time and start over from the top."

"Okay." GQ cleared his throat again. "Hello, everyone, I'm the starting right fielder for Channel Thirteen News and—oh, that doesn't make any sense, does it?"

GQ broke out with a case of the giggles, and Clarisse joined him for a moment.

"It's alright, honey," she said. "It happens all the time."

Roger and the cameraman exchanged glances.

"Whenever you're ready," Clarisse said, "just start over."

GQ coughed and started in once more. In successive takes he claimed he was the starting Clyde Voorhees, the replacement introducer, the reporting right fielder, and live with the Toronto Jay Blues. After six attempts his hair and face were damp with sweat, his voice was husky from all the throat clearing, and he hadn't yet gotten past the third sentence of his TV broadcasting debut. When the cameraman said "still rolling" for the seventh take, GQ started to speak but then fell silent, shaking his head, his face a bright crimson from frustration. He seemed about ready to punch someone. I was hoping it would be Roger.

"Let's stop here for now," Clarisse finally said. "I'll bet you're going to need some time to get ready for the game."

"I don't know what's the matter with me," GQ said, turning from side to side as if he was searching for something. "It's just every time I look at that camera, I get so self-conscious."

"I wouldn't worry about it." Clarisse took the microphone from GQ with one hand and put her other arm around his shoulders. "Maybe we can try again some afternoon when you have more time. I can tell you have a natural affinity for television."

The two walked slowly down the left field line together, Clarisse rubbing GQ's back with a comforting hand. At one point in their walk, I saw her write something on her clipboard and then tear off a small strip of paper to give to GQ. He put it in his back pocket and nodded his head. When they made it back to the dugout, GQ walked down the clubhouse tunnel to change into his game jersey and Clarisse herded Roger and the cameraman up into the stands, where they could get some shots of the game about to start.

GQ never did find his rhythm that afternoon. He made an error on an easy fly to right and struck out twice in his two at bats, the second coming on three pitches. When the coaches switched him out of the game in the sixth, he refused my offer of a spot on the bench and stood at the dugout railing instead, alone among thirty-two of his teammates. For one full inning he remained motionless, standing with his elbows on the rail, his chin resting in a palm. Before the start of the seventh, just as I was grabbing my glove to take over for Appleby, I saw GQ pick up his gear and head down the clubhouse tunnel.

When he hadn't come back to the bench by the bottom of the ninth, I started to get a little worried. I knew there would be no one in the clubhouse and I didn't know what GQ might be up to. I walked down the tunnel, but when I reached the locker room, all was silence. I couldn't see any sign of him and I didn't have much time to look since I was third up to bat that inning. As I was about to go back up the tunnel and return to the bench, I heard someone in the showers. Sure enough, it was GQ, his voice muffled by the flow of water from the showerhead he stood under.

"It's a beautiful afternoon, sports fans, with hardly a cloud in the sky, making this a perfect day to head on out to the ballpark. If you're not already on the way, I'd say round up the kids and pile in the car, for it's certain to be another great one here at Dunedin Stadium. In the meantime, don't turn that dial, because after these brief messages I'll be back with the starting lineups and the first pitch right here on the Toronto Blue Jays' Radio Network."

Brian had made himself scarce during the couple hours we spent at the stadium for the voluntary practice Thursday afternoon. I didn't see him take BP in the cage, and I know he never came down to the weight room while I was in there with Lenny Longo and a few other guys. As I was getting undressed to take a shower, he appeared in the locker room long enough to say he was heading back to the hotel with Folgers. I had spent so much of the day doing my own thing without him that it caught me by surprise when I heard his key in our hotel room door around eight thirty that night.

"Standen," he said as he walked in. "I'm glad you're here. I need to ask a favor. What are the chances I can catch a ride from you in the morning?"

That struck me as an odd request; I had been giving him rides pretty much every morning since we left Columbus six weeks ago.

"Where do you want to go?"

"I want to go home, but if you could just get me as far as the airport I can make it the rest of the way from there."

"Wait. What?" I needed a second to process what he was asking. "You're leaving?"

"There's a flight from Tampa International at eleven fifty. If you can drop me off by ten thirty, that should give me plenty of time to make the gate."

"Don't you need, like—tickets and stuff, to get on an airplane?"

"The hotel manager helped me make a reservation down at the front desk about two hours ago. I've been saying good-bye to some of the guys since then."

"Isn't it super expensive to make last-minute reservations like that?"

I didn't mean to badger him about mundane details like tickets and reservations, but I was still trying to wrap my head around the idea of him leaving so suddenly, and my mind does lean toward logistics whenever there's a late change in plans.

"I put the ticket on my credit card. I figure by the time it shows up on my statement next month, I should have my signing bonus from the Blue Jays, so it'll work out fine."

"What did the coaches say? Did you even talk to them?"

"I talked to Didier and Assenmacher at the stadium this afternoon. They were really understanding, wished me luck and everything."

"But Tall Boy, how can you just leave? We're three days away. Sunday night. We've almost made it."

Brian sat down on the bed across from mine and pursed his lips for a moment, as if trying to find the right words. Finally, he just shook his head and shrugged.

"I don't want you to take this the wrong way, Standen, but we're not three days away from anything. No matter what happens this weekend—whether they work out a settlement with the union guys or let the replacement teams play—even if nothing changes between now and next week, we haven't made it to jack shit."

"What are you talking about? We worked our asses off to be here—right here and right now. How can you just leave? This is what we've dreamed about our whole lives."

"That's exactly what I mean. You and I always dreamed of being major leaguers, but even if they let us play the Mariners on Monday, we won't be playing in the Major Leagues. We'll be playing on a replacement team, against a replacement team, with replacement coaches and replacement umpires, on a replacement field in a replacement city. This isn't the real thing, Jake. This is never going to be the real thing."

"So that's it? You're going to walk away for, what—a lack of authenticity?"

"I'm going to fly back to Ohio because regardless of what she says on the phone, Karen needs me, and because she's about to have a baby who is going to need a father."

The way he finished his sentence reminded me that they had specifically asked their ob-gyn not to tell them; Brian and Karen still didn't know if they were having a boy or a girl.

"I don't expect you to understand this, Jake—you don't have any kids; you've never been in a committed relationship—but at a certain point you have to decide what's most important to you. Once you figure it out, it's not that hard to put away childish things and get serious about what you want to be for the rest of your life. I want to be the man my wife hopes she married, and I want to be the best dad my kid could have. I can't be either of those things from a hotel room in Florida. I can only do them in person. I need to go home, and I want to be there tomorrow."

I'd be lying if I said his words didn't sting. It made me wonder if maybe he and I had been drifting apart for longer than just the half week since our argument. I'd never once heard Brian refer to professional baseball as a childish thing, and he'd played professionally four years longer than I had. What's more, he knew next to nothing about Sadie, and he seemed to know less about me than he thought. Before I could put any of that into a reply though, Tall Boy stood up and walked to the door.

"I still haven't talked to Hack or GQ, and I'll want to pack before bed, so I better get on it. The hotel manager said it's about a half hour from here to the airport, so let's shoot for leaving by ten, if that's okay with you."

Brian opened the door and stood there until I realized he was waiting for me to look up. When I made eye contact, he smiled and said, "Easy hops?"

I still didn't understand what sense it made for him to leave so close to Opening Day, but it was clear there would be no talking him out of it, so I didn't try.

"No holes," I answered, and together we mimed a long-distance fist bump.

He stepped out into the hallway, then turned and glanced back at me. In that second before he closed the door, I was surprised at the look on his face. All of the worry I'd noticed around the edges of his mouth, the conflict he seemed to be struggling with even when he was sitting alone, that middle-distance stare he'd been carrying around for the past several days were gone. In their place was the look of someone who'd come to a decision and was happy to be done with the burden of deciding. Brian looked like a man completely at peace with himself.

If nothing else, at least this answered the last spring training question about the Blue Jays. When I drove him across the bay on the Campbell Causeway and dropped him off curbside in the departures area of Tampa International the next morning, the team was officially at the league-approved limit of thirty-two replacement players. I was all but assured a spot on the Opening Day roster.

We won our third in a row today, something we hadn't done all spring, 7–6 at home against the Phillies. I played the whole thing, went one for four with a single, walked, scored a run. In the top of the seventh, two out and a man on third, I got a chance to make my signature play. The batter hit a lazy fly down the left field line, maybe eighty feet behind me. With Appleby playing short and Longo in left, I knew that if I didn't get to it, nobody would. I made a clean turn and went flying after it.

To chase down a dying quail as you sprint at full speed, you have to run on the balls of your feet. If you allow your heels to hit the ground it jars your head too much, and you won't be able to track the baseball's trajectory. I got a good read as it came off the bat, but there was a wind blowing right to left that was pushing the ball toward the fence in foul territory. That was good news in that if I missed it the ball would probably land foul, but bad news because there's a pitching rubber in foul territory along the left field line for relievers to get loose in-game. Wouldn't you know it? Just as the ball was twenty feet from the ground and falling fast, I felt the earth rise under my right foot as I stepped on the slope of the warm-up mound. If you ever wondered how disorienting it would be to get scooped up and tossed around inside a tornado like Dorothy in the *Wizard of Oz*, try sprinting back while looking up at a ball traveling over your head and tailing right to left as the ground rises unexpectedly beneath you. I knew I only had one more step before I tumbled ass over tea kettle, so I planted my left cleat and launched myself across the warm-up mound as I lunged toward the ball with my glove.

We've had three umpires assigned to our games all week. The ump working the left side hustled the whole way out and was standing in perfect position to make the call when I finally popped back up, glove in the air, baseball sticking out the top like a new moon. He signaled the batter out, out, out with a flair that got all the fans on their feet. Longo pumped a fist, and Appleby made the detour to pick up my hat as we jogged back toward the bench. You'd have thought I hit a game-winning grand slam the way everyone on the team was lined up to give me high fives at the top of the dugout steps.

To play great third base, it's not enough to be ready on any given pitch; you have to want the ball to come to you—and want it with every fiber of your being. If that ball goes to someone else, you're useless, a spectator, holding your breath until the play is made. But you can't trust anyone else. They're all slipshod, clowns, worthless and weak. Who knows how many plays they've blown that were way easier than this one? The ball has to come to you because you're the only one you can trust to make the play. The only catch is, you have to make the catch. If I can get through tomorrow's game clean, I'll have made it the entire exhibition season, at least fifty chances total, with just the one error. I damn near always make the catch.

We heard in the clubhouse after our game that Sonia Sotomayor, the federal district judge who took the case between the owners and the NLRB, ruled in the players' favor this afternoon. She said the evidence suggested that the owners hadn't bargained in good faith with the players during the labor talks that fell apart last year. As a result, she issued an injunction reinstating the old labor rules until the two sides can agree on a new collective bargaining agreement. The Players' Association promptly declared their strike over. As quick and surprising as all that was, it still doesn't decide anything where our situation is concerned. The threat that the owners would lock the players out after last season ended, thus forcing the players to sign off on a new agreement more favorable to the owners, is what caused the players to go on strike midseason last summer in the first place. The owners announced that they'll hold a vote over the weekend to decide if they will lock out the players, starting immediately, until a new CBA is reached.

Day after tomorrow, we're legit.

Despite all the news about the union guys ending their walkout, and whose turn it was to do whatever next, I felt strangely confident that Friday wasn't going to be our last game, and here's why: not once in all my years playing ball had I ever been on a team that won a meaningful final game. One year in Little League we were tied for first with another team at the end of the season but then lost the game that decided who went to the city tournament. Senior year when we won the league and then district and then regionals, we lost in the state semifinal. One year at OSU, we came within six outs of winning the Big Ten title. All of those teams were winners; we just never won the last game. You could call my logic backward and faulty, but our victory over the Phillies Friday made me certain we'd still be there when Saturday rolled around.

The only championship I ever got to celebrate on the field was in the fall after I turned seven. That year the Clippers won the International League West and were leading 2–1 in the best-of-five championship headed into the weekend. A friend of my father's who had retired from Western Electric got a job working as an usher at Cooper Stadium. When we ran into him at the grocery store one evening, he told us to look him up the next time we went to a game and he would get us down into the box seats if he could. Never one to pass up a free upgrade, my father decided that we should give it a try that Saturday night.

We got to the stadium a half hour before first pitch, then made sure we ran into my father's friend to say hello before taking our seats in general admission. To his credit, the friend took note of where we sat, and while the players changed sides in the middle of the fifth, he waved a hand to catch our attention and motioned for us to come down to his section.

"I know the couple who bought these season tickets," he said as he led us down the stairs. "If they aren't here by the fifth inning, that means they're not coming tonight."

The seats he took us to were choice: fourth row next to the aisle, just above the visitors' dugout. We were so close I was able to notice that one of the Syracuse players, while he got loose in the on-deck circle, was wearing one black stirrup sock and one dark-blue one.

The Clippers jumped out to a three-run lead in the sixth, and the excitement grew in the stands with each passing inning. By the time our side took the field for the ninth, we were up by four and only three outs away from the Governors' Cup. When Syracuse got two outs with still no men on, my father's friend walked down the stairs and took a position beside the little gate that separated our section of seats from the field. I assumed he was standing guard against people jumping the rail after the Clippers got the last out, but when the batter popped up to the right side and the first baseman settled under it to end the game, my father's friend opened the gate and stepped down onto the field himself. The crowd erupted as the first baseman gloved the ball and the players converged at the pitching mound. I was too busy yelling and clapping to notice, but my father nudged me to get my attention. His friend was holding the gate open and letting anyone from our section who wanted to jump down onto the field to join the celebration.

"Go, Johnny," my father said. When I hesitated, he added, "I know you want to."

I joined the fans rushing down the aisle, and in a few seconds I was on the field, running toward the mound, whooping and waving my arms in the air. One of the Clippers players saw me coming and greeted me with a sweeping high five. I assumed my father had come down right behind me but when I looked back, there he was, still standing at his seat, eyes on me, clapping and smiling as if I had helped the team win the game. Jumping around on the field, high-fiving the players, celebrating a title-clinching victory in front of a stadium full of raucous fans—you could say I spent the next eighteen years of my life trying to feel exactly that way one more time.

I didn't yet know what a shit he was; I hadn't yet been made aware that he was the kind of man who would abandon his wife and only son at the first sign of a setback. At seven years old, all I knew was that this was a joy I had never experienced before, and I was sharing it with my dad. I meant it when I told Sadie making that double play from left field was my favorite childhood memory. If I was allowed to pick two memories, though, that game the Clippers won for the championship, when I got to celebrate on the field as my father watched from the stands, would be the other moment in my life I'd want to relive.

I got back to the hotel after Friday's game to find the message light on my phone blinking. It was Sadie saying her VW had developed a weird noise, and while her mechanic said it was nothing and promised to stay as late as it took to get it fixed tonight so Sadie wouldn't have to be without her car all weekend, she wasn't sure how long it would take, and she'd rather try again tomorrow night if I wanted to get together. It looked like I was on my own for the night.

I grabbed a quick something from a drive-through for dinner and brought it back to the hotel, but with Tall Boy gone our room felt too quiet and empty to stay there all evening. Appleby had mentioned in the locker room that he and a few of the guys were having a Friday-night poker session in his room, and I considered walking up to the second floor to look for them, but I finally decided that I didn't feel like playing cards tonight. By nine o'clock I found myself down in the hotel lounge, which was empty except for a couple people in business casual having a drink at a table in the corner. The TV above the bar was turned to CNN. The federal judge's decision and the MLBPA announcing the end of their strike seemed to be the only things they wanted to talk about. At one point they interviewed Tom Glavine, his team's union rep and an All-Star pitcher for the Atlanta Braves before the strike.

"It is frustrating not knowing what's going on," he told the interviewer.

"Welcome to my world," I told Tom Glavine.

A few beers after I sat down, the lounge door opened and Folgers walked in.

"There he is," Folgers said, clapping me on the shoulder as he took the next seat over. "How the hell did you come up with that ball in the seventh this afternoon?"

"They call me Golden Jake, third base. I am the walrus. Goo goo ga joob."

"I don't know what the fuck that means." Folgers laughed. "But I'm glad you're my third baseman all the same. Hey, any word from the man?"

"Who?"

"Brian. Did he make it back home today?"

It hadn't occurred to me until just then to wonder about his flight that afternoon.

"I never heard."

"I guess we can assume no news is good news on that front, right?"

I always enjoyed Folgers's company and I would've been happy to share a drink with him tonight, but Tall Boy leaving the team forty-eight hours before the opening game of the season was about the last thing I wanted to discuss at that moment.

"Don't worry about Brian," I told him. "He's good at looking out for number one."

"We'll miss him sorely. Tall Boy sure left us some big shoes to fill up the middle."

"We'll be fine. Shit, he almost cost us the game Wednesday, standing there with his head up his ass on that rundown. Plus, he was a distraction, always yelling out from the bench at the other team. You won't miss him, and neither will anybody else. We're better off without him. Maybe now we can carry this winning streak into the regular season."

He had ordered a draft, but when the bartender brought it over, Folgers placed the mug on a coaster next to the beer I was drinking.

"Know what?" he said. "Next one's on me. Keith, let me just get twelve to go."

He put some money on the bar and got up from his stool. When the bartender handed him a twelve-pack, Folgers clapped me on the shoulder again.

"Last game of spring training tomorrow. Give me a call if you want to carpool over."

With that he leaned a hip into the lounge door and headed down the hallway toward his room. I finished my beer and picked up the draft he'd just bought for me.

I hadn't meant to sound so negative about Tall Boy. I would've liked to have heard from him, if only to find out that his flight had gone well and he was back in Columbus. I hoped he knew he could still count on me if there was anything I might do, whatever help I could offer from Clearwater, Florida, anyway. I also wanted Brian to know that I really did understand his point about how being a father started with being there in person. I didn't need to look further than my own family to appreciate that any moron could become a baby daddy—more than a few accomplish it while drunk and by accident—but only a man stays involved for the next eighteen years to be a father, too.

Even when we were kids, Brian had always been good at anticipating my moods and making sure I was doing all right during tough times. I remembered how he and Mrs. Sloan had called on my eighth birthday to insist that Mom and I come over for hot dogs on the back grill. Mrs. Sloan gave us both a hug at the door, telling my mom, "I thought you might not have time to put anything together, but we wanted to make sure he had some fun tonight." There were cupcakes and a present on the kitchen table when we came in. After we ate our hot dogs and I blew out the candles, Mom stayed in the kitchen to talk with Brian's parents while he and I went out to look for something to do in the backyard.

"Want to listen to the Reds game, Johnny?"

"Don't call me that," I said. "Don't call me John, either."

"Why not?"

"I just don't want to be called that anymore."

Brian already knew I hated when people called me "Johnny Junior," but now with my father gone I'd decided that maybe I wanted a new name altogether, one that was only mine.

"Okay," he agreed. "What do you want people to call you?"

I hadn't thought it through that far. "I don't know. What do you think?"

"I've heard that guys named John go by Jack sometimes."

I'd never heard that before. What I had heard, in the last few weeks of school before summer let out, was some of the sixth-grade boys calling each other Jack Off on the playground. I wasn't sure what that meant, but I knew it wasn't something you wanted anyone to call you.

"No," I said. "I don't want to be Jack."

"Hey, how about Jake—like Jake the Snake?"

There was a pro wrestling show that came on after the Saturday morning cartoons. Based on the way wrestlers kept showing off for the crowd during matches and turning their backs on their opponents at exactly the wrong time, we figured the wrestling was probably fake, but we liked the wild costumes they wore and the funny things they said about each other during the prematch interviews. A few weeks before, we'd watched Jake "the Snake" Roberts throw another wrestler clear out of the ring and onto a folding table, which collapsed under the weight. When his opponent couldn't recover from the fall inside a ten count, the ref waved the match over and declared Jake the Snake a winner. I liked that name. It sounded fast and strong.

"Yeh," I said. "From now on, I want people to call me Jake."

Brian shook my hand as if we were meeting for the first time. "Everybody will."

After I came back from the restroom, the bartender pointed out that it was twenty till two and asked if I wanted a last call. I wasn't sure how it had gotten so late so fast. I was pretty buzzed, but it seemed like I'd only been there a couple hours at most. I ordered one more draft and tried to focus on the TV. CNN was replaying some of its earlier coverage on the day's baseball strike news.

For the last few days I'd been carrying around a picture in my mind of Sadie raising a child—a daughter, in fact. I don't know why. She had never talked about wanting children, or not wanting them. The topic had never come up between us, but for some reason the idea had gotten stuck in my head. And I knew as an elemental fact, the same way you know that it's the weekend the moment you first wake up on a Saturday morning, I knew Sadie would make a great mom.

I could see them walking through a park or getting a pretzel from a sidewalk vendor in the city somewhere. They would both be wearing skirts and sneakers, but they wouldn't be matching outfits; Sadie wasn't into kitsch. She would know just the right way to act and talk around her daughter, never treating her like a child but more like a woman in training. And of course the girl would idolize Sadie, hoping to grow up to be every inch as pretty and sophisticated as her mother. She would practice walking like Sadie, and take note of the way she dressed and spoke.

Honestly, I almost wanted it to be true. If I let my mind wander, I would start to think up scenarios, different ways Sadie might break the news to me. "There's something important I have to tell you," she would start, and it would end with a pretty little thing, a miniature version of her mother, walking out from the kitchen in Sadie's house. Crazy stuff, really—and the craziest thing of all was that I would welcome the news.

I've never fully embraced the idea that one day I'll have children. People always say, "Having a baby changes your priorities completely"—as if that in itself is a sensible reason to have kids—but losing both legs would also change your priorities completely, and I've never heard anyone say I should be more open-minded toward elective double amputation. About the time I graduated high school I realized that kids are loud, needy little brats who sap all your strength and demand all your attention from the moment they're born. You may have been wild and crazy once upon a time, but as soon as a baby shows up, you go from freelance fellow to somebody's parent, and that remains your title until the day they put you in the ground. So if I'm not convinced I want any kids of my own, why the hell would I want to help raise someone else's? Simply finding out that a woman already had a kid has always, instantly ended my interest in her, but here I was daydreaming about Sadie having a daughter, and liking the idea. It's funny, some of the stuff you come up with when you spend an evening inside your own head.

I don't really recall walking back to my room that night but when I woke up the next morning, my jeans and polo were neatly folded over the back of the desk chair. The clock radio above the TV read 10:26. After a shower I hustled over to the stadium so I'd have time for a quick bite to eat from the snack table before our pregame warm-ups.

SATURDAY, APRIL 1

We lost 6–3 against Montreal this afternoon to close out the exhibition season at 9 and 18, last among teams in the American League. Not that anyone was counting. I sat out the whole game, meaning I finished the entire spring training schedule with one error at third. Again, not that anyone was counting.

No word yet from the owners' meeting in New York about whether they'll hold up the regular season until a new CBA can be reached. I caught the end of an ESPN segment where one of the talking heads said that by league rules twenty-one of twenty-eight teams, a 75 percent majority, would be needed to reach a decision, but I never heard if that threshold was needed to lock the players out or to accept them back.

They announced a start time of 1:05 p.m. for our game versus Seattle Monday. Tickets went on sale today: nine dollars for reserved seats, five dollars for general admission. Someone told me those are the same prices they charge when Toronto's single-A team plays in Dunedin Stadium during their regular season. No one seems to know exactly what they'll do if we're still here when the single-A season starts.

For all of the other teams, tomorrow will be a travel day, spent flying either to their home cities or to the cities where they'll start the season with a series on the road. Since we'll be hosting the Mariners and playing our home games here, we're the only replacement team in the league that will spend Sunday right where we are. The coaches told us to treat tomorrow like last Thursday. The facilities will be available for voluntary BP and anyone who wants to work out, but no team activities are scheduled.

In twenty-four hours, this time tomorrow, the Florida Marlins will officially open the regular season against the New York Mets, and when they do, my name will be listed on the active roster of the Toronto Blue Jays Major League Baseball Club.

I was actually fine with the coaches' decision not to start me for Saturday's game. I was still a little ragged from the previous night, and though I knew from experience a little physical exertion would help me sweat out some of my hangover, I was happy to take it easy on the bench that afternoon instead. Just as important, Coach Assenmacher called Lenny Longo and me over to a corner of the dugout an hour before game time.

"I just wanted to let you boys know," he told us as he stuck the lineup card on the wall beside the bat rack. "We had a coaches' meeting earlier. We still don't know any more about the strike than you do. That being the case, we're going to give some different guys all the playing time this afternoon. Longo, you're our regular left fielder going forward. Standen, you'll be at third. That means your backups are playing today. Enjoy your day off."

I really loved the way he said "your backups."

There might never have been two guys in the history of baseball as happy to be sitting on the bench the last Saturday of spring training as the Player to Be Named Later and me. We even came up with a song to celebrate our sedentary positions, to the tune of the Doors classic.

Riders on the Pine

Riders on the pine, riders on the pine
Into the game went nine.
None of their names were mine.
Like a porn star with no wood
The coach thinks we're no good.
Riders on the pine

There's a killer on the mound.
He's puttin' hitters on the ground.
Take a long holiday.
Let your backups play.
If he throws one at your head
His family will dread
The riders on the pine.

Coach said I ain't in today
So I watch the starters play.
If you give this pitch a ride
Then I won't be so snide.
Riders on the pine, riders on the pine

I got back to the hotel a little after six but decided to hold off getting something to eat because I planned on taking Sadie out to dinner. She'd said she would let me know as soon as she figured out her weekend, but when I still hadn't heard anything by seven thirty I called her house and got the answering machine. I had left several messages over the last month, but I must have always let my mind wander after I recognized her voice at the beginning, so I'd never paid much attention to what she said in her outgoing message. Had she always started it with the sentence I heard when the machine kicked in? "Hi, you've reached the Holders, but Don and Sadie can't come to the phone right now." It sounded strange, like I was hearing that part for the first time.

After the beep I said I was hungry and hoping to take her out, then turned on the TV to check for the latest update. The CNN Headline News channel had a "SportsTicker" crawling along the bottom of the screen that read: "Still no resolution in MLB impasse. Owners meeting tonight to decide next move."

It seemed like ages since I'd talked to Sadie, and I had a lot to tell her tonight. Not only would she enjoy the story about GQ's TV debut but she still didn't know about Tall Boy leaving for home and how that meant I was guaranteed to make the Opening Day roster. I tried to think of a subtle way I could remind her of the five grand I'd be getting as a result—above and beyond the league minimum salary, $115,000 per year, that I'd start making as of Sunday night—and how she wouldn't need to work so many overtime hours from now on.

She was sure to have a story or two for me as well, between her work and her glitchy car. I hoped she hadn't gone for some wild new hairstyle when she went in for her appointment at the salon. I was a fan of exactly the way she looked the last time we were together, when she saw me off to work Wednesday morning at her house. I'd given her one of the warm-up jerseys from my locker, a dark-blue T-shirt with a white "Toronto" arcing in all caps across the front. It was about three sizes too big on her, and she wore it like a nightshirt, with nothing underneath, when she kissed me good-bye at her front door.

The more I thought about it, the more it struck me as odd that so much had happened in the last couple days and yet Sadie and I had only traded a few phone messages since midweek. I had no cause to question her reasons for us not getting together the last three evenings; every one of them was perfectly routine. Still, if the situation had been reversed, there's no way a late shift, a haircut, and a squeak in my wheel well would have prevented me from seeing Sadie for three nights straight. All three happening on the same day wouldn't have kept me from a chance to be with her. When she still hadn't called by eight o'clock, I decided to skip our game of phone tag and just head over to her house without waiting for an invitation.

On the drive there I realized I had no business blaming Sadie for the last three nights. If anything, my own fear and hesitation were why I was so willing to accept her reasons for us not getting together sooner. I'd spent the whole week hoping for the perfect moment to tell her what I really felt, but it just never seemed to come, and even if it had, I wasn't sure I would've known what to do with it. How do you say something and keep it from sounding tired and corny when the thing you have to say is as old-fashioned as it gets? Is there a new way, a way nobody has thought of yet, to tell someone that you are tits over ass in love with them? Can you just come out and say to a woman that she really is the last thing you think about when you go to bed at night and the first thing you think of when you wake up in the morning, without running away like a coward, or dying from exposure? There must be a rule somewhere for how long you should wait, for just the right mood and just the right moment, to say to the most wonderful person you've ever met: "I want to pick up the pieces of my life like so many broken bats and rebuild my world around you." No matter what else we did, I promised myself I was going to tell her tonight.

Sadie, both arms hugging grocery bags, was just bumping her car door closed with her butt as I pulled up to the curb in front of her place. I know she saw me wave, but the bags were full and looked heavy. She only nodded her head in response. I hustled up the drive intending to help, but Sadie had already climbed her porch steps by the time I caught up, so the best I could offer was to hold the screen door open. She must have only gotten a trim at the salon; I couldn't really see any difference in her hairstyle.

"I was just going to call you after I put these away," she said as she walked to the kitchen.

"Have you eaten yet?" I pulled her keys from the front door lock. "I'm starving."

"I had a late lunch, but . . ."

I heard the refrigerator door open, followed by the sounds of jars being placed on the glass shelves inside. I carried her keys with me down the hall, listening for Sadie to finish her sentence. When I reached the kitchen, the puzzled look on her face suggested she'd gotten lost in thought. She seemed to be studying a can of green beans.

"Is that a yes to dinner?"

"Oh." She looked up. "I guess we could eat. I've been running errands since I got off work, though. Can you give me ten minutes to freshen up?"

Her pantry door stood open. I could see another can of green beans on the shelf just inside. I took the can from her hand and put it beside the other in the pantry.

"I'll wait here."

"I'll just be a minute," she said, and hurried up the stairs to her room.

There were still a few cans in one of the bags, so I put them in the pantry wherever there was space. Then I folded up the bags and stuck them in a corner beside the trash can, where she had stowed some other bags from a previous store visit. If there had been more mess I would've continued straightening, but the woman kept a clean house. I sat down at her kitchen table to wait.

Sadie must have gotten her mail and brought it in when she first unlocked the front door. Scattered on the table were several advertisers and an electric bill. I collected the various items and made a tidy pile. In among the mail was a bright-red envelope, the kind that comes with greeting cards. There was no name or address on the envelope though, and it wasn't sealed. Sadie hadn't received that card today; she'd bought it. Of course I looked. On the front of the card, a cartoon woman's hand was sticking out from behind a shower curtain, wiggling a finger as invitation for the reader to join her. The preprinted message inside mentioned a previous shower and the hope that "we can do it again soon!" Sadie and I had never taken a shower together. That card had not been bought with me in mind.

The new outgoing phone message, the haircut that wasn't, the way she'd barely made eye contact from the moment I got out of the car— now it all made sense. A sudden, constricting tightness in my chest convinced me that sitting in that chair, at that table, holding that card, was the last place I wanted to be if I ever hoped to take a full breath again. I needed to go, and right away. I was almost out of the kitchen before I realized the key ring in my hand felt too heavy and full. I looked down to discover I'd grabbed her keys. Mine were still in my pocket. I put her set on the counter beside the stove, then closed the front door as quietly as I could on my way out.

By the time I reached my car, the strangest thought had lodged in my head. During the years I played at OSU, the upperclassmen made the freshmen learn a set of school songs by heart as part of an initiation ritual. Every day after practice a different freshman had to sing one of the songs in front of the team. Regardless of the confidence one had in his own voice, it was made clear to the freshmen that not knowing the words to the song you had to sing would bring far bigger consequences than singing poorly in front your teammates. My favorite was "I Want to Go Back to Ohio State, to Old Columbus Town" because it had some great lyrics, especially toward the end:

> And when we win the game
> We'll buy a keg of booze,
> And drink to old Ohio
> Till we wobble in our shoes.
> Ohi-o! Ohi-o!
> We'll win the game or know the reason why!

That final line had always puzzled me. If you lost the game, what the hell difference did the reason make? But as I sat in my car, gripping the steering wheel between both hands, that lyric popped into my head, and for the first time I understood it completely. I'd driven to Sadie's house with no plan more important than to finally tell her exactly how

214

I felt. Was I really going to leave without seeing her face when I said the words? Not only would I lose the game; I wouldn't even know the reason why.

Sadie opened her front door before I'd reached the top porch step. "Are you feeling okay?"

"Can we talk for a minute?"

"Of course." She moved out of the doorway to let me in again. "What's the matter, Jake?"

By the time we sat down, me on the couch, Sadie in the armchair, my heart was pounding so loud I was certain she could hear it from across the coffee table.

"What's the matter is, I can tune out an entire stadium full of people yelling and clapping, but somehow I can still hear your voice when you call out, 'How you doin', Third Base?' When I'm in the batter's box, I keep forgetting to look down for the coach's sign because I'm too busy wondering if you're somewhere in the stands that day."

I wasn't sure how to read the fact that she was looking down at her hands. She seemed to be fiddling with something between her fingers.

"I don't understand," she said. "Do you mean I'm a distraction in your world?"

"No. I mean, yes—but the other way around. My world is the distraction. You're the one I want to focus on. Today, tomorrow, forever. Do you get what I'm getting at? I really think this is it. I mean, I think you are. You're it."

"I'm what, Jake? Tell me what you want."

"You're the most amazing woman I've ever met. There's so much uncertainty in my life right now, between the union guys and the owners and the media and the strike. The only thing I'm sure of is how crazy, stupid in love with you I am. What do I want? Sadie, I want you."

She looked at me for the first time since we sat down, then untangled her fingers to place her left hand on top of her right in her lap. On her ring finger was a gold band with a diamond in the middle.

"I'm sorry, Jake," she said simply. "You can't have me."

I wanted to add a thousand things. I wanted to tell her that I would spend the rest of my life taking care of her. With me she would never know need or want, have nothing to fear. Whatever it took to make her happy I would swear to provide in outlandish, conspicuous abundance. Anything, everything, all that I have is hers.

But weren't those things understood in between what I actually did say? What else could I add to what I already told her that wasn't simply a garnish, a side dish at best to the main course of my love? I had served that main course—stuttering and with discomposure, it's true, but I did set it down there in front of her—and she had answered by showing me her wedding ring.

"It's all my fault," she said. "I meant to tell you tonight. I know it was wrong for me to—"

"I probably should go."

"You don't have to," she started to say, but I was already at the door.

Sadie had made it out onto the porch by the time I reached my car. My back was still turned when she called out, "Jake? Good luck tomorrow. Good luck with everything."

She was right. Her standing there holding on to the screen door while I got in my car with my back turned, that was no way for us to end. At the very least, we should wish each other luck.

"Thanks," I said, turning to face her. "You, too. Good luck."

"I'm so sorry, about everything."

"Don't be. I'm not."

"I wouldn't blame you if you did, but—please don't hate me."

What a funny thing to say. I thought we'd just made it perfectly clear to each other that the reason I had to leave and never come back was exactly the opposite.

"I won't," I promised, and it's a promise I've kept ever since.

When I got back to the hotel, I tried to lie down and wash the evening from my mind. After an hour of staring at the ceiling, thinking over every word of my conversation with Sadie and then getting angry with myself for my inability to think about anything else, I finally gave up and pulled on a pair of shorts. There was just one way I was going to quiet my pounding heart and shut my brain up for the night, and only one person I could think of who might be able to help.

I didn't hear any noise the first time I knocked, but when I knocked a second time and said, "It's me. It's Jake," I heard a rustling inside. A moment later Folgers opened his door, blinking at the harsh light from the hallway but smiling gently through the glare.

"What can I do you for, partner?"

Of course he kept a supply of sleeping pills, and he didn't ask why I was wondering. He just nodded and disappeared inside his dark room, reemerging again at the door with two blue gel caps in one hand and a bottle of beer in the other.

"They work a little faster if you wash 'em down with one of these."

I reached for the beer and the pills, but he pulled his hands back to make sure I'd look up.

"Just the one beer, though. Okay?"

After we wished each other pleasant dreams, I padded up the hallway back to my room, and an hour later, that's how I got to sleep Saturday night.

If Tall Boy had still been around, I'm sure it would have happened differently. We would have turned on the news when we got up, or bought the Sunday paper for something to read over breakfast, or listened to one of the sports talk stations on the radio as we drove to the stadium. Instead I slept until ten, felt too groggy to pay attention to anything more demanding than the sensation of water falling on my head, and went straight for the bathroom. After a hot shower I got dressed and decided to make my way to the ballpark around ten thirty.

On the drive over I pondered the best way to spend the evening. I vowed not to spend a single minute obsessing over what had happened between Sadie and me last night. There would be plenty of time to work through all that in the days to come. Instead, I would focus my attention on the big night ahead. My first thought was to invite some of the guys over to watch the Mets-Marlins game in my room. Then I remembered that the hotel lounge had a big-screen TV, and since it would be a night worth celebrating, things would be easiest if we all just met in the bar to begin with. It wasn't until I turned into the stadium lot and saw all the cars that I realized something had happened.

I don't recall specific scenes or what occurred first and what took place next after I'd walked into the clubhouse. In my mind it's just a series of moments, random images with nothing to connect each to the others except that I was there to witness them: Hack Hennessey walking the length of the locker room, Sharpie in hand, stopping by each locker to ask guys if they would sign the practice jersey he wore. Lenny Longo holding a duffel bag, trying to stuff things from his locker into it. He kept missing the opening though, and for every piece of equipment or article of clothing he managed to get into his duffel, another fell and added to the pile of his belongings already on the floor. One of our catchers sitting on a chair, feet spread before him and arms draped over his knees, facing the center of the room. "Jesus!" he kept exclaiming, and, "Can you believe this shit?" He wore a helmet turned backward on his head. He had put a stretch of tape across it that read, "No Fehr." One of our relief pitchers, arms loaded with baseballs he'd pilfered from a stash in the equipment room, took a detour by my locker as he made his way toward his own. "I'm coaching my boy's Little League team this year. I bet they'll get a kick out of knowing we'll be practicing with big league balls." He turned to walk away and then stopped to add: "You should grab you some of these. What are they gonna do, fire us?" GQ sitting in front of a TV tuned to CNN with the sound off. As the anchor mouthed details of a story no one in the room could hear, the ticker at the bottom of the screen scrolled the same message over and over: "Baseball owners vote down lockout. Commish Bud Selig, players' union chief Donald Fehr agree: MLB strike officially over."

For the guys who had turned on a TV back at the hotel, or heard the news on the radio, or saw the front-page headline on the Sunday paper, there was really nothing left to do but come to the stadium and get your things out of your locker. That's why everyone else showed up around the same time I did.

The union had neither gained nor given any concessions. The owners hadn't agreed to share a larger portion of their profits with the players. The old CBA had been reinstated, and the labor dispute was in the exact same place on April 2 as it was when the strike started, 232 days before. The only thing that had changed was that they'd agreed to disagree until a new CBA could be hashed out, and now they would start spring training all over again with the union guys. Every front office of every team in the league had been instructed to terminate all replacement contracts at 11:59 p.m. Saturday night, to leave no doubt that none of us qualified for the Opening Day roster bonus or termination buyout. We replacements were only in the way now, and it was time for us to go.

I never kept much stuff at the stadium to begin with, so it didn't take long to collect my things. In fifteen minutes I'd cleared out my locker and worked my way through the clubhouse, shaking hands with all the guys. Eventually I walked the tunnel to the field, to make sure I hadn't forgotten anyone. Assenmacher was standing on the grass in front of the dugout. When I reached the top of the walkway, he turned, saw me, and nodded.

"You boys got a raw deal," he said. "I'm sorry, Standen."

I was surprised at the edge in my voice when I replied, "What are you sorry for, Carl? You didn't do anything."

He came down the dugout steps with his hand outstretched.

"You're one of the most teachable ballplayers I ever met. I'm sorry I didn't get a chance to work with you five years ago. If I had, who the hell knows? Maybe you'd be one of the guys coming back right now, instead of one of the guys leaving."

I knew what he meant. He wasn't saying I had Major League ability. He was saying that he thought I had enough talent to make it worthwhile finding out how far dedicated coaching in a professional league could have taken me. He was saying I deserved a better shot than the one I'd been given. By now though, no pro team would waste the ink needed to sign a weak-hitting third baseman in his mid-twenties. There would be a hundred guys just like me graduating high school or finishing their college seasons in two months. My time had come and gone.

When I shook his hand, he said, "Godspeed to you, son."

Assenmacher walked down the tunnel toward the locker room, but I had already said good-bye to all the guys in the clubhouse, so I decided there was no point in following him. Instead, I walked out onto the field to stand on the dirt beside third base and take one more look around. Call it instant nostalgia, but the grass never looked greener, the seats of Dunedin Stadium never looked a more appealing shade of deep blue than when I looked around that last time. A few minutes later I hopped the railing and climbed the reserved-section stairs, heading for the walkway that led to the customer exit. On the concourse leading out of the stadium I found Folgers, duffel bag at his feet and arms on his hips, staring at the "Players from Dunedin to The Show" sign. He looked up as I approached, nodding toward the long list of player names.

"You know," he said. "I didn't realize how bad I wanted it until today."

I held out my hand, but for the one and only time since we met, Folgers ignored my offer of a handshake.

"You take care now, you hear?" he said, and gave me a bear hug.

Folgers was still standing in the concourse, looking at the wall of names, when I got into my car and pulled out of the parking lot.

By the time I made it back to the hotel I had briefly visited every emotion I would spend the next two months processing: fear, envy, despair, rage, melancholy. My mind was numb from thought. My ears were ringing with grief. When I opened the door to my room, the first thing I saw was the message light flashing on the phone.

Of course Sadie would have heard the news by now. I couldn't imagine her phoning me to gloat, even though she had realized the hopelessness of my situation long before I did. Was she calling to offer some kind of condolence? I had heard her say the words "I'm sorry" enough the previous night to last me a lifetime. The thought of hearing her say it again today filled me with a sadness I couldn't bear to see through to the end. I decided just to ignore the blinking light.

My only remaining obligation was to get my belongings together and check out at the front desk by noon, to make sure they didn't charge me for an extra day. In the time it took to pack my bags, I decided there was nothing Sadie, or anyone else for that matter, could possibly say that would make me feel worse than I already felt. With my bags zipped and sitting beside the door, I punched the required sequence of numbers and waited for the hotel's phone-answering system to play the message.

It was Brian. His voice sounded tired and strained, as if he'd been up all night.

"Hey, Standen. Jake? I just heard. Channel Six even broke in on the Sunday sermon crap to tell the big news. The union guys are back, huh? Fuck 'em all, man. Come home.

"Karen's been asking about you. You should've seen her last night; she was the champ. She's in bed asleep right now, but she's doing great. She's worried about you, Jake. We're all thinking about you, buddy. Come home.

"You've got a new godson here you need to see. I know you don't like kids, but he's gorgeous. Eight pounds, seven ounces. I'm thinking center fielder. Just got here half past two, and already he wants to meet you. Come home.

"I don't know what you'll do about a job, but we'll think of something. Worse comes to worst, I can always put in a good word for you over at Pepsi. They're taking me back, so you know they ain't picky. It'll all work out. It's okay. Come home."

And that did it. There on the floor between the beds in room 136 of the Clearwater Howard Johnson, I couldn't hold it back another second. I cried for my best friend's joy and my own sorrow. I cried for the father I'd been given and the little brother I had not. I cried for every lover I had scorned and every lie I ever told, for every time I'd been a coward when I needed to be bold, for every promise I had broken and every friend I had betrayed, for every hope I ever lost and every wish I ever made. I cried for the baby seals getting clubbed in the Arctic and the children going hungry in China. I cried until I had washed all the parched lands and ended every drought. For the love I could not have, for the future I'd never know, for the only dream I'd chased my entire life that was now and forever out of my grasp and beyond my reach, I cried.

SUNDAY, APRIL 2, 1995

It's over. It's all over.

We never really stayed in touch with any of the guys after the strike. Brian and I received a letter from Folgers late in the summer of '95. He wanted to know if we'd be interested in a reunion of sorts, to get together with any other replacement Blue Jays who could make it to Dunedin in the fall. We wrote him back saying we'd come if we could, just tell us where and when, but that was the last we heard about it.

A card arrived for me at my mom's house that Christmas. I have no idea how Sadie discovered Ma's address or knew that we were related, but she always had a talent for finding out things that would have stumped me. The return address label on the envelope says it's from "Mr. and Mrs. Donald Holder." One of these days I'm sure I'll work up the courage to open it and see if she wrote a message for me inside.

For a time after I got back from Florida I resented what happened between us, but eventually I realized the only thing I regretted was the way I had assumed that, when we were together, Sadie felt lucky, too. I always believed what Hollywood movies want us to believe—that there is a perfect someone in this world for everyone. I just never thought to ask the obvious next question: What if you find her, but that turns out not to be enough? To this day the worst thing I can think to say about Sadie Holder is that she didn't feel the same about me.

I should give credit where credit is due: I've heard all my life that the St. Louis Cardinals run one of the classiest organizations in baseball. Not long after the strike ended, I read somewhere that the Cards, along with the Florida Marlins, went ahead and paid their replacement players the $25,000 they would have gotten if the strike had gone one more day. That same article said several other teams gave their replacements between two and five thousand as severance payment. The Blue Jays didn't offer us anything.

It seems fitting that the Baltimore Orioles, the one MLB organization that never bothered to field a replacement team, would provide both the worst reason and the best example of why we replacements should have been allowed to play. In September of '95, Cal Ripken Jr. played in his 2,131st consecutive game, breaking Lou Gehrig's iron-man record that had stood for fifty-six years. The excitement surrounding that game, and the classy way Ripken achieved his historic milestone with grace and humility, helped bring a lot of people who had ignored baseball that summer back to the game. If replacement teams had been allowed to play even one regular season contest, Ripken's streak would have ended a full season before he got to the record. In another game played almost exactly a year later in '96, during a dispute over a strike call, the Orioles' second baseman Roberto Alomar spit in the face of home plate umpire John Hirschbeck. There was a joke going around the Grapefruit League just before the strike ended: "How can you tell the replacements from the regular major leaguers? The replacements are nice to the fans and respectful to the umpires."

Beyond that, I'm not sure what else I should say.

Should I confess that I feel screwed by how the owners used us replacements as a minor bargaining chip against the union players? I do, because they did. You know who got screwed the most by the strike, though? Canadian baseball fans. When the strike started, the Blue Jays were two-time defending World Series champs. In the six seasons following the strike, they never finished higher than third in the AL East. They had perhaps the most dominant roster of any team in the late '80s and early '90s, but by the end of the strike that talent had aged and dissipated to a point that it may take a couple generations of new players before the Jays reach those heights again. What's more, the Montreal Expos were leading the NL East by six games the day the strike started in '94. They haven't finished closer than eight games behind the first-place team since the strike ended. Now there's talk that, to save the team from falling attendance and disengaged ownership, the MLB suits may buy the franchise and sell it to new owners who will relocate to Washington, DC. If that happens, Montreal baseball fans will have gone from first place to losing their team in the span of a decade.

Here's one thing the strike made me realize: Pete Rose should be in the Hall of Fame. Rose was banned from baseball for "conduct detrimental to the integrity of the game." I don't care if Rose made his bookie rich with a lot of stupid bets or if some of those bets were on baseball. Hell, I don't even care if he bet on the Reds, as long as he bet them to win. If Rose ever bet against the Reds, then not only should he be held out of the Hall, but they should press charges and take him to court just like the Black Sox players had to stand trial in 1921. But Rose never once said he bet for the Reds to lose, and nobody ever found evidence to prove that he did. Rose was already betting his job as manager, and his reputation as a baseball whiz kid, that he could lead the Reds to victory from the bench. His betting the contents of his wallet on the same outcome was just an extension of what he already had on the line as team skipper. How were those bets as detrimental to the game's integrity as what this generation of owners and players did when they canceled half a season and a World Series in a dispute over profit sharing?

In the handful of years following the strike, the owners and players combined to do even more damage by pretending not to notice how performance-enhancing drugs were altering the game. PEDs allowed aging hitters to obliterate home run records and aging pitchers to heal faster and pitch longer, extending careers that might have already qualified them for Hall of Fame consideration. Instead, several players wound up with numbers so inflated that we fans can't trust which accomplishments came from pure talent and dedication and which numbers resulted from pills, liquids, and creams. I've heard the argument that it shouldn't matter. If we pay players to entertain us, then who cares if they're willing to risk long-term health issues to take drugs that allow them to play longer and at even greater levels? But I still believe it's every bit as difficult today for the world's best hitters to bat .300 versus the world's best pitchers as it was when Babe Ruth was in uniform. If you allow PEDs that were unavailable to Ruth, then you lose the ability to compare the achievements of today's players with any other era except their own. In other words, PEDs ruin the conversation about which players were the best of all time. I've always thought one of the greatest things about baseball is how, through its rich history and meticulous statistical record, the game's past can speak directly with its present, and eventually to its future.

I know you're too young to read this now, but soon you'll be old enough to ask about our time in Florida and mature enough to understand the answers. You're already smart enough to figure out that the big-barreled red plastic bats are for babies and only real hitters use the skinny yellow Wiffle ball bats. I had to laugh when you asked last night if I ever saw Babe Ruth play, and when I answered no, you asked if that made me mad. Brian and I have talked about it and we're pretty sure that between us we'll be able to coach next summer's Little League team. If you can learn everything your dad and I have to teach you, I won't have to say I'm sorry that I never saw Ruth play. Instead I'll be able to brag that I helped the next Ruth learn the game.

Maybe I was dumb or naive to think I would ever be allowed to play on a Major League team in a game that counted. But how many people get to say they came within a day and a half of realizing the biggest dream of their life? I'll admit that I was dumb and I was naive, but I'll never apologize for the fact that the stretch of days in the spring of 1995 I spent playing for the Toronto Blue Jays became six of the most thrilling weeks of my life. I haven't stopped feeling sad about how things ended, but I have gotten used to feeling sad about it whenever the subject comes to mind. That's probably as close to closure as I'm going to get.

After all I've come to understand and everything I've since been shown, I realize that if I missed out on anything during the replacement spring training in Florida, it can all be condensed into a single moment. Even now, if I sit quietly and let my thoughts drift, or in those fleeting seconds at night as I float between consciousness and sleep, I can still conjure the moment and imagine what it might have felt like to be there when it arrived. I follow in my mind's eye as two white lines, call them hope and destiny, stream in from infinity to converge at a home like no other, a powerful place where trepidation turns to resolve, where lust turns to love, where the dream becomes you. And the dream remains the same for the Hall of Famer, the rookie, or even a scab: to catch on with a big league club and find your name among the Opening Day nine; to catch that copper-shaded game, its season turning green like a stretch of infield grass; to catch that dying quail down the left field line, over the shoulder, one handed—I go back, back . . . back.

And I'm gone.

Born and raised in and around Columbus, Ohio, BRETT BAKER claims he was working on his MFA degree at the University of Alabama throughout the 1994–95 Major League Baseball strike. He currently lives where the Rhine meets the Main in Wiesbaden, Germany with his wife, Melinda; stepdaughter Lydia; and Clochette the cat.